MAN OF MY DREAMS

DAPHNE JAMES HUFF

ONE

You dream it, and I'll make it happen . . .

The familiar words, spoken so close to her ear, pulled Bree out of a deep sleep. Looking around the room, her heart pounded in her chest.

Where was she?

Instead of familiar venetian blinds and small windows, there were large panes of glass covered in frothy pink curtains that let in an enormous amount of light. Too much light for this time of day.

A few blinks cleared the fog, and she flopped back into the unfamiliar bed. The scent of mothballs invaded her nose.

She was in Aunt Agatha's New York City apartment. Bree's apartment now.

Bree wiped away the tear that trickled down her cheek and sat up again. Her laptop was still open on the bed, where she'd fallen asleep watching *Escape to New York*. The voice that had woken her up was Hayden Carmichael's during one of her favorite, swooniest parts in the movie.

The superstar's first big hit was almost twenty years old, but it was what had planted the seed of moving to the city in her middle school brain. That seed had grown over the years into a dream, a massive bundle of desire like one of those gigantic topiary houseplants that took over an entire bookshelf with its tendrils and twists.

With a yawn, she closed her laptop with the movie still playing, then stretched slowly as she looked around the room. She'd barely taken it all in last night when she'd arrived, exhausted after two delayed flights and a very expensive cab ride she was sure should have cost at least half as much as she'd been charged. Between her Minnesota accent and her wide-eyed exclamation of joy at seeing the Statue of Liberty, the cab driver had assumed she was a tourist.

Except thanks to Agatha, Bree's first trip to New York wasn't as a tourist, but as a resident. A grin spread across her face. This was the first day of the life she'd always dreamed of.

Sleep still clung to the edges of Bree's eyes, and she rubbed them while stifling another yawn. She needed coffee. Immediately. Then she'd head out into the city.

Though dulled by her exhaustion, excitement was making its way through her system. She wrapped herself in her worn terry cloth robe and slipped on the new sheep's wool slippers she'd splurged on at the airport.

She stood up, and her shins banged into the night table. She turned, banged her knee on the bed, then tripped over her suitcases that were still piled in a heap, wedged in between the bed and the wall.

The smile slipped from her face as she half climbed, half limped out into the hallway. The bedroom had seemed enormous last night in her half-conscious state of mind, but in the morning light, it was tiny.

Stumbling over creaking floorboards, she walked five steps into the kitchen. It was just as small, and even worse . . .

"Where's the coffee?" she asked the empty room.

Bree hadn't gone without some form of caffeine in her body within minutes of waking for over fifteen years. One of the perks of being a barista for as long as she had was that she knew how to make a good cup, no matter what she had on hand. Instant, whole beans, whatever kind of milk was available. Big cups, small cups, no cups. She could make anything work.

No coffee at all, however, made it impossible to even get started. A frantic search through the cupboards and drawers confirmed that, unless she wanted to make her morning cup out of mouse droppings and dead roaches, she was out of luck.

Did Birdbrain Bree forget to bring any food to an apartment that's been empty for forty years?

The mocking voices echoed in her ears as Bree took a few steadying breaths. She reminded herself that her forgetfulness was what Aunt Agatha had loved most about her. It was even in the letter accompanying the surprising announcement from Agatha's lawyer that she'd left Bree a Manhattan apartment in her will.

To my darling Bree, with a heart full of dreams and her head in the clouds, I hope this leads you to your happily ever after.

"No coffee." She closed a dusty cupboard and tightened the belt on her robe. Sunlight and the sound of honking horns filtered in through the kitchen window. "That's fine. Plenty of coffee in New York."

If her best friend, Leigh, were here, she'd look up the closest and best-rated café in the area. Bree was much happier to wander around and see what she could find. It always yielded the most interesting results. Bree trusted fate way more than Google for these kinds of things.

Before she could let fate do her thing, however, she had to get dressed. Leggings and a tank top might have been okay for a quick run to the store back home, but this was New York City.

She could be anyone she wanted to be here. It was her chance to reinvent herself.

She dragged one of her suitcases into the living room, bumping into the couch and the coffee table. Heat was starting to pool under her arms. She took a quick sniff. Did she have time for a shower?

No, coffee was more important. Whatever she pulled out first, she'd wear. She'd only brought her favorite clothes with her and sold the rest, along with her car. With a little luck, she'd have enough funds for a few months before she'd need to worry about finding a job.

As if to make up for the lack of coffee, the most perfect sundress fell right into her hands the second she opened her suitcase. A smile lifted the corners of her mouth, her shoulders dropped, and her body relaxed. It would be okay. This was the perfect dress for what would be the most perfect first day of her new life.

Ten minutes later, she was putting on a pair of strappy sandals when she heard a thump from the hallway. A stream of curses followed. It sounded like an old woman. Like Aunt Agatha. Bree's shoes clicked as she went to the door and peered out the peephole.

It *was* an old woman, cursing up a storm. Her papery-thin white skin was deeply lined. She'd dropped what looked like an entire library's worth of books and was bending slowly to pick them up, one by one, to replace them in her overturned shopping caddy.

Bree didn't even hesitate. This was clearly someone meant to be in Bree's life.

After opening the door, Bree stuck her head out into the hallway. "Hi there, looks like you could use some help."

The old woman turned to look at her and raised an eyebrow. "Ya think?" She turned back to her books.

A real New Yorker, Bree thought with an excited quiver in her stomach. The old woman was a bundle of mismatched clothing. Green knitted leggings peeked out from below a long purple skirt. A light-gray puffy jacket was zipped up tight. It seemed like an odd combination for mid-May, but older people were often colder than others.

Bree stepped into the hallway and bent to pick up a few books. It wasn't that easy with the sundress, which turned out to be shorter than she'd remembered, and the sandals were hard to balance on. This was more of an outfit to be seen in than to help people in.

The woman didn't say anything but did grunt a bit when Bree managed to totter over and place a few books into her caddy.

"I just moved in."

Another grunt.

"It was owned by my aunt." Bree tucked the hair that had escaped her braid behind her ear. "Well, not really my aunt, but someone I knew my whole life who taught dance in my town, and I would go there after school and—"

She clammed up when the old woman paused and peered closely at Bree. Without a word, she went back to the books. There were only a few left now, and it took Bree a single unsteady swoop of her arms to gather them up and dump them on top of the rest.

It was a staggering amount of books, really, and Bree wasn't sure how the old woman planned on getting them all downstairs. They were only on the second floor, but there were at least twenty stairs. Last night they'd felt like a million, lugging her suitcases behind her at midnight.

"Do you need some help down the stairs?"

With a silent eye roll at Bree, the old woman pulled her cart down the other end of the hall, toward a gilded doorway Bree hadn't noticed. Smiling smugly, the old woman opened the door and stepped into an elevator. The clanking of the machinery was earsplitting, but it still would have been preferable to banging her suitcases up the stairs last night.

Hypnotized by the slowly fading elevator noises, Bree shook her head.

The old woman hadn't talked to her at all. Not even a hello, never mind about asking her name. Back home, that would have been the height of rudeness.

New York is home now. The smile slipped back onto her face.

Brushing off her skirt, Bree turned back to her door to retrieve her keys and phone before heading out into the city.

The handle wouldn't turn.

With her pulse pounding in her ears and sweat on her palms, she tried to open the door again, knowing before she even touched it what the outcome would be.

She was locked out.

A familiar flutter made its way up her chest. This was clearly a sign to explore, to discover the city in the spontaneous way she knew would lead to amazing things the way things like this always did.

Thanks to her restless spirit and taste for adventure, Bree had traveled all over the country, where she'd met endlessly fascinating people, collecting their stories while waiting for her own to start. Now it finally was, and she wasn't about to let getting locked out of her minuscule apartment ruin her perfect first day.

The elevator clanged from the back of the hallway, drawing her eye. If all her neighbors were like the old woman, Bree would have better luck getting someone in the street to help her call the building's super.

Without wasting another moment, she walked down the stairs and out the door to see what her new city had in store for her.

The tree-dappled street her apartment building was on led to a wide avenue with a familiar name. Seeing the "Broadway" street sign brought to mind theater marquees and neon lights, but here it was all bright awnings and graffitied trucks. The beep of car horns mingled with the chatter of pedestrians. Words in languages other than English mingled with the unfamiliar and delicious smells that wafted out food carts and open doors.

Dodging people and telephone poles, she weaved in and out of the crowd, taking in every new sight, every new sound. The buzz of far-off construction floated on top of everything.

"Holy cow." Bree had never seen so many people before. It was almost enough to make her remember that she was phoneless and wallet-less.

It was also chillier than she'd expected, but she was from Minnesota. All the shivering her body insisted on was because of her excitement, not the cold.

At least now the old lady's warm clothes made sense. Bree's floaty sundress gave her about as much protection from the biting wind as tissue paper. Several people she walked past gave her slightly raised eyebrows beneath their hoods and hats protecting them against the unseasonably cold May weather.

Ignore them. Just like she did back home whenever her unusual outfits clashed with everyone's small-town sensibilities. Minnesota Bree was flighty and flaky and forgetful. "Birdbrain Bree," as her family liked to call her with a chuckle. She, of course, always laughed along, clinging to whatever unique identity they wanted to pin on her. It was better than not being thought of at all.

New York Bree would be different. She shook back her hair and puffed out her chest, determined to walk in the confident, catwalk stride like people in the movies as they moved along busy New York sidewalks.

Holding each person's eye gave her a small thrill, a sense that despite the rocky start, her dream New York life—her dream New York self—was totally possible. Nothing bad happened when she made eye contact with people, except she almost ran into a few others going the opposite way. Even so, no one shouted at her, and a few people even smiled.

Smiled! Sure, they could have been laughing at her poor wardrobe planning, but through her optimistic eyes, they were all smiles of welcome.

After a few blocks, however, an unfamiliar, uncomfortable heaviness settled in her chest. Her stomach gave a growl loud enough that a dog barked at her from the backpack he was being carried in.

Her eyes flitted from one storefront to another. A gym, a shipping store, clothing for dogs, shoes for humans, a grocery store that took up half a block . . . She should go into one and explain her situation, but which one? It must happen all the time, people losing their phone.

If things got very desperate, she could always go to a police station. Someone in this teeming mass must know if there was a police station inside one of these white-stoned buildings. Someone would help her.

Her attention shifted back to the people streaming past her on the sidewalk. Everyone looked so serious, on their way to work or school, sipping from to-go cups of coffee that Bree tried not to salivate over. Back home, she'd have known at least half the faces and they'd have all gladly helped her.

Except some of the people streaming by did look familiar. Not in a super famous way, more like in a social media influencer way. Like they were all professionally good looking and were paid a lot of money to look that perfect all the time.

Hayden Carmichael lives in New York. The cold left her body, and heat crept up her neck. It was just like the movie she'd been watching last night. A girl, new to the city, bumps into him. He spills his drink all over her new dress . . .

Bree shook her head. The lack of coffee was making her lightheaded. It was a city of eight million people. Even if he did live in her neighborhood, which she had no way of knowing, that only narrowed things down by a few million. Out here on the sidewalk, Bree had literally never seen so many people in her entire life.

Except, suddenly, there he was, walking toward her.

The shock of it made her stumble. Shivering as she straightened, she blinked and focused her gaze on him, trying to ignore the pounding of her heart in her ears.

Dressed in gym shorts and a hoodie, Hayden Carmichael's short hair was wet like he'd just showered. His eyes were partially blocked behind round glasses, but there was no mistaking that face, that scruff, those cheekbones. That perfect pout of a mouth that was tugged down in a concentrated frown instead of the wide grin he was usually photographed with, no matter what he was doing.

Bree stopped for a moment, stumbling again when someone plowed into her from behind and cursed at her. Afraid to take her eyes off him, she let her head swivel, looking back. Her heart almost stopped when his head turned, he looked back at her, and their eyes locked.

Was Hayden Carmichael *staring at her?*

A gasp got caught in her throat. This was absolutely the most perfect day.

Letting out her breath in a sigh, Bree picked up her pace, nearly skipping in delight.

I can't wait to tell Leigh what happened. She'd never believe it. Bree turned her head to look in front of her again, just in time to see a door swing open and to run smack into it.

Everything went black.

TWO

Aiden was used to the stares. Through no fault of his own, his face was famous, even if he wasn't. Most days, in the midst of his familiar routine—gym, clients, animal shelter, studying—he didn't even notice the stares.

Did he occasionally stare back? Of course. New York was full of beautiful people. If they wanted to look at him, he'd enjoy returning the favor.

Things never went past looking, however. It took people all of two minutes with him to realize he wasn't the movie star they thought he was. When women gave him the googly heart-eyes the way this one was, he would hold their gaze for a moment, let them wonder, then go on with his day.

Today, however, he looked again.

There was an aura of pure sweetness radiating from her, like she was a fairy who'd stepped out of an enchanted forest and had no idea how she'd ended up in New York. Her long, dark hair and bright-blue eyes hinted at both mischief and warmth. She was impossibly beautiful and improbably dressed.

When Aiden turned his head for another look, a frown

tugged at his lips. Was she shivering? Had she not checked the weather before leaving the house in that tiny dress?

Their eyes met again, and time slowed, Aiden's heart beating a staccato rhythm he hadn't felt since those early days in the city a decade ago. His heart stopped entirely when her face smashed into a door neither of them had noticed.

A curse flew out of his mouth that earned him a few more stares.

Before the woman's head had even hit the pavement, Aiden was at her side.

His hand found her pulse the way he'd been trained to do, and he was careful not to touch her or move her in case anything had been hurt that he couldn't see. His stomach gave a lurch when he considered just what kind of injuries she might have.

She was lying on the sidewalk like an extra in a superhero movie who'd been tossed to the side by the bad guy. Without hesitation, he stripped off his hoodie and laid it over her, thankful he'd been on his way to the gym and not on his way home, so it smelled like fabric softener, not sweat.

"Is she okay?" someone asked. A crowd had started to gather behind him, but he paid them no attention and focused on handling the situation in front of him.

Taking a deep breath, he went through the mental checklist of what to do when someone hit their head. She was breathing, and there was no blood. Next, he should see if he could wake her up.

"Miss? Can you hear me?"

There was a flutter of eyelids and a sharp intake of breath that had his pulse racing. Her blue irises were edged in black, and they were now looking up at him with that same intense gaze from before she fell.

"I had a dream about you." Her voice was strong, and loud.

There was a tittering of laughter behind him. Aiden ignored

them and the drop in his stomach, staying focused on the woman.

"Oh yeah? What was I doing?" Keeping her talking was good. Head injuries were serious things, and he'd seen quite a few in the various jobs he'd had. Though he felt more confident treating animals than humans, he had the treatment steps memorized for both.

She blushed. "I don't remember."

Her blush suggested otherwise, but it also meant she was reacting relatively normally. He checked his watch, quickly updating his schedule for the day. Just a bit longer. Then he'd have to be on his way, or he'd be late. "What's your name?"

"Bree."

"Brie? Like the cheese? Or is that short for something?"

"I'm not cheese." She frowned.

Despite the tension in his chest, he let out a small chuckle at how vehement her answer was, the lilt of a midwestern accent turning the irritated words into a song.

She shifted slightly beneath his hoodie. "It's short for something, but I'm not sure what. Everyone just calls me Bree."

Uh-oh. Memory loss was never a good sign.

"Bridget?" He guessed.

Another frown and his breath hitched. The puckered skin between her eyes was inexplicably adorable.

Her blue eyes blinked up at him, a little too bright. "You look really familiar. Do I know you?"

Aiden hesitated. She did, but not in the way she thought she did. "You've never met me. I would have remembered someone like you."

She flushed again at this, and he cursed his unexpected candor. Unplanned words didn't often leave his mouth. He got back to his head trauma first-aid checklist.

"Does anything hurt?"

"Um . . . my head." She reached up to touch the rising bump on her forehead and winced.

He gently pulled her hand away, ignoring the tingling in his fingers at the feel of her skin on his. "You fell. It'll hurt for a while. Anything else?"

She shook her head, then her face tightened, and she groaned.

"Don't move, just say the words. Are you sure nothing else hurts?"

"No."

"Can you wiggle your fingers and toes?"

"You said not to move."

Aiden's heart thudded at the slight teasing edge to her voice and the small quirk of her lips.

There were murmurs and movement behind them, and Aiden glanced over his shoulder. The crowd was dispersing, apparently convinced he had it under control. One man hung back, however, and squatted down next to them.

"Should she go to a hospital?" His silvery eyebrows drew together. "That fall looked pretty nasty. And she can't remember anything."

"No hospitals." Bree sat up. Aiden's hoodie dropped away, and her dark hair fell down her back in a tangle of wild waves and half-done braids. She shivered.

An attentive ache rushed through him, and Aiden draped his hoodie around her shoulders again. "Why no hospitals?"

Bree looked around and frowned, pulling the hoodie tight against her body. "I don't know."

"That's okay. At least you remember your name."

A corner of her lip turned up. "Only part of it."

Oh hell, she was too cute for her own good. Every protective instinct inside of Aiden was on fire in a way they hadn't been in a long time. Maybe it was the way her hair fanned out around her head, wispy and cloudlike. Or the way her accent brought to mind wholesome images like cornfields and crystal-clear lakes that were incongruous to the dirty, smelly city that surrounded them.

The city that had literally just knocked her on her ass.

"Can you remember where you live?" It was the other man who spoke, and he kneeled next to them on the sidewalk.

Irritation flickered across Aiden's skin. He had this under control. This wasn't the first time he'd had to use the first-aid certification he'd gotten in college.

Did this guy have that? Did this guy keep it updated every year the way Aiden did?

"No. I remember him though." She tilted her head and looked at Aiden, frowning again. "I don't know from where, but I definitely know you somehow."

A familiar dread dropped heavy and low in his abdomen. The older man looked Aiden up and down before recognition lit up his eyes.

"So, are you really a doctor, or do you just play one in the movies?" A smirk spread across the guy's lips.

Aiden sighed. "I'm a personal trainer and I used to be a vet tech, so I know emergency injury procedures."

Unlike you, he added silently.

He turned back to Bree with what he hoped was a calming look. "You probably have a concussion. You should really let a doctor check you out."

"No doctors."

Did he have time to convince her otherwise? A glance at his watch told him no, though it took effort to calm down the voice screaming in his head to haul her away to a hospital immediately.

"Fine. Can we call someone? Where's your phone?" Aiden looked around, but there was nothing on the ground.

"Someone probably grabbed it when she fell," said the other guy with a shrug.

Aiden ground his fist into the rough sidewalk. Yet another of the many reasons he hated this city. Leave your stuff unattended for two seconds and it gets stolen.

"I don't think I had one," said Bree.

"You don't have a phone?" Aiden tried to keep the shock out of his voice but did a poor job of it.

No last name, no phone, no doctors. Panic was slowly starting to take over, hot stickiness clinging to the blood in his veins. His mind searched for a solution, some plan that made sense in this totally unprecedented situation.

Instead of an enchanted fairy, maybe Bree was a demon sent to torture him. It wouldn't be the first time New York had turned something he thought was good into something terrible.

"Why don't we get you something to eat?" The older man smiled gently and got to his feet. Aiden did the same, relieved to have a next step to follow, and he reached out his hands to help Bree up.

She was unsteady, and his hoodie fell off her slender shoulders. As he bent to pick it up, he got a whiff of flowers and sugar. Her hair, maybe, or her skin. It smelled just like you'd expect a mythical creature wandering around New York without a phone to smell like.

Whatever it was, it went straight to the calming section of his brain. The anxiety took a small step back, and he could think almost clearly.

Aiden coughed, put the hoodie back on her shoulders, and moved away. "Do you know if you have any allergies?"

She scrunched up her face. "No?"

He exchanged a glance with the other man, who raised his eyebrows and named one of the gluten-free, sugar-free, organic, superfood chains that were more and more prevalent in the city these days. "I think there's one on the corner."

Aiden nodded. "No sense giving her an allergic reaction on top of a concussion."

The older man checked his watch. "It seems like you've got this under control, and I need to get to work." He hurried off before Aiden or Bree could say anything.

Aiden bit the inside of his cheek. Of course he'd be left to clean things up on his own. He didn't have time to babysit. This woman was nothing to him, just a stranger he'd happened to be near when she'd hurt herself.

Most people in the city were friendly enough, and Aiden knew if he hadn't stopped, someone else would have. But he hadn't been able to resist. The unshakable sense of duty and discipline that got him to his goals was sometimes very inconvenient.

Standing next to Bree, the phone-less fairy, Aiden found he didn't mind so much right now that he was the one who always took charge of a messy situation.

"Where's that guy going?" She turned her wide eyes to his, as if she couldn't believe someone would just walk off when someone was hurt. "Do you need to go to work too? I'm sorry, I've messed up your whole morning."

She'd messed up a lot more than that, but Aiden couldn't very well say it when she was looking at him like that. Then someone on the street rushed past, bumping into her, and sent her flying into his side.

Without thinking, he wrapped his arms around her, the sugary, floral scent overpowering whatever logical part of his brain had considered leaving her to fend for herself like anyone else would.

"Don't worry about it. I won't leave you on your own."

THREE

The café wasn't far, but they took their time, staying close to the buildings to avoid the busier, faster part of the sidewalk. To keep her from getting jostled too much from the rush of people and being pushed into him again, Aiden put himself between Bree and the flow of pedestrians.

She was looking around like she was lost or confused or both. Panic pulsed in his chest.

"Does any of this look familiar?"

She shook her head, wisps of her feathery hair floating around her face. "I don't think I've been here before."

He inhaled slowly and let it out through his mouth. "Here, like this street, or here, like New York?"

A car horn blared and she started. Pulling the hoodie tight, she looked up, then across the street, and finally, behind her. "I'm pretty sure I live in New York. But that could also be from my dream."

Oh yes. The dream starring Aiden. Or, much more likely, the movie star she thought he was.

Aiden was fifteen the first time someone told him he looked just like Hayden Carmichael. *Escape to New York*, the movie that launched the superstar's career, had just come out, and all the girls in Aiden's class were obsessed with it. The baby-faced actor had just the right mix of sweetness and danger to be irresistible.

Aiden, like any self-respecting teenaged boy, thought of himself as all danger and no sweetness, and therefore saw no similarities.

It happened more and more as Hayden Carmichael's star continued to rise. The movies weren't exactly Oscar-worthy, but they were everywhere, and so was his face. When he got to college, Aiden started asking people to call him AJ, but it didn't do much to stop the wide-eyed stares and excited whispers from following him everywhere.

At least he'd gotten some peace when he'd moved to New York. The city had its countless downsides, but celebrities walked around here relatively undisturbed, unless they were there for public events. The kind of events where Hayden sometimes hired Aiden to distract the paparazzi out front while he snuck out the back.

Today, on a random block of Broadway not near anything important, barely anyone even glanced his way as he led Bree across the street to the café.

When they reached it, Aiden held the door out for her, and he caught another whiff of whatever smelled so amazing about her. He was tempted to ask her what shampoo she used, but not only was that not an appropriate question to ask someone you've just met, she probably wouldn't remember.

"Do you know what you like to drink?"

"Coffee."

The response was so immediate, Aiden drew back in surprise before he walked in behind her. The café was mostly empty, the stark white walls and metal chairs colder than the weather outside.

"Looks like that part of your brain is doing okay."

"This is a deep and abiding love. I don't think I could ever forget it."

Smiling, Aiden stepped up to the counter and ordered his drink, then turned to let her order. She fumbled at her sides, frowning, as if looking for a bag or wallet.

"Don't worry, I've got this." He held out some bills to the barista, who stared at him for just a second too long. Giving the young woman a conspiratorial wink, he tucked the twelve dollars' worth of change into the tip jar. He couldn't really afford it, but he didn't feel like he had much choice since he wanted to avoid someone saying Hayden Carmichael was a cheapskate.

Bree bit her lip. "Thank you. I can't remember if I even had a phone and bag with me."

"Why would you leave the house without them?" Aiden couldn't imagine that happening to anyone. It had certainly never happened to him.

They moved down the sticky counter to the pickup area.

"I don't know. But would someone really take them while I was lying there?"

"This is New York, of course they would."

"You say that like New York is a bad place."

"It's a terrible place."

Another frown. The way it pulled her eyebrows together did something to Aiden's stomach. A swirling, jittering kind of anxiety that would only be calmed when Bree was relaxed and happy. He hadn't had this kind of reaction to someone he'd just met in a long time. Which, of course, only made him even more anxious.

Bree swept a hand through her dark waves, her fingers not even pausing when they snagged on the undone braid, but tugging at it until it fell apart entirely. "Do you not like New York?"

"I hate it."

This seemed to shock the frown off her face. She continued to stare at him, wide-eyed and open-mouthed, while he picked up their drinks and led the way to a table.

They sat down and she was still staring. He wiped the table with a napkin before setting down his biodegradable cup. Even if she couldn't remember where she lived, she couldn't have been in the city that long. Everyone loved it at first, including him.

But after a decade of living in this dirty, expensive, exhausting city, there was too much pain for him in New York. Enough to erase the handful of happy memories and fuel his plans to leave as soon as possible.

"How can you hate a city?"

"How can you not remember your name?"

The harshness of his words was clear as soon as they left his mouth, and hot guilt spread over the back of his neck. He rubbed the feeling away with his hand.

"I'm sorry, that was inexcusably rude. You fell and hit your head. It's not your fault."

"It's okay, and I'm the one who should be sorry. I'm the one who interrupted your morning. It's really nice of you to take care of a stranger like this." Bree took a sip of her coffee and made a face. "This is not making me feel better though. Yuck."

Aiden took a sip of his own and silently agreed with her. This place wasn't on his list of regular coffee places, it had just been the closest.

"Other than the terrible coffee, how are you feeling?" Aiden reached out a hand and held it above her wrist. "May I check your pulse?"

She nodded and extended her arm. Her pulse was steady

beneath the warmth of her smooth skin. He withdrew his hand quickly and nodded once.

"It's been about thirty minutes, so you shouldn't be too fuzzy anymore." Unless she'd hit it harder than she'd realized.

"It still feels a bit . . . soupy up there."

Soupy did not sound good, but there was only so much he could do to convince a total stranger to seek medical advice she clearly didn't want.

"Do you remember a friend's name? Someone we could call?"

Her eyes suddenly lit up. "I remember the name of a café. I think I used to work there."

"Great." Relief washed over him, and he took out his phone. "Let's give them a call."

When she gave him the name, however, there was nothing in Manhattan or Brooklyn or even the state of New York. Taking a deep breath, he thought through the logical possibilities of where she might be from.

"Minnesota?" That would make the most sense with her accent.

"Oh yeah, that's where I used to live," she said with such certainty, he wasn't sure if she'd known the whole time and he just hadn't asked the right question.

A muscle twitched in his jaw. "Let's give them a call and see what they know."

The phone rang three times before a woman with the same cheery accent as Bree answered, "Campbell's Café, Leigh speaking."

"Hi, I'm sorry to bother you, but did you have a woman named Bree working for you?"

"Bree! Oh my goodness. Is she okay?"

The woman on the phone was loud enough that Bree's eyes lit up from the other side of the table.

"She ran into a door."

"Oh geez, that's a new one. Usually she's calling for bail or bus money home."

That was . . . not totally unexpected based on his impression of Bree so far. "She can't remember where she lives or her full name."

"What happened? Can I talk to her? Do I need to fly out there?" The concern in Leigh's voice was bordering on panic.

"We're in a café. She's drinking coffee. I'll let you talk to her."

He handed over his phone and watched with rapt interest as Bree asked question after question of her friend, trying to sort out what was a dream and what was real. The door to the café opened and a group of tourists walked in, their voices echoing in the small space. He scooted his chair a little closer to Bree's.

Even with only hearing one side of the conversation, he could tell this must be her best friend from the way her shoulders relaxed and her eyes lit up. The swirling anxiety in Aiden's stomach finally settled to see Bree so calm, finally satisfied that he had done his duty and his overpreparedness had once again saved the day.

Good thing, since it's your fault she got hurt.

He frowned at the mean voice in his head, but Bree must have thought he was angry with her.

"Leigh, I have to go. I've already used all of this guy's niceness for probably the next year."

"It's fine, don't worry—"

But she'd already disconnected the call and handed him back his phone.

"I do live in New York, but I just moved here yesterday," Bree said and leaned back in her chair. "I must have left my keys and phone in the apartment and locked myself out."

Thinking about someone being that forgetful gave Aiden a stomach cramp.

"Do you do that a lot?"

Bree shrugged, looking completely unconcerned.

"I'll find a pay phone eventually to call the super."

With a sigh, he held out his phone again, but she ignored it.

"Did I hear you say before you're a personal trainer? I didn't make you late for a client, did I?"

He shook his head. "Just a workout." One of two he did in a day, and now the second would have to be pushed super late. It had been worth it to make sure she was okay, though he wouldn't be completely at ease until he knew she got home safely.

"So my full name is Brianna Peterson." She held out her hand. "Thank you for your help today . . . " She raised her eyebrows.

For some reason, the formality of her words and posture made him smile. He barely knew her but could already tell it wasn't her natural way of doing things. There was a dreaminess about her, a slight disconnect from reality that was both infuriating and intriguing.

It was time for him to go.

Instead of shaking her hand, he stood up and pushed his chair back with a loud scrape. "AJ."

Her lips turned slightly down at his sudden move to leave. "Ok, well, nice to meet you AJ. I hope the rest of your day goes better than mine started."

His phone beeped, and he looked down at the reminder he was supposed to already be at the gym. "I hope you enjoy living in the city, Bree."

"Thanks."

She gave him a smile, the first he'd seen from her, and it lit her up. Every muscle in his body rebelled against the direction to step away from the table, but he was nothing if not in total control of his muscles. They were his livelihood and, along with his accidentally recognizable face, his ticket out of the city. He wasn't looking to start anything with someone, especially not a woman who apparently regularly locked herself out of her apartment.

"There's a pay phone on pretty much every corner of Broadway. They don't look like those old phone booths though. They're just big screens. Calls are free."

There, that was all he could do for her. He allowed himself only the shortest of hesitations, to linger on a face he'd probably never see again, not in a city of eight million. Then he did the only sensible thing. He said goodbye and walked out of the café.

Other than doing a shortened version of his planned workout, Aiden's day followed its regular schedule. After his workout, he had a few clients at the gym, then he had lunch with his friend Tony. They talked about movies—but none starring Carmichael.

It made it easier to avoid feeling guilty for not mentioning the incident that morning to his best friend. As hard as he tried not to think about Bree, his brain was intent on going through every word and every glance they'd exchanged. Not even the chaos of the animal shelter where he volunteered was enough to keep her out of his mind. The familiar rhythm of his day allowed space for his mind to drift, and it always landed on her.

Had she found a phone? Had she managed to call her super? Where did she live? Why could he still smell her sweet, floral perfume even though he'd showered at the gym?

It wasn't until Aiden was heading home from his shift at the shelter that he got the distraction he'd been hoping for. Unfortunately, it was in the form of a message from the people checking out from the short-term-stay apartment he owned.

He'd been renting it out for years, and it never failed to

amaze him just how ridiculous humans could be in a space that wasn't theirs. The rental website kept the worst offenders away, but no one could guarantee people knew not to flush eight rolls of toilet paper and expect things to not overflow.

Today's incident was slightly less damaging than that, but only slightly. These clients had decided to wait until after they left to tell him that the door to the bedroom had come off its hinges. He'd installed the rolling barn door a few years ago to give the listing a bit of a boost, something to set it apart, but honestly, it was more trouble than it was worth for the extra booking or two per month.

He came right out of the subway station he'd just entered and crossed the street to hop on the train going uptown. The minutes ticked by as the train chugged along, robbing him of his only free afternoon this week to just relax and play video games until his mind went numb and one of his roommates took pity on him and ordered food.

Just like he did every time there was an issue with—or caused by—a client, he reminded himself that the apartment was still worth it. He was so close to paying it off, to finally being free of it and of the city. Every time he considered selling, he got that panicky feeling that it wouldn't be enough unless it was fully paid off first.

It was part of the reason he'd started doing look-alike work for Hayden, but there hadn't been a gig in ages. It wasn't a reliable source of income, not the way this apartment was supposed to be.

By the time he got to the Upper West Side, it was early evening, and his mood had dropped to the absolute worst. It was probably good the clients had waited until they'd left. He wasn't sure he'd be able to hold in his anger, even if it meant a low host ranking.

The temperature had fallen, and he dug his hands into the

pockets of his shorts, remembering only now he'd left his hoodie draped around Bree's shoulders. He hoped she was warmer than he was right now. Helping Bree had felt good, like a peek into the life he longed for away from the city.

Not that he hoped people would run into doors around him on a regular basis. But staying calm in a crisis, reassuring a scared and injured patient, that's when he felt the most like himself. Even if he wanted to do that with animals as a vet, he'd have to deal with the owners, too, delivering bad news in a gentle way.

He wasn't sure he'd succeed in that with Bree. She'd looked so disappointed that he'd only said his name was AJ, no last name. No way to find him.

It's what was best for both of them, but it was the final nail in his bad mood, souring him beyond recognition. He'd never see her again, and the thought bothered him more than the tourist who'd just sneakily snapped his picture as he walked by.

Lost in brooding thoughts, when he finally got to the apartment, it took him a full minute to realize that Bree was sitting on the front steps.

FOUR

Bree stood on shaky legs to face the man who'd helped her that morning.

"Oh cripes, you're Hayden Carmichael." She'd spent the whole day wondering why AJ looked so familiar, but now that she saw him again, everything clicked into place. "I didn't recognize . . . I mean, I'm such a fan. No wait, that's not what I wanted to—"

She snapped her mouth shut. In all of her dreams about this moment—of which there'd been more than she'd even admitted to Leigh—she always knew the right thing to say to make Hayden fall in love with her instantly.

With a tightening of her throat, she realized that ship had sailed hours ago when she'd opened her eyes and told him she'd had a dream about him.

Could this day get any worse?

Underneath his tight t-shirt, his chest was rapidly rising and falling. Though his expression was blank, his eyes darted from her to the door behind her.

"What are you doing here?" His voice had the slightest tremble.

Apparently, her day *could* get worse. She not only managed to knock herself out in front of a gorgeous guy who turned out to be a movie star, but now he thought she was stalking him.

"I live here," she said, with as much conviction as she could muster while shivering under the hoodie—*his hoodie*, she remembered with a rush of blood to her face.

A slight frown pulled at his perfect lips, but the tension in his body lifted and he took a deep breath through his nose.

"Do you live here too?" The wind blew her hair into her face, and her heart thundered in her chest. Her perfect, dream New York life may still have a chance, even after the horrible start to everything. She was neighbors with a celebrity. Maybe they'd even become friends.

Not good friends, obviously, she wasn't important enough for that. But he'd say hi to her in the hallway, maybe ask her to check his mail or water his plants while he was off filming.

"I'm not him." He scrubbed a hand over the scruff on his chiseled jaw and sighed. "My name is Aiden Johnson. Aiden with an A, not an H."

That had to be the name he used when he was in the city, when he was trying not to draw attention to himself. Out of habit, her teeth worried at her lower lip, then she stopped. Whether he was telling the truth or not, he was still one of the most attractive men she'd ever laid eyes on. Torn up and chapped lips was not the look she was going for.

"Should I call you AJ or Aiden?"

A scooter zoomed by on the street behind him. "If you live here, why are you sitting outside?"

She frowned and brushed back her hair from her face. Maybe he hadn't heard her question. "I'm waiting for the super."

When she'd spoken to Leigh with AJ's—Aiden's—phone earlier, her very organized and responsible best friend had promised to call the super for her, as long as Bree promised to find a clinic to get her head checked out and tell them to send Leigh the bill. Apparently she'd kept Bree on the café's health insurance through the end of the month, just in case.

Because of course Leigh would do that, and of course she hadn't let Bree leave Minnesota without getting a copy of all the details of where she'd be living, or without making note of where the closest hospital was. It was the one constant whenever Bree went off to follow one of her spontaneous ideas—Leigh got all the information in case something went wrong. Which it usually did.

For other people, it might be their parents who worry that way, but Bree's family had long ago decided it was easier to roll their eyes at her misadventures than spend time fretting about them. It's not like she'd ever change.

And so far, nothing had, based on the hundreds of dollars in medical bills she'd racked up and the hours Bree had spent alone on the steps, waiting for someone who may or may not show up. She had no doubt Leigh had called, however. Unlike Bree, she was very reliable.

"Are you sure you actually live here?" Aiden shoved his hands into his pockets and looked her up and down. "I don't mean to be rude, it's just . . . " His lips twisted into a deep frown. It didn't detract even a fraction of how beautiful his face was. "I'm not Hayden Carmichael, but I do get quite a bit of attention from some of his, er, fans."

Bree felt the heat creep up her entire body. *Fans* clearly meant stalkers, which is what he thought she was. It definitely looked bad, sitting on the front steps of his building, wrapped in the hoodie he'd forgotten to take back this morning.

"I moved in yesterday."

"Nothing was for sale here."

"I inherited it from my aunt, who passed away."

"Oh." His eyebrows drew together in a concerned expression Bree had never seen Hayden Carmichael make. "I'm sorry."

There was nothing to say to that, other than "thank you." Which she did.

They stared at each other for another few moments, until Aiden offered the one thing she'd been hoping for but hadn't dared ask.

"I can let you into the building."

The smile that split her face almost hurt, but she was so grateful, she didn't care if she looked a little unhinged. "That would be amazing, thank you."

He blinked at her, as if taken aback at her elated reply, or not used to such enthusiasm. Or both.

When he opened the door, she hurried behind him into the vestibule, relief thrumming in her veins. This New York adventure was back on track. Things worked out how they were supposed to, and Aiden was proof of that. Her tremendously attractive neighbor had come to her rescue twice in less than twelve hours. Forgetting her keys this morning hadn't been stupid of her, but destiny putting her on the right path.

He stopped to check his metal-faced mailbox engraved with the letter and number 1B. She wanted to let him know that she was in 2B, right above him, but that would probably not help with the stalker vibe she'd only just managed to get rid of.

"How long have you lived in the building?" she asked.

There were only eight apartments, two on each floor. While the larger building next door had a nonstop stream of people going in and out, no one had even come down to check their mail while she'd been out on the steps for hours.

"I don't really live here. I rent out the apartment to tourists."

"That must be pretty lucrative."

He gave her a wan smile. "You'd think so, if they didn't manage to break something every other month."

"So why don't you just sell it, if it's so much hassle?"

She thought it was a simple question, but his already chilly attitude turned ice-cold in an instant. A mask went over his features, transforming them into a totally neutral expression. "Why don't I give Paulie a call to see when he plans on getting here."

"Oh, okay. Thanks."

As he spoke into the phone, Bree took the opportunity to study his face a little closer. While he was remarkably similar to Hayden Carmichael, there were a few little differences besides his first name.

Aiden's beard was short and scratchy, the way Hayden usually wore it between movies, but the hair didn't quite grow in the same pattern and was a slightly lighter brown than Hayden's. There was also a mole right in front of the ear not covered by his phone. She found herself staring at it, fascinated that this was all that separated Hayden from Aiden.

Her stomach dropped. Maybe Aiden was right to worry she was a Hayden Carmichael stalker. For Pete's sake, she had apparently memorized the man's facial hair and moles.

"Paulie won't be here for another hour at least." Aiden put his phone back in his pocket, leaned against the wall next to the mailboxes, and sighed. "He's stuck in traffic on the bridge. But he said you could call a locksmith if you really need to get in."

"How much would that cost?"

"Not as much as you might think." He raised an eyebrow, and hesitation flickered across his face in a very un-Hayden Carmichael way. "I know a guy if you want me to call him."

Bree's racing heart finally slowed down as reality sank in. This wasn't her dream man, just someone who looked incredibly similar. There was a stiffness to him that was the total opposite of Hayden's open, easy personality. Aiden was just a normal guy who'd been nice to her when she needed it, her shy and awkward sort-of neighbor.

She ran a hand across the raised 2B on her mailbox. "You've already done so much to help me."

He blew out a breath and pushed himself off the wall.

"It's a phone call. It's fine." He started walking down the hallway. After a moment, he seemed to realize she wasn't behind him and turned to look back at her. "Are you coming?"

"Where?"

"You're not just going to stand there in the entryway. Mrs. Wilson will probably call the police on you if she sees you hanging around for much longer." He glanced up the stairs. "Actually, I'm surprised she hasn't called already."

Bree hurried to follow him. "Does she live on the second floor?"

"Yeah."

"I met her this morning. She had a bunch of books in her shopping caddy."

As he turned to unlock the door to his apartment, she saw the corners of his lips lift a little. "Must have been on her way to the library. She'll be out for most of the day then."

"How do you know—oh!"

Bree was left momentarily speechless at how cute and cozy the inside of his apartment was. She'd expected something like the inexpensive rentals she stayed at on her wanderings. Tidy and clean but minimal comfort with nothing fancy.

This was luxurious, yet comfortable. The pieces were clearly expensive, but rather than cold and sharp the way a lot of modern furniture was, the warm colors and soft fabrics invited you to stay awhile. Maybe even curl up on the couch with one of the blankets that were folded neatly in a wicker basket by the fireplace.

Though their apartments had the exact same layout, Aiden's seemed so much bigger. Ideas started sprouting in her head about how to rearrange things and what she'd need to buy to make her space a little less squished. It would be expensive, but totally worth it to make it her own. She couldn't have the perfect New York life without the perfect New York apartment.

"Are you okay?" Aiden asked.

Heat rushed to her face when she realized she must have sighed out loud when she walked in. "Yes, just admiring your style. It's beautiful in here."

"Thanks." His cheeks tinged pink. "It didn't always look this nice."

"How long have you had this apartment?" She followed him through the living room, letting her hands trail over the back of a squashy armchair and fiddle with the tassels on a curtain.

"Ten years."

"Wow." Her eyes lingered on Aiden as he walked into the kitchen and leaned against the counter. He had to be about her age—Hayden Carmichael's age too—so to have already been here that long meant he'd bought it right out of college.

How much did he make to afford something like this? It would have cost less a decade ago, but even then, New York real estate, especially the Upper West Side, had never been cheap. The only reason Aunt Agatha had property was because her parents owned it first. Agatha had moved to the Midwest in the 1970s and almost never spoke about her time living in New York. Bree hadn't even known about her apartment until the lawyers had handed her the letter and a giant folder full of paperwork.

Leigh had taken her through it all. While the mortgage had been paid off decades ago and Agatha had taken care of the estate tax, Bree would need to pay the property taxes and condo fees.

"What do you do for work?" Her face heated again. "Sorry, that was rude."

"If you're going to live in New York, you'll need to learn to be a little rude." He folded his arms across his chest and smirked. "Don't worry, it won't take long to rub a little of that midwestern niceness off you."

His eyes met hers, and a different kind of heat whipped through her body.

"You think I'm nice?"

He dropped his arms and turned, brushing away invisible crumbs on the counter he was leaning against. "Too nice for a place like New York."

She swallowed hard. What was the universe throwing her way now? A gorgeous, helpful guy who said lovely things about her.

It wasn't the first time a man had come to her rescue and sparks had flown. But this was the first time she was actually planning on staying in the same town. This wouldn't be something casual she could drift away from like she usually did.

Maybe it still could. After all, he didn't actually live in the apartment. He might not be here that much. This could be the universe telling her to have some fun.

He looked up and she took a step forward into the kitchen, eager to see what fate had in store for her.

FIVE

With a regretful twist of his gut, Aiden took a step back, breaking the weird simmering tension between him and Bree.

She was way too cute and innocent for her own good. Aiden knew that kind of fresh-faced optimism, had been full of it himself years ago, before the city had stripped it all away, inch by inch, until all that was left was his raw, bleeding heart on the sidewalk, trampled flatter every day.

Except she wasn't some doe-eyed coed clutching a fresh art history degree in her fists, but a grown-ass adult. For some reason, this made his protective urge rise even higher. She'd managed to come this far in life without her bubble burst about New York.

That had to be why he kept helping her. He knew what lay ahead of her, and only the truly heartless would wish that on anybody. He couldn't trust anyone else to take care of her the way he could.

Not that he wanted to take care of her in any permanent way, of course. He was on his way out of the city, not looking for another anchor to weigh him down the way this apartment had.

It took more effort than it should have, but he took another step back, toward the fridge, and his hand groped for the handle. "Can I get you something to drink?"

"Do you have any coffee?"

He nodded. "I should, unless the last booking drank it all in addition to breaking my door."

He rummaged in the cabinets for a minute, not remembering exactly where everything was. There was a company who came to clean and restock in between guests. All the repairs, however, he did himself, or got Tony to help.

"I usually have a few cups in the morning," Bree said from somewhere near the couch. He must have imagined her coming closer to him before. "That's where I was headed when I ran into that door."

"So that explains the inattention."

"Well, I was looking around too. It's only my first day here."

He peered around a cabinet door to look at her. "You moved here without having ever visited?"

"I've seen movies, but it's not the same."

No, it wasn't, he wanted to say, but held back, rifling through the cabinet instead. Five hundred packets of sugar but no coffee. It wasn't his job to tell her there was no Santa Claus and that New York was a stinking cesspool of a city.

"I remember the first time I saw *Escape to New York*, and it was like . . . " She shook her head and walked over to the small table between the two windows in the living room. A mirror hung above it, and her fingers traced its gilded edges, her hand peeking out from the depths of his hoodie's sleeve. "This feeling deep in my chest, like it was the most beautiful thing I'd ever seen."

He tried not to roll his eyes at the mention of Hayden Carmichael's first movie. What she was probably remembering was her teenaged self falling in love with the actor the way millions of others had that summer.

Luckily, just then, his hands landed on the coffee pods, and he didn't say any of the less than flattering things running through his brain about the actor's early films.

"Ah, here we go." He popped one into the machine on the counter and grabbed a mug from the hooks along the wall. "Are you sure it's not too late in the day for coffee? I have decaf."

She waved that away, then tugged at the hoodie's drawstrings and wandered over to the couch again to sit on the back of it, facing the kitchen. She looked way too good in his clothes, in his apartment.

"I worked at a coffee shop for ten years, so my blood is practically pure caffeine. I could drink it at midnight and fall asleep a minute later."

"Meanwhile, I have one sip after noon and I won't sleep a wink." He gave her a smile as he handed her the mug. Her eyes were a little wide, and he toned down the smile.

He'd have to prove he wasn't Hayden soon or the poor woman was going to hyperventilate. It tugged at him in a very uncomfortable way, how much he wanted her to like him, Aiden. Which was ridiculous, since the very last thing he wanted was for her to feel anything about him other than neighborly gratitude.

He handed her a mug. "Why don't we give the locksmith a call?"

It only took a half hour for the locksmith to show up, and Bree said goodbye somewhat hesitantly. Aiden knew he should be more neighborly, offer more assistance, but he'd reached his limit for the day.

Finally alone in his apartment, he took a picture of the broken door and sent it to his friend Tony, who was a contractor. Only ten years older than Aiden, Tony had started out as a client at the gym, but their sessions quickly turned into discussions about real estate and the ways Aiden could improve his listing on the short-term rental market.

A few hours later, Tony was there with his tool belt, and Aiden had ordered food to arrive at the same time.

Tony wrinkled his nose when he saw what he'd ordered.

"Salads? Really?" Tony pouted. "I'm about to lift five hundred pounds of door, and you feed me lettuce?"

"Pizza and beer will make your workout tomorrow miserable."

"But it will make me happy now, which is what you want if you're expecting me to help fix the door."

"The door was your idea."

Tony waved this away. "You didn't have to. I just told you it was a cool thing to do. Not that it would work."

Aiden rolled his eyes and pulled a carton of ice cream—real ice cream, not sugar-free organic coconut milk stuff—from the freezer.

"Will this keep you happy enough?"

Tony's eyes lit up and he licked his lips. Actually licked them like a cartoon character.

"Yup, that'll do."

Within an hour, they'd gotten everything back on track. It wasn't hard with the two of them, but there was no way Aiden would have been able to do it himself.

"Thanks for your help."

Tony waved his gratitude away and held out his empty bowl.

"No, really." Aiden scooped some ice cream for his friend, then grabbed a banana for himself. "I don't even want to think about how much that would have cost me otherwise."

"I thought things were going okay, that it was all booked up," Tony said, his voice thick with chocolate mint.

"It was, but then I had a few cancellations, and I'm just not getting the traction I used to."

"You know if you put your pretty face on your host account—"

"Absolutely not." He shoved the banana peel into the trash. There were limits to what he was willing to use his accidentally famous face for. The memory of Bree looking at him, speechless and starry-eyed, made his stomach turn.

Tony held up a hand in surrender. "Fine, fine. Do it your way."

Aiden ran his hands through his hair and dropped onto the couch with a heavy thump.

"I'm just so close, you know?"

Tony knew about his plans, though he didn't fully understand the reasons behind them. Like a true New Yorker, Tony didn't get why Aiden would want to live anywhere else. Tony had lived in the city his whole life, had grown up here, and would never leave.

"Would it be that bad if you had to stay another few years?" Tony asked as he helped himself to more ice cream. "Go to school in Long Island instead of somewhere far away?"

Vet school had been his dream since he was a kid, but it had been on hold for years. His father had expected Aiden to follow in his footsteps and go into finance.

Which had worked out about as well as his relationship with Margot had.

Aiden's stomach twisted. "I just . . . can't stay here any longer."

He only had two years left on the mortgage and just enough saved to pay a company to manage the property for him during that time so he could go to school anywhere other than New York. It was the light at the end of a decade-long tunnel that got him out of bed every morning.

Spoon and bowl in hand, Tony leaned against the counter. "Plenty of animals here in the city."

"Yeah, and they can go to the doctor. I want to be a vet."

The bad joke he'd told a hundred times got a weak chuckle from Tony.

"At least the next few months should be interesting with your new neighbor." Tony waggled his eyebrows.

"How do you know about Bree?"

"I passed her on the sidewalk on the way in. She asked if I was one of her new neighbors. That accent was something else." He grinned mischievously and took a bite of ice cream. "Bree, huh? So you've met her too."

"You could say that." He told him about how he'd helped Bree after her fall, then how he'd found her on the steps.

Tony set the bowl onto the counter and crossed his arms. "Please tell me you didn't call her a stalker."

Aiden brushed away some dust on the coffee table and didn't answer.

"You are the worst. It's like you don't ever want to find a girl."

"I do, just not one here."

Tony made a face but held his tongue for once. At least until his next thought. "So you won't mind if I go over and introduce myself properly."

"What?" Aiden whipped a glare at his friend. "Why would you do that?"

Tony shrugged, his lips twisted up into a rakish smile. "She's hot. I'm hot. It's clearly destiny."

Aiden glared at him. "She's my neighbor."

"You're never here. You rent this place out to tourists."

"Well, not right now." In an instant, the decision was made, and a new plan for the month took shape. "There's more work I need to do."

"Oh? Work that you just conveniently forgot to tell me about?"

Tony gestured around the pristine living room and raised an eyebrow.

"It's little stuff, like painting baseboards." Aiden had a list a mile long, but he knew it wouldn't take more than a few days. "Besides, I need a break from my roommates."

A few guys who worked at the gym had a house in Jersey City, where he'd been crashing for the past few months. They were right out of school, used to living in shared spaces, and didn't mind the extra help with the rent. But it was exhausting living with people so much younger than him.

"You know you can always stay with me, if you need to," Tony said.

He'd offered before, and Aiden had always said no. It wasn't that he didn't think he'd like living with Tony, but the opposite. He'd like it too much, and then he'd stay. Part of the reason Aiden always got slightly annoying roommates was to ensure he never got too attached to anyone or anywhere. It was a strategic move on his part that had made sense a few years ago, but he was getting too old for that kind of hassle.

At the end of a long day, like today, he just wanted to be in a nice, quiet space. Like this apartment he'd bought ten years ago with a girlfriend who'd split and left him with a massive mortgage payment.

"Thanks, but I'll be fine here for a while."

From behind his front door, they heard someone come into the hallway, drop their keys, and say, "Oh, for cripes' sake" in the most adorable Minnesota accent.

Tony smirked. "I'm sure you will be."

SIX

After the kind of busy, full day she loved, a long, lonely evening stretched out in front of Bree. She sat on the couch, the rough fabric scraping along her legs as she drew them under her, and considered her options.

She had no Wi-Fi, and her data plan was running dangerously low. She had her laptop and DVDs, but was that really how she wanted to spend her first night in New York?

Exploring the city was what she should be doing, but her first twenty-four hours had been very spendy, even for her.

Aiden's locksmith had shown up five minutes before Paulie, the super. In the end, no replacement lock was needed, but she'd had to pay the guy anyway.

Then, she got some groceries, and they'd cost what she'd thought would last her at least two weeks.

Even the thrill of now being the kind of person who "ran to the bodega for a few things" was tempered by a low-level worry about money. It wasn't an immediate issue, not with everything she'd gotten from selling all her stuff before she'd moved, but what would be enough six months or more in Minnesota was looking like it would last two months in New York, max.

Financing her adventures was usually easy on her barista salary since she either lost interest after a few weeks or just came home when she ran out of money. Birdbrain Bree wasn't known for her financial savviness.

Because she was the best friend a girl could have, Leigh chose that exact moment to call her.

"I don't think I can do this." The words were out of Bree's mouth the second she picked up the phone.

"Hello to you too." There was a smile in Leigh's voice. In the background, Bree could hear the chatter of her two girls getting ready for bed.

"I'm serious. This is too much." Bree leaned back on her hard and uncomfortable couch—who would ever choose this as furniture?—and choked back a sob. "Everything is going wrong. The weather hates me, the apartment is tiny, the old lady across the hall barely said two words to me when I helped her with her books, the coffee is terrible, and I'm going to run out of money in a week."

"Not to mention this morning's run-in with the door."

"See, proof this isn't the right place for me." Bree swiped at her eyes.

"It's been one day."

"One miserable day."

"You've quit too many things. I won't let you quit this."

Bree propped her head on her hand and pouted. "Why not?"

This wasn't how Leigh usually responded to Bree's whining. Normally she just offered to pick her up wherever she was or sent her money for a bus home. When Bree needed an out, Leigh gave it to her.

"Because this has been your dream for so long." There was the sound of her girls singing some silly song, and Bree almost started crying again, she missed them so much. "It's not like getting your pilot's license or becoming a scuba diving instructor."

Both had been very intense but short-lived obsessions for Bree that she'd never seen through to the end. "No, this is like everything else. I just realized sooner it's not for me."

"The whole time I've known you, only two things have stayed the same. Hayden Carmichael and New York City. This is where you're supposed to be."

This was true. In a family of seven, you had to find your niche. Her older sisters had sports and law, her younger sisters had science and teaching. Other than her reputation for having her head in the clouds, Bree was known for her love of Hayden Carmichael and New York City. They were what made her more than just the forgettable—and forgetful—middle Peterson sister.

Bree let out a dramatic sigh and leaned back on the couch again, grimacing and staring at the monstrous easy chair across the room. At least it looked somewhat comfortable, but she didn't have the energy to move.

"But I miss you," Bree whined.

"I miss you too, but you need to stay." Leigh was using her 'serious mom' voice. "The dream might not look exactly the way you thought it would, but it can still work. You have to give it a real chance. It's what Agatha would have wanted."

Even though Leigh couldn't see her, Bree squirmed and pouted. "Fine. I'll stay. But if one more totally ridiculous thing happens, I can't guarantee I won't be on the first plane home."

"Give it at least five more ridiculous things."

"Two."

"Four."

"Three."

"Fine, three," Leigh said. "But they have to be truly terrible things, not like locking yourself out of your apartment."

"That was totally terrible."

"For crying out loud, you do that all the time. Just give a key to a neighbor in case it happens again."

Bree's stomach dropped. She hadn't told Leigh that the guy who'd helped her that morning was also her neighbor . . . and a stunningly gorgeous man who looked just like her favorite movie star. And she wasn't about to bring it up now, or Leigh would use it to negate all the bad stuff that had happened today.

"That is . . . not a terrible idea."

The smile in her friend's voice was audible. "I am known to have those from time to time."

"Any brilliant ideas on what I should do tonight?"

"Just rest. Go to bed early. Tomorrow will be a new day."

Bree grumbled at the much-too-reasonable suggestion. "And what should I do tomorrow?"

"Go find a perfect little New York café. Make it your mission."

Sitting up a little straighter, Bree perked up at that. "I can do that."

Leigh laughed. "I expect a full report by this time tomorrow."

They hung up, and Bree felt better than she had ten minutes ago. Looking around the tiny living room in the fading evening light, she had to believe that life for New York Bree would be different, that she could be different here. The gift from Aunt Agatha had been more than just an apartment. It was Bree's chance to show everyone they were wrong about her.

Starting tomorrow.

Bree woke up to the sound of the rain pouring down outside.

Dragging her feet, Bree drew back the curtains to find the fat drops splattering against the window and blurring the view of the street outside. Amazingly, it was still teeming with people and cars. It was impressive how energized they all seemed, when all Bree wanted to do was curl up under her covers for another few hours rather than face whatever unpleasant surprises the city had in store for her second day in New York.

Pushing the curtains closed again, Bree considered what rain meant for the day's activities. She'd promised Leigh she'd find a good café, but surely the weather was a sign she should stay inside, wasn't it?

"Coffee first," she muttered to herself, and plodded into the kitchen.

The can of instant powdered coffee was all she'd been able to find at the bodega last night, and it was worse than she'd imagined. It quickly became clear that she'd need to venture out into the downpour after all.

With a sigh, she wandered to the living room—just took a few steps really, the apartment must be shrinking somehow—and flung open her suitcase with much less enthusiasm than the day before. She picked out her most boring jeans, the simplest t-shirt, and rummaged around until she found the plain gray rain jacket she'd thrown in as an afterthought. Her dreams of living here included a magnificent wardrobe, but today didn't seem like the right time to go out and get one.

Though her clothes were on the plainer side, Bree spent a bit of time brushing out her long, dark hair. As the only brunette in her family, she seesawed between loving her hair and hating how it made her different from her sisters. All four of them were tall, blond, and accomplished, while Bree was the short middle sister muddling through life.

Already thinking of changing your plans, Birdbrain? Surprise, surprise.

Bree took a deep breath and set her brush down on the edge

of the sink. It tumbled to the floor, and she blinked away tears. New York would be different. It had to be.

A renewed sense of purpose struck her. She sent a quick text to Leigh, who she knew would be busy with the morning rush, to let her know she was setting off on her mission.

After checking and double-checking she had her keys and phone, she grabbed an umbrella and headed into the rainy city. Her feet sank into a puddle almost immediately outside her apartment. The urge to run back upstairs was a tug right behind her heart.

"I'm New York Bree." She gripped her umbrella tighter. "It's just a sign I need rain boots."

With her wet socks squelching only slightly less loudly than the rain pounding on the sidewalks, she went two blocks in one direction without finding a café, then turned left and went three more blocks without anything other than an entrance to Central Park.

Dry socks suddenly seemed much more essential to this adventure, so she tried to circle back to her apartment, but went the wrong direction and didn't notice for five blocks. By now she was so cold and wet, she would have even gone to a Starbucks, if only she could find one.

The city was a grid and should be easy to navigate. She had the entire map of her twisty little town memorized since she was six, could drive off in any direction and always find her way home, and had never gotten lost in any other city she'd been to. There was no reason for New York to be this tricky.

It was the rain, she decided. Everything was harder to see in the rain. The streets looked nothing like they had yesterday, the colors muted and the tops of the buildings melting into the gray sky.

Hope leaped into her chest when she turned the next

corner. A café appeared, and she squished toward it so quickly she nearly caught her umbrella on others that she passed.

She stopped inside and soaked in its rain-free warmth. It was full of the nutty coffee smell she associated with happiness and Leigh.

Bree collapsed her umbrella, then snuck a quick picture to send to her best friend, wishing she could have been there with her. But running her own café and raising her two kids on her own was not something Leigh could put on hold to come to New York on short notice. She'd promised to visit once Bree got settled, and the thought was a comfort.

Another comfort was the warm mug that Bree had in her hands within minutes of arriving. It must still have been the morning rush, and the small space was filled with the chatter of customers and the drumming of the rain against the windows. There were people stationed at tables with their laptops. Remote workers probably. Leigh liked having them at her café, said that it was good for business and made it look like her café was popular.

If that was how you measured it, then this was the place to be. Bree took a seat at a table along the long wall that faced the large window to the street and took in everyone around her. There were all the same types of people as back home, and she smiled into her coffee.

Bree briefly closed her eyes with her first sip, but they popped back open almost immediately. The sigh that escaped her turned into a gag. Of course the coffee would be terrible.

Across from her, a bushy-bearded professor-type with patches on the elbows of his blazer pushed up his glasses and leaned closer to peer at something on his screen with a frown. A few tables away was a hoodie-wearing student, his back to her, bent over a large textbook, his screen open to the picture of the anatomy of what looked like a dog. On tall stools at the long, high counter along the window sat two professional women, all sleek hair and expensive pantsuits. Next to them, a young dad was tapping away on his laptop while his baby slept in a stroller next to him.

Even if the coffee wasn't great, for the first time since she'd gotten to the city, something felt familiar. She never wanted to leave the comfortable sights and smells of a café. With a trickle of excitement, she realized she could, in fact, stay here all day. She could do whatever she wanted.

The endless possibilities sent a familiar release of tension through her. The day was in destiny's hands now. For the moment, she was happy with drinking this horrendous coffee and eating whatever pastries they had that didn't cost more than her electric bill back home.

Back in Minnesota, she corrected herself. New York was home now. A happy bubble of excitement filled her stomach. If there could be more moments like this—with slightly better coffee—then it really could be home.

The bubble slowly evaporated, however, the longer she sat there. Nobody made eye contact with her. Everyone kept their heads down, looking at their phone or laptop.

Back in her small town, she wouldn't have been able to sit for more than five minutes without someone coming over to chat. There was a coldness to the space that had nothing to do with the rain. Even the baristas ignored her as they cleaned up the empty tables around her.

Tears pricked the corners of her eyes, and she took a miserably cold sip of the dregs of her substandard coffee. She grimaced and stared at the quickly emptying tables around her. Only the student in a hoodie remained.

Bree was just about to get up and leave when the student turned away from his textbook, pushed down his hood, and ran his hand through his hair. Her stomach gave a sideways lurch.

It was Hayden Carmichael.

Wait, no. She scanned his features more carefully. It was Aiden Johnson, her neighbor. Now her stomach twisted in a tight spin right up into her chest.

The embarrassment from yesterday still fresh in her mind, Bree scrambled to gather her things, heart pounding. He'd think she was stalking him again.

A slightly more reasonable voice—the one that always sounded like Leigh—cut into her thoughts. This was a random café she'd walked into completely by chance, without a plan in mind. It was perfectly normal that she was here.

That didn't mean she wanted to be here when he spotted her.

Unfortunately, her rotten New York luck wasn't done with her yet. Aiden stretched one way and then the other in his chair, his eyes roaming the crowded room until they landed on her.

After a blink of recognition, he raised a hesitant hand in a halfhearted gesture of hello. She gave a small wave back that, even to her eyes, was way too excited for the dread that was pooling in her chest.

Leigh's voice echoed again in her head.

Might as well talk to him. It's not as if you could make a worse impression than you already have.

Fat chance, said her own voice right back.

SEVEN

He could have just left it at a wave. But something about Bree's pursed lips and shifting eyes made her look sad, which was way too uncomfortable. Before he could think about it too hard, he stood and made his way over to her, pulling his hood up as he went.

Her eyes finally landed on him when he got to her table. His hands flopped awkwardly at his sides, so he folded his arms and leaned against the table next to hers.

"How's day two in the city treating you?"

Her lips turned down. "Well, I haven't run into any doors yet."

"Sounds like a good day so far then." The words that he'd meant as a light joke came out flat and harsh. Her frown deepened, and his arms squeezed tighter against his chest.

She gestured to his open laptop and book. "What are you studying?"

"Hm?" His eyes looked back and widened. "Oh shoot, let me close that."

He launched himself back to his table and did just that.

Then, inexplicably, he came back to actually sit in the chair across from her.

The body he was normally fully in control of was following some other plan for the day he wasn't aware of. "It's nothing."

"It was definitely not nothing." Bree raised an eyebrow. "Normally, I'd be too polite to pry, but someone recommended I should try to be ruder now that I'm a New Yorker."

The delight at seeing her smile made his own lips mimic hers.

"That someone must be a smart guy."

He thought she'd drop it, but some mix of curiosity and loneliness shimmered in her eyes. An empty coffee cup sat in front of her, and she ran her finger along the edge of it. "You mentioned being a vet tech in addition to a personal trainer. Are you studying to be a vet or something?"

Time for him to be a rude New Yorker. "Or something."

His eyes darted to the counter, where a barista was giving him a wide-eyed glare. He pulled the hood further down over his head and leaned forward.

She leaned in as well, and her voice dropped. "You're not trying to be an actor?"

The horrified face he made got a laugh out of her, and her whole body relaxed. Her shoulders dropped and the tiny lines between her eyebrows smoothed out. The amount of time and brain space he used to observe Hayden Carmichael in order to imitate him was now coming in handy to observe Bree's various moods.

Seeing her happy was his favorite so far.

"Are you?" He raised an eyebrow. "You check all the boxes: works in a coffee shop, rich relative has property in the city . . . "

Bree giggled and shook her head. "I'm just taking a break from it all. Living my New York dream."

Dread trickled into his stomach at that. Nothing about living in New York was a dream. "Good luck with that."

From her expression, his tone wasn't as light as he'd intended. The turned-down lips were back, and now her eyes were shifting away from him.

"Well, I've got to get going. A lot to do to settle in." She stood, then her eyes lit up. "Oh, I forgot. I still have your hoodie. I'll drop it off when I get back to the apartment."

If it were up to him, she'd keep it forever. He waved a hand. "No rush. If I'm not there, just stuff it in my mailbox or something. Don't worry about it."

"I never do."

With another smile and a wave goodbye, she headed back out into the rain.

Aiden stayed another fifteen minutes, trying to get back into the rhythm of studying, but it was no use. His mind was on Bree. Where was she off to today? Would she be safe? Did she have her keys?

What he needed was a workout, but it wasn't in his plan for the day. Shifting his entire schedule for the week felt like too much effort right now. Instead, he could get started on some of the work he'd told Tony the apartment needed.

The fact that he'd be able to hear when Bree got home had absolutely nothing to do with his decision, of course.

That plan now adjusted, he made his way in the rain back to his apartment, mentally going through the list of supplies he'd need to pick up later. When he noticed the tinted windows on the luxury SUV parked out front of his building, he didn't even bat an eye. The city was full of cars like that.

He did notice, however, that a movie star was loitering in the hallway next to his door.

"Hey, man, looking good."

Aiden blinked, completely clueless as to why Hayden Carmichael would be here at his apartment. Look-alike gigs were booked through Aiden's agent, and they were as unpredictable as the actor himself. It had been a particularly quiet period for double work since Hayden was performing on Broadway. There had only been a few decoy situations over the winter, so Hayden could sneak away to . . . wherever it was he snuck away to.

He put out a hand and Aiden shook it.

"You just caught me. I'm on my way to the gym."

"Gotta stay in shape, I get it." The star tapped his stomach, which Aiden knew was sculpted into a perfect six-pack, the same way his was. "Can we talk?"

"Sure." Aiden led the way into his apartment, curious as to why Hayden was brimming with way more energy than usual. Which, for him, was saying something.

They'd spent a fair amount of time together, especially before Aiden's first time playing paparazzi distraction, so that he could learn all of Hayden's mannerisms. They weren't friends, but because Aiden had gotten access to him without cameras around, he'd seen what a lot of people didn't. The fidgeting, the snapping fingers, the drumming of his hands on every available surface were the little signs that the actor was feeling uncomfortable.

Today that energy was turned up to eleven.

As the two men stationed themselves at opposite ends of Aiden's kitchen, there was a gigantic goofy grin on Hayden's face. It was the total opposite of his typical smooth, sleek smile that Aiden spent hours practicing in front of the mirror.

"Want anything?" Aiden held up a mug and raised his eyebrows, a silent offer of coffee that he knew Hayden would turn down. The guy only drank kombucha and Perrier. Aiden poured himself a cup, grateful he'd never had to impersonate him during a meal.

Hayden shook his head and held out his phone. "There was a picture of me in the paper yesterday, but it wasn't me."

Aiden put down his mug and took the phone. It was a fuzzy shot, taken from a bit of a distance, of Aiden kneeling next to Bree as she lay on the sidewalk after walking into the door.

SUPER HAYDEN TO THE RESCUE, read the headline, referencing his upcoming movie.

Aiden's stomach twisted. Was Hayden upset? Had he come to tell Aiden in person they couldn't work together anymore?

Though unpredictable, the look-alike work was lucrative and helped smooth things over during months the apartment rented less. Aiden quickly calculated how much he could raise the prices on his listing to make up for the loss and still be able to stay on track with the final two years of his mortgage payoff plan.

"I'm so sorry." He handed back the phone with a slightly shaking hand. "I hope it didn't cause you any trouble."

Apologizing for something he couldn't avoid was ridiculous. It wasn't Aiden's fault his face looked like it did. Sure, he could grow out his beard and hair. Most of the winter he did, but he'd gotten a haircut last week, and the scruff he'd had yesterday had just been shaved off this morning. If there was one thing more miserable than New York in the stifling summer months, it was summer with a beard and long hair.

Of course the month he cut everything off would be the month Hayden Carmichael's first superhero movie came out. Plastered all over the city was the mirror image of Aiden's now beardless face.

"No trouble at all, my friend." Hayden took back his phone and slapped him on the back. The tension in Aiden's shoulders relaxed a little, but not completely. "In fact, it's perfect timing. I have just fallen in love with the most amazing woman on the planet."

He beamed at Aiden, clearly expecting a response to this.

"Uh, congratulations."

"She's in the business, but she's not an actress, so she really wants us to keep things quiet. I, obviously, want to make her happy."

There was a pause and Hayden tilted his head, waiting.

"Oh, right, of course." Leaning back against the counter, Aiden nodded, then crossed his arms and kept his attention focused on Hayden. The actor loved a captive audience, and Aiden knew from experience it would be better to just let him tell whatever story he wanted to without interruption, even if it took a while.

Today was no exception. Rather than continue right away, Hayden did a slow walk around the kitchen, drumming his fingers along the edge of the counter and then the cabinets.

He opened a few, took out a glass, put it on the counter, then turned back to Aiden. "I want to take her away for a few weeks, really make sure things are solid before we go public."

"That sounds nice." Honestly, anything not in the city sounded amazing.

"Yeah." Hayden wandered into the living room.

Aiden peeked at his watch. There was no plan today other than to work on the apartment, but that didn't mean he wanted Hayden hanging around for hours. "What does this have to do with me and Bree?"

"Oh, so you know her? That's even better." Hayden plopped onto the chair that faced the kitchen, placing his feet on the coffee table. "When my publicist called me to see if I wanted to make a statement about this sidewalk rescue, and didn't even realize it wasn't me, it gave me an idea."

Dread sank into Aiden's stomach. There was only one direction this could be going, and he didn't see any way to stop it from getting there.

"You could go around the city with this Briar chick, take her to restaurants and stuff. The press will be so focused on that, they won't think to go looking for me and my lady love anywhere else."

"Her name is Bree, and I don't think that's a good—"

He held up his hands. "I know it's a lot, which is why I'd pay way more than the other times you've helped me out. What's it been, six years we've known each other?"

"Seven."

Someone at Aiden's gym had noticed the similarity, and their sister worked in casting. When she'd arranged a quick meeting on set and even the crew had gotten the two mixed up, the movie star had asked Aiden to distract the paparazzi on his way home. What was supposed to have been a one-time thing had evolved into something more frequent.

But it was stuff like coming out the front door of a restaurant to walk to a car so Hayden could sneak out the back. Not spending weeks pretending to be the actor.

"Seven years and no one's ever noticed. That's clearly a sign we should do this."

Aiden tried not to roll his eyes. It wasn't a sign, it was just New Yorkers knowing how to keep their cool around celebrities. "I'd love to help, but I have my job and this apartment and—"

Hayden interrupted him with a number that almost stopped Aiden's heart in his chest. He grabbed the edge of the counter, not quite believing what he'd just heard.

It was enough to pay off the rest of the mortgage on the apartment with some to spare.

Aiden had already dipped into savings to get his associates to be a vet tech, then again when he'd done a few internships to get the needed experience to apply to vet schools. If he did this gig, it would be enough to get him through all four years of school without needing to work, without needing to worry about something happening to the apartment and derailing everything. He could sell as soon as the job was done instead of two years from now.

It was enough to be free.

"That's . . . really generous." He was proud of how calm his voice sounded.

"No, helping me get some quality alone time with my soulmate is generous." Hayden leaned back in the chair and put a hand over his heart. "She's everything to me."

Aiden wasn't sure how that could be true if he'd only known her for a few months. Thinking of the potential payout, he bit back what his usual response would be if a friend had said something so ridiculous and cheesy.

"That's wonderful you've found someone."

Aiden wasn't jealous, only incredulous that this would last. If things fell apart—like they always seemed to with Hayden and his leading ladies—it wouldn't be Aiden's fault.

Still, it would be prudent to make sure there was a clause in the contract that guaranteed he got paid at least a portion if things blew up during their romantic, month-long escape.

"So, do you have her number?" Hayden asked. "Brandy?"

Before Aiden could answer, there was a knock at his door.

He looked through the peephole, and his heart jumped into his throat. It was Bree.

EIGHT

Aiden analyzed the choices available to him, silently weighing the pros and cons of each.

He could pretend he wasn't here, and Bree would leave his hoodie on his door. He could sneak out into the hall so she couldn't see who was in her apartment.

But he knew what a Hayden fan she was. Meeting him would make her happy—something he was inexplicably and illogically very concerned with ensuring happened as often as possible.

Based on everything she'd shared so far, surely Bree would jump at Hayden's proposal. Why wouldn't she want a chance to make some money pretending to hang out with her favorite movie star? Especially if the request came directly from Hayden Carmichael himself.

It wasn't really much of a choice.

He shot a closed-mouth smile at Hayden. "Speak of the devil."

When he opened the door, Bree was standing in the hall-way, his hoodie in her hands, positively brimming with forest-sprite energy. She shifted her weight from foot to foot, her words tumbling out a mile a minute.

"Hi, here's the sweatshirt. Sorry I kept it. I wasn't trying to be weird. I just wanted to wash it, but I didn't know there wasn't a machine in the building. Then I had to go find a laundromat, but I didn't have change or any bills to make change at the machine, so I had to go find an ATM and—"

Aiden took the hoodie from her hands and smiled. "Thanks. Do you have time to come in for a minute?"

Bree's eyebrows shot up, and he noticed again how pale-blue her eyes were, the irises surrounded by a black ring. The contrast with her dark hair was breathtaking in a way that Aiden didn't want to think about right now. All that mattered was that, yes, she could absolutely fit the part of a celebrity's girlfriend.

Now the question was if she would be willing to.

"Sure, I have all afternoon. I've just been trying to figure out how to get Wi-Fi in my apartment. No one's had a phone up there in years. The cable company isn't even sure if there are the right hookups, and no one can come out until next week—"

"Just use my Wi-Fi." He grabbed the sticky note from the bulletin board next to the door that held all the information for guests.

Her eyes met his in a grateful disbelief, and Hayden Carmichael had to clear his throat to get her to look at him. It was probably the first time in Hayden's life that someone hadn't noticed him immediately when walking into a room, and Aiden felt an odd surge of triumph at being the focus of Bree's attention, albeit for a brief moment.

"Hey there, you must be Aiden's mystery damsel in distress."

Bree's eyes went from soft and grateful to wide and shocked in less than a second.

"I . . . he . . . I mean, yes." Two red spots appeared on her cheeks. Combined with her Minnesota accent, it was maximum adorableness that even a golden retriever puppy couldn't beat.

Hayden seemed to notice as well, his eyes lighting up as he stepped forward, hand outstretched. "Hi, I'm Hayden."

Bree stared at his hand as if it were going to bite her.

Hayden withdrew it, running it through his hair instead. "Do you live nearby?"

"She lives upstairs." Aiden saved her from needing to put words together.

Hayden flashed his famous smile, the sleek and smooth one, not the goofy one he'd had earlier. "Perfect. This will make things so much easier."

"Make what easier?" Bree found her voice, though it was quieter than Aiden had ever heard it. He took a step closer to her, ready to jump to her aid in case she fell.

"Whenever I'm looking to take a bit of a break, Aiden here helps me out by distracting the paparazzi." The actor reached over and slapped Aiden's shoulder, harder than was necessary. "This time, since I'll be away longer than usual, I thought it would be a good idea to have me—Aiden here, I mean—be seen escorting some lovely lady around town."

Hayden grinned and Bree trembled visibly. She leaned against the couch to hide it, and Aiden took another step in her direction.

"So you want me to date Aiden?" Her eyes flicked to his, then down to his feet. He stepped back.

"Fake date. No need for things to go anywhere you don't want them to." Hayden gave her a wink that had her lean ever further onto the couch, like her legs wouldn't hold her up anymore. "Since someone took a photo of him helping you out when you fell yesterday, there's already a great baked-in story the press will go gaga over. It doesn't need to be real, just real enough to fool them."

Bree's gaze turned to Aiden's, as if to see what he thought of the whole situation.

"It's a paying gig," Aiden said.

"I don't need the money."

Aiden raised his eyebrows at that. Unless she'd inherited a pile of cash along with the apartment or had come with years of savings, there was no way she'd say no to the kind of money Hayden was willing to pay.

"I mean, I won't say no to money. Who would, heh." Her face paled when an awkward chuckle left her mouth. "I've just never done anything like this before, so I don't really know—"

Clearly picking up on Bree's reaction to him, the actor's eyes lit up. "What if I took some time after my trip to hang out with you a little, to thank you for what a great job I'm sure you'll do?"

"You-you'd want to hang out with me?" Bree's voice pitched up an octave on the last word, and Aiden's stomach dropped. "What would we do?"

Hayden gave a casual shrug, the one that Aiden had spent hours learning to imitate. "Whatever you want. I'll take you to some of my favorite places in the city."

"That would be amazing." Her words rushed out in a single breath, like a sigh.

"You dream it, and I'll make it happen."

At this, one of Hayden's most iconic lines from *Escape to New York*, Bree visibly swooned, and Aiden's hands clenched into fists at his sides.

Then Bree inhaled, and her eyes flicked between him and Hayden. "Could I think about it? I'm not an actor, and I don't really know Aiden."

"Of course, no worries." Hayden flashed his smile at them

both with a subtle wink at Aiden. "Why don't I head out and let the two of you talk about it? I'll have my people work on the paperwork and get it over to you both later tonight so you can see what it'll involve."

"So soon?"

The look of pure astonishment on Bree's face was identical to the one Aiden had seen right before she'd walked into the door yesterday. It was the same adoring gaze she'd had when she'd opened her eyes lying on the sidewalk.

Except now it was directed at the real Hayden Carmichael. Hoping he was being inconspicuous, Aiden took a few deep breaths, trying to loosen the tightness in his chest.

She wouldn't do it for the money, but she would do it for an hour with the charming and captivating Hayden Carmichael. She'd put up with weeks of awkwardness, of Aiden's stiff and uncomfortable manners, just for a chance to bathe in the aura of her favorite movie star.

"The sooner the better," Hayden said. "Aiden here knows the ropes—he's done it plenty of times before for me. It'll just be a few well-timed outings with a tipoff to the paparazzi about where you'll be, and they'll be so busy writing stories they won't even think to look for me."

"You really think I can do it?" Bree's voice was breathy, low, and unsteady.

"A gorgeous, smart girl like you? Of course."

Again, her eyes turned to Aiden's, as if seeking his help, his confirmation. The softness of them, the vulnerability, urged him to give her what she wanted. Yet the pain in his chest made him want to deny it to Hayden.

But that wasn't logical. That didn't fit into his plan. The thousands of dollars Hayden was willing to pay him, however, fit perfectly into his plan, whereas feelings for Bree did not.

So he smiled at her and gave her a reassuring nod. "It'll be fine, don't worry. I'll take care of everything."

Bree glanced between the two men, taking in their identical faces, their identical expressions of eagerness and reassurance.

Then she turned on her heel and ran out of the apartment.

NINE

There were some things you had to discuss with your best friend before you could make a decision, and fake dating your movie star crush's look-alike was one of them.

It was agony waiting until early evening, when Leigh's coffee shop would be closed. Her usual go-to rainy day activity of watching Hayden Carmichael movies was obviously not an option, so she did her best to pass the time cleaning her shoebox apartment and unpacking a few things. Nothing major, nothing permanent, but the things she always took with her when she traveled that felt most like home.

She was half expecting Aiden or—holy cow, she'd really met him, hadn't she?—Hayden Carmichael to come up to talk to her, but no one knocked on her door all day. That could have been a sign she shouldn't do it.

More likely, they were just giving her space to decide. It was clearly important to both of them, but Bree got the impression Aiden would have preferred someone else.

He said he'd take care of everything. In less than two days, he'd picked up on the same thing her family and friends in Minnesota already knew.

Bree was a total disaster, couldn't be relied on, and generally screwed things up. She needed someone else to take care of things. Why would he want to do something this important with someone like her?

Naturally, her best friend knew that something was wrong the second she picked up the phone.

"Hi," Bree said, in what she was sure was her normal voice.

"Oh no," said Leigh. "Did the café mission not go well? Have we already gotten to three terrible things?"

"Not exactly?" Bree collapsed onto her couch, a flowery patterned love seat that must have been there long before Agatha had been born. Everything in here had that old, antiquey feeling. It was all nice, way nicer than anything Bree had ever owned, but ancient. She felt terrible thinking about it, but she wondered how much she could get for it all. Maybe enough so she wouldn't need to fake date Aiden to survive longer than a few months in New York.

"So, something good happened?"

"A few good things actually." Bree hesitated. This was a big bombshell to drop. She should ease into it. "My neighbor gave me his Wi-Fi password. So I don't have to worry about calling the phone company quite yet."

"That's so sweet of him." Leigh sounded genuinely happy for her, but she also had a tired edge to her voice.

"I'm sorry, you must be beat. We can catch up tomorrow."

Yes, that would be better anyway. She'd have time to think things through on her own, convince herself it had really happened. What if she'd hallucinated the entire thing? No sense getting Leigh's input on something that might not even be real.

"Oh no you don't." Leigh's 'mom voice' had been activated. "You said a few good things. That was just one. You're not getting out of this so easily."

"Well . . . I met Hayden Carmichael."

It sounded like an explosion had happened on the other side of the phone.

"Are you serious! What the heck, Bree? Talk about burying the lead."

Bree could picture the way Leigh was probably shaking her head right now. "There's more."

"If you tell me he asked you out on a date, then you are literally the worst friend ever for making me feel even a tiny bit sorry for you."

"Not exactly. He was in my neighbor Aiden's apartment. They were talking about him doing a look-alike thing, a decoy job."

"Wait, your neighbor's named Hayden too?" Leigh sounded confused.

"Aiden, with an A, not an H."

"And he looks like Hayden Carmichael?"

"Uh, yes."

There was a pause, then more of Leigh's mom voice. "Is there a reason you didn't mention this when you talked about him before?"

"Well, he told me his name was AJ, and he doesn't look exactly like him." Bree stood up, then sat down again, crossing her legs in the opposite direction. "He has a mole behind his ear that Hayden doesn't have."

The other end of the phone was silent.

"Uh, Leigh? Still there?"

"Yes, I'm here. Just looking up how soon I can get a flight out there so I can smack some sense into you in person."

Bree snorted, then Leigh giggled, and that's all it took for the two of them to start laughing. It felt good to laugh with her best friend, to have one familiar thing in the midst of everything that had happened in the past two days.

"Okay, so they were talking about a look-alike gig," Leigh said, a bit out of breath. "For like a movie or something? Did they invite you on the set? I could definitely time my visit for that. No smacking, I promise."

"No, Hayden Carmichael wants to take a break, go off the grid for a while." Bree leaned back on the couch, trying to keep the envy out of her voice. Flying away somewhere new sounded like heaven right now.

"Makes sense. His new movie is coming out soon, and he's doing that play on Broadway. He must be exhausted."

"He asked Aiden to pretend to be him for a few weeks and said that, with a girlfriend, it would be even more convincing."

Bree ran her hand along the rough fabric of the couch and let Leigh connect the dots. It didn't take long.

"That's absolutely bonkers."

"I know, right?" She stood up and walked the three steps into the kitchen. The dishes and leftovers from her bored day inside covered the counter. "There's no way I can do it. I barely know my neighbor. That would be so weird, to pretend to date him." She picked up a bowl and put it into the sink.

"Would you have to kiss him?"

She almost dropped the glass in her hand. "Leigh, is that really the first thing you thought of?"

"How is it not the first thing you thought of? How long has it been since you were on a date? I've been on more than you in the past few years."

Bree gripped the glass, then set it carefully into the sink.

"That was on purpose, so that when I moved to New York one day, I wouldn't have to either convince someone to come with me or leave them behind. Which was a good idea, apparently."

Of course, there'd been fun and flings while roaming all over. But never anyone in Minnesota, never anyone she'd have to leave behind. Being known as the flighty Peterson sister in a small town wasn't easy for lots of reasons, but in this one way, it had been a blessing.

"So you agree with me," Leigh said. "You should do this."

"I didn't not date for years just so I could fake date a Hayden Carmichael look-alike." Especially one who, at this point, had already figured out what a disaster she was.

"You're frowning right now, aren't you?"

Bree dropped the expression and picked up a sponge. "Geez Louise, are you sure you're not psychic?"

"Only with you and my girls." Leigh paused. "And for when it's going to be a really rough day at the café."

"How was your day?" Sponge abandoned, she headed back into the living room.

"Oh no, don't even try to change the subject. You're doing this."

"What if I do have to kiss him?" The thought had her heart pounding. Aiden was gorgeous, but there was no sign he thought the same of Bree.

"Make that one of your conditions. Don't agree to anything you don't want to do. There'll be a contract or something, right?"

Bree leaned against the couch and looked around. Was the apartment smaller than it had been yesterday? "I guess, but I kind of ran off before they could give me details."

Leigh chuckled, and Bree found herself smiling a little, too, before she realized something.

"I'll probably have to sign an NDA. I won't be able to talk to you about it."

"NDAs don't apply to best friends," Leigh said confidently. "Besides, I already know about it now. What's the offer exactly?"

"It's a ton of money, which will be nice, but Hayden said he'd—that we could—you know, hang out when he was back from wherever he's going." Her hands traced the flower pattern on the couch.

"Make sure that's in the contract, then. Don't let yourself get swindled by these Hollywood types. Your neighbor's done this before, so he should know what to pay attention to."

"I don't think he's ever done anything like this. He didn't seem to want Hayden to ask me about it." Bree let out the words she'd been feeling all day. "I don't think he likes me very much."

"That's good." Leigh's voice was the brisk and professional one she always used with vendors. "No risk of falling for each other or anything silly like that."

Silly. Yes, it would be, wouldn't it, to have a crush on your kind and generous neighbor who looks just like your celebrity crush. It would be a very Birdbrain Bree thing to do. Not something New York Bree would do.

"Enough stalling. You wanted a sign to stay in New York?" Leigh chuckled. "This is it. Now get down there and work out the details to make your dreams come true."

TEN

Aiden was just finishing up some trim on the living room baseboards when his phone dinged with a new email. A quick swipe of his fingers revealed the contracts had arrived.

Paintbrush still in one hand, he rocked back on his heels. Even after thinking about it all day, he hadn't decided whether he wanted her to agree or not. It wasn't that he didn't think Bree could do it, but it would mean spending so much time with her when he knew that was a dangerous thing.

He put away the paint in the hall closet, then paused to consider the mirror she'd so carefully touched yesterday. It wasn't real gold, just something he'd picked up cheap at a flea market, but she'd looked at it like it was something special. Almost like how Hayden had been looking at her.

His reflection in the mirror frowned at him.

Hayden had left soon after Bree had, telling Aiden how perfect her "bright-eyed ingénue" look would be for the gig, already assuming she'd agree. Hot, petty jealousy had Aiden hoping Bree would say no, just to prove the cocky celebrity wrong. Now that he had the contracts, he had no reason not to go upstairs and talk to her.

Just as he grabbed his key from the dedicated hook by the door, there was a knock. Aiden opened the door to find Bree, her face lined with worry.

His heart sank. She wasn't an actor or an impersonator. She might be free-spirited, but that didn't mean she was willing to do something that thrust her into the public eye, with no training or preparation.

"I think I want to do it."

He stepped back, and the door swung open.

"Really?"

Bree *did* want to be attached to Hayden, after all. For her, this wasn't about the money but about the chance to spend time with the movie star. For Aiden, it was about having enough money to pay off the mortgage and cut ties with New York forever.

That was the image he tried to keep top of mind when he smiled at Bree. "Great. Come on in. I just got the contracts."

Then she gave him the hint of a smile back, brushing past him on her way in to let her flowery scent waft over him. His heart raced, and his stomach gave a traitorous churn.

Bree paced around the living room a bit before finally sitting on the easy chair across from the couch. Clearly, she was nervous and didn't want to sit too close to him.

His stomach twisted in knots at the thought that she wasn't even a little attracted to him.

"You'll have to learn to look more comfortable around me if you want to do this." With his tone, he tried to make it a joke, but it didn't seem to translate.

"I mean, I think I want to do it." Her fingers twisted around a lock of dark hair. "But I'm still not sure I want to do it."

He breathed in slowly and leaned back on the couch. That was probably the single most confusing thing Aiden had ever heard. "Isn't it what you always dreamed of? Spending time with Hayden Carmichael in magical New York City?"

She shot him a look. So the joke she missed, but the sarcasm she heard.

"I haven't had the best introduction to the city. I was honestly thinking of going home just this morning."

His body lurched, and he grabbed the back of the couch to steady himself.

No, no, no.

Aiden knew how Hayden could be, and he said he only wanted her. If she did leave, he'd be stuck with this apartment another two years. Now that he knew there was a way to go to vet school without worrying about paying off the last of his debts, he couldn't let that slip away.

"It's only been two days. You got hurt yesterday, and it was raining today."

"Exactly. It's not like this place has been the most welcoming." She looked down at the trinkets arranged on the coffee table between them. She took a candle in her hand and sniffed deeply, then lifted her eyes to meet his. "Well, you've been really nice. Thank you."

He waved that away. As if he could have been anything other than nice to her. "I know we don't know each other that well, but I've been here a long time. I can show you the nice parts of the city. Introduce you to it the right way."

"All while pretending to be Hayden and his new girlfriend?"

"I mean, this way it'll be free." Aiden gave his best true smile, not his Hayden impersonation.

At this, she did laugh, and Aiden's shoulders relaxed.

"Let's make sure that's in the contract." She scooted forward in the chair and looked at him expectantly. "Do you need my email to send them?"

"I should probably get your phone number too." He leaned toward her, stretching himself across the coffee table, and cleared his throat. "Even if we don't do this, you can always call me if you have any trouble with your apartment."

She rattled off both with the ease of someone who lived in a small town and knew everyone.

"I hope you don't just give those out to anyone who asks. This isn't small-town Minnesota."

"I know." Her cheeks flushed, however, setting off the bright-blue color of her eyes. They were wide and trusting, hopeful and eager. Just like he'd been all those years ago. Except she was an adult who should know better.

At least she seemed to know how to read a contract. Within a few minutes of opening the document on her phone, she'd asked several sharp questions that Aiden wondered why he'd never asked before.

"You're really good at this."

She flushed again, this time her eyes sparkling with pleasure. "I've helped Leigh out with the coffee shop's paperwork sometimes."

"Have you ever thought of becoming a lawyer?"

"Why?" She looked up from her phone, and her eyebrows drew together. "I liked my job at the café. I got to talk to people all day, help them, and be involved in the community. It was great."

"A lawyer does that too."

"At my age, I'm not looking to go to school for a million years and pay hundreds of thousands of dollars just to have a few extra letters after my name." Her eyes widened. "I mean, it's awesome if that's what you want to do. The vet thing, I mean. Is that what you'll use the money for?"

Though the couch was soft and solid under his legs, the

world shifted, and his stomach dropped. She remembered that detail about him?

"Yes." It was more complex than that, but at the end of the day, it's what the money would allow him to do.

"Why a vet?"

"Why do you want to know?"

She scooched to the edge of her chair and tucked her hair behind her ears. "I'd like to know a bit more about you if we're going to do this together."

He leaned back on the couch. That wasn't a terrible idea. "We had a dog when I was little. She got sick, and the vet was able to operate on her. I just thought it was so cool that you could save animals like that."

It wasn't the whole story, but there was no way to put it all into words. How hard it had been for him as a twelve-year-old to see the dog he'd held on to as he learned to walk no longer able to make her way up the stairs. How pitiful she'd been, sitting in her dog bed, whining but unable to play the way she used to. How scary it had been to see the stiffness in her joints after just a short walk around the block.

"There's more to it than that. I can tell." Bree's curious gaze was like a hot brand on his face. "You don't have to tell me if you don't want to, but I can tell there are details inside your head that you need to say out loud for me to understand."

A horn blared outside, and Aiden's eyes flicked away from Bree to the window. The busy street outside was blocked by curtains, but muted sunlight still filtered through. Margot had always gotten angry with him whenever he held back on details. It seemed unfair to compare her to Bree, who was ten years older. Aiden certainly wasn't the same as he'd been a decade ago.

Though in many ways, Bree reminded him of his younger

self. Full of energy and excitement. The person he'd been before the city had worn him down to his rough and raw edges.

He swallowed thickly past the lump that had appeared in his throat and looked back at her. "Well, I'm going to use the money to become a vet. You could use it to do whatever you want."

Bree shook her head, and he leaned back even more into the couch to avoid getting another intoxicating whiff of her hair. "I wouldn't even know where to start. You're really brave to go for it and smart to have it all planned out, but that's just . . . not me."

"What are you talking about? You were brave and smart to make this big move."

She rolled her eyes. "I inherited an apartment, then bought a plane ticket."

"You saw an opportunity and took it. Sounds pretty smart to me."

She raised a shoulder, and her gaze wandered to the same window he'd just been staring at. "I'm nothing special."

He set his hands on his knees and leaned forward. "Trust me, you've got what it takes to make it here."

The plans were already forming in his head on how to make sure she loved this city, make sure she never left. Make sure they'd get to the end of this contract so he could finally leave.

"Brave, rude, smart . . . anything else a newbie New Yorker needs to know?" She bit her bottom lip.

"I can teach you all that, too, if we do this thing together." He gestured to their phones, which they'd both forgotten in their conversation. "I hope you'll agree. You're much easier to talk to than some of the actors I've been around."

She waved away the compliment and looked back at her phone. After scrolling through the contract again, her eyes flicked back up to his. "What's he like?"

He didn't have to ask her who she meant, but he wasn't sure

how much she really wanted to know. Telling her the real reason Hayden wanted this break wouldn't help anything. She was still hoping to hang out with him, probably even date him for real. This wasn't about the money for her.

"Actors are . . . " He rubbed the back of his neck and tried to think of the right words that were true, but not too true. "They don't live in the same world we do. Image is really important to them. It has to be. Your job at the coffee shop was helping people, but you could be yourself when you did it. Their job is looking and acting a certain way."

"Are you saying he's self-centered and shallow?" She let out a short, choppy laugh that hit him right in the chest. "What guy isn't?"

I'm not, he wanted to say, except he kind of was.

Between the personal training and the impersonating, his work required him to look a certain way, act a certain way. A not-so-insignificant amount of mental energy was spent on counting his macros and remembering to book his next waxing appointment.

That would be fine if that were his goal in life to be a famous actor or a social media influencer or something. But he didn't want that. He wanted a simple life in a small town, working with animals. Animals didn't care what you looked like or how much money you had.

"Hayden's been famous since he was fifteen and was doing theater and commercials before that. He had a way different childhood than most people."

The actor had shared some of his upbringing with Aiden, and they'd bonded over what terrible dads they'd both had. But that wasn't something Bree needed to know to make her decision.

Aiden ran a hand over his jaw. "Is his ego slightly larger than average? Sure, but he's not a bad guy."

"Not a bad guy?" Bree repeated with an arched eyebrow. "I'd love to hear how you talk about people you don't like."

Her eyes went back to the contract on her phone, and she pointed out a few more inconsistencies and parts they could ask to have clarified. It was more complicated than his normal impersonating contract. It asked for at least one public appearance per week, and that they should appear "close," but that wasn't defined. Bree caught that immediately.

"Can we have them specify what we will and won't do?" She flushed. "Like no kissing?"

"Of course," he said, even as disappointment swept over him. "I won't sign anything unless you're totally comfortable with it."

She was quiet for a moment. "Thank you. I'm not used to anyone worrying about me, except for Leigh."

Fire flickered in Aiden's chest. Was that all she had?

"No family back in Minnesota worried about you being on your own in New York?"

"Not really." Her fingers tangled in the ends of her hair. "My family's expecting me to turn around after a few weeks, and they're probably right. I'm not known for sticking with things for very long."

He inhaled slowly and let out the breath through his nose. Signing this contract with Bree was even more dangerous than he thought. She was practically promising him she'd bail on it. There was the risk he'd put his personal training on hold for weeks and not get the full payout of the impersonating gig. He'd be worse off than when he started. He couldn't let that happen.

"Even with the promise of hanging out with Hayden at the end of it?"

Her eyes lit up at this.

"It's something I never dreamed would be possible," she said with a sigh that had his heart sinking.

It shouldn't matter if she preferred the movie star over him. No woman on earth would pick Aiden over Hayden.

Besides, he wasn't interested in Bree. So what if she could read a contract and smelled like flowery heaven and was fearless and brave. It didn't change who she was. She was chaos personified. No plan, all vibes.

The opposite of what he wanted in his life.

"I do have one more question for you." Bree bit her lip and looked up at him, her eyes anxious, and he held his breath. "Why do you want to do this with me?"

The soft fabric of the couch slid under him as he shifted around and exhaled slowly. "Why wouldn't I want to do this with you?"

Bree lifted a shoulder. "Oh, you know. Because you're . . . you." She waved her hand toward herself. "And I'm, well, me."

Aiden inhaled deeply through his nose, his chest rising even as it constricted into a tight little ball. "I wouldn't want to do this with anyone else."

There was a sharp intake of breath, and a smile played on the edges of her lips.

"Then I guess we're doing this."

Their eyes locked, and something passed between them, a shuddering kind of hesitancy. Like if he wrapped her in his arms, she would stay there forever.

Then he blinked, and it was gone, whatever it was.

"I guess so."

ELEVEN

Day three in New York dawned sunny and bright, and Bree managed to make her way to the coffee shop without getting lost. It was a small victory, but she savored it, along with the slight glimmer of recognition in the barista's eyes when Bree gave her order.

No more Birdbrain Bree.

Warm to-go cup in hand, she stepped out onto the sidewalk and breathed in. Optimism settled over her like pulling on a favorite jacket. The start of her new life might have finally arrived, one full of routines and familiar faces, just like it had been in Minnesota.

Unlike in Minnesota, this life involved getting ready for a date with a movie star.

She took a sip of her drink and walked toward the crosswalk. Her eyes slid over the faces she passed, and she sighed at the lack of recognition in their return gazes. It wasn't really a date, of course, and Aiden was a look-alike. Who didn't want to do this gig with anyone else.

A woman wearing giant headphones with a level sticking out of her backpack looked at her twice, a quick flick of her eyes up and down, and a thrill went through Bree. If they did their job well, people would look at her like she was a movie star's girlfriend. Like she was someone important.

With a spring in her step, Bree walked another block, the sunny day stretching out before her like a blank canvas, waiting for inspiration to strike. She turned a corner and the green railings of a subway appeared. A plan for the day materialized in an instant.

If people were going to be looking at her like she was Hayden Carmichael's girlfriend, she'd better dress the part.

She hurried down the stairs, recognizing that even she shouldn't be this excited about her first subway ride. In the dozen or so times she'd been to the Cities, she'd taken the light rail to get around town, but this was the New York City Subway. The Metro in Minneapolis St. Paul only had two lines. New York had . . . well, she didn't know exactly, but definitely more than two.

Warm air blasted her face, and she choked on the thick, metallic smell it carried. She stumbled on the stairs but righted herself quickly. People passed her without stopping or even glancing at her, as if someone standing at subway entrances gagging was a regular thing.

Pushing aside the rising sense of unease, she ran a hand over her braid, checking for flyaways, squared her shoulders, and continued down into the tunnel tinged orange by the incandescent lights.

A MetroCard shouldn't have made her so happy, especially after the fight with the machine it took to get it, but Bree clutched it tight like it was a golden ticket to a magical candy factory. She ignored the people who flowed behind her while she stared at the subway map, until one of them muttered something about tourists and hot embarrassment flooded her cheeks. Quickly settling on her lucky number six, she decided she'd pick a train at random and get off after that many stops to see what New York had in store for her.

After only three stops, however, she almost got off, wondering if she was on some kind of prank show.

In that short time, someone almost sat on her, a couple had a screaming match right in front of her, and a group of guys swung from the poles in a packed train. This was on top of a smell that she was pretty sure meant someone had used the train as a bathroom recently.

Her adventures across the country up until now should have prepared her for things like this, but discomfort was easy when you knew you could leave whenever you wanted. What would have been a hilarious story for Leigh on the long drive home from the bus station was now her daily life.

No one else seemed bothered, and if she wanted to be a New Yorker, it couldn't bother her. So, she stuck it out and stayed on the subway, even though every part of her was itchy with the familiar need to escape. She held her breath and kept her eyes glued to an ad for an energy drink for the next three stops until she could escape and bolt out the doors.

Breathing in fresh air at last at the top of the stairs, she considered calling Leigh to tell her all about it. Or she could save it until their video call they had planned that night.

Thanks to Aiden sharing his Wi-Fi, she didn't have to worry about using up too much of her phone's data. Her lips turned up in a smile. He was incredibly thoughtful.

The neighborhood she'd walked out of the subway into was completely different from the quiet, tree-lined street of her apartment building. It buzzed with a different kind of energy, the crowds thicker, the buildings taller. The streets were lined with clothing stores, big brands she recognized and some she'd only seen online. Everyone was either in a hurry or stopping to take tons of pictures.

The smile on her face widened, and she quickly snapped a selfie before eagerly continuing down the block. Wherever her random subway had taken her, it was clearly somewhere people wanted to be. She'd made the right choice.

The feeling of rightness only got stronger when she turned a corner and there, across the street, was the same place teenage Hayden took his love interest shopping in *Escape to New York*.

Bree only briefly wondered if thirty-something Hayden's girlfriend would shop at Macy's before hurrying across the small plaza in front of the entrance and through the doors. The smell of perfume mingled with flowers and the hundreds of bodies milling around the white marble floors.

She breathed it all in, then set off to find the perfect outfit for her date with a movie star.

Three hours later, the novelty of a New York shopping spree had worn off. It wasn't quite the same as a movie montage. Her arms were tired, her feet hurt, and the sales people had been few and far between. There'd been no giggling best friend or brooding crush to give her input, so she'd sent pictures of things she wasn't sure of to Leigh, and reminded herself that she could always return things if she tried them on again at home and didn't like them.

She frowned as she maneuvered around people on the packed sidewalk outside the store, looking for a cab. Getting on a packed and smelly subway right now was the last thing she wanted to do. If she could even find a station. That first one had just appeared for her.

She looked up and realized she didn't see Macy's anymore, and nothing looked familiar. A quick look at her phone revealed it had gone dead. Had she forgotten to charge it overnight? Probably.

The thrill of flagging down her first cab was quickly squelched by the driver informing her he was headed downtown. Why that made a difference, Bree would never know, since he drove off before she could ask him. So she wandered to the other side of the street and tried there.

It shouldn't be this hard, she thought, even as she managed to get a cab going in the right direction. This wasn't a vacation. She was living here now. If this was where she was supposed to be, shouldn't things be easier?

Her gut was still roiling by the time she was dropped off at her building, however, and the rest of the afternoon stretched out before her, totally empty. Back home, she'd have either just been finishing or just starting a shift at the café. Leigh would be catching her up on whatever her girls were doing, and the regulars would have their stories to share as well. Maybe she should look for a job sooner than she'd planned.

Except she didn't need the money. Aiden's agent had negotiated more than what was in the original contract, which had already seemed like a fortune to Bree for just walking around New York with a hot guy. Money wouldn't be a problem for a while.

She walked up the stairs, trying to think of what to do with the rest of her day. Her arms and legs were sore like she'd just worked a double at the café, and the shiny excitement she'd had that morning had vanished. Regret and doubt trickled into the echoing hallway, and not just because she'd forgotten there was an elevator.

What if none of the clothes she picked out were right for whatever Aiden had planned? Should she have asked his opinion on them? Maybe she should see if he was downstairs. She turned, bags still slung over her arms, but the thought of that adorable apartment, with the coordinating colors and effortlessly cozy style, stopped her in her tracks.

He said he wouldn't want to do this with anyone else, but that didn't mean he really wanted to do it with *her*. Why would he? Birdbrain Bree couldn't even handle the subway or shopping on her own. Buying clothes to make her look like someone Hayden would date wouldn't change how Aiden saw her, and he was the one who'd have to put up with her for the next four weeks.

What if he changed his mind and canceled the contract? Then she'd never get her picture in the paper, never get to hang out with Hayden Carmichael. All her New York City dreams would disappear.

She turned back to her apartment and opened the door. Taking in the faded couch and bulky furniture, the sign was as clear as the sky outside: she needed to redo it all. Now.

She loved Aunt Agatha, and hated the thought of getting rid of anything in her parents' apartment, but as she squeezed by the oversized love seat with all her shopping, she knew she couldn't live like this long term.

As far as Bree knew, Agatha hadn't been back since she left in her early twenties. The apartment had to feel like Bree's, since it was hers now. More importantly, it had to feel like the apartment of someone responsible enough that Aiden would want to work with them.

Bree set her shopping down on the couch to put away later and turned in a slow circle to see where she might be able to get started. Now that she really looked at everything, nothing really stood out as "Aunt Agatha." The old woman's style had been much sleeker and more modern.

Relief settled in Bree's chest. If any of this had been important to Agatha, she'd have shipped it out to Minnesota. Nothing had to stay that Bree didn't want or need.

A few minutes later, she was dragging a dining room chair into the hallway, ignoring the ache in her arms. She didn't need eight, and probably didn't even need the table either, but that was too big to move on her own. The door across the hall opened up.

"What do you think you're doing?"

The old woman glared at her, her accent so classically New York that Bree smiled despite the harsh tone.

"Ope, sorry, didn't see ya there." Bree stood up straight and stepped out from behind the chair to extend a hand. "I didn't get to introduce myself the other day. I'm Bree Peterson."

She didn't move, just glared at Bree from behind a pair of thick-rimmed glasses. "I know who you are. I didn't ask that. I asked what you think you're doing with that chair."

Bree swept a hand over her hair, smoothing down the sweaty flyaways around her face. "I thought I'd put a few out on the street. I don't need this many."

"They're a *set*. They can't be separated."

"Alrighty then. I'll put them all out there. A set is a bit much for just me on my own."

It felt good to say it. Decisive. The kind of thing Aiden would notice and appreciate.

The woman was staring at her as if she'd just said she was going to start throwing puppies out the window. Bree stepped back behind the chair again.

"Not even here a week and getting rid of Agatha's family's things?" The woman emerged from her doorway to stick a finger out and point it at Bree. "You should be ashamed."

"You knew my aunt?" Bree perked up at this. Judging by her age, she must have known Agatha when she was a girl, before she moved to Minnesota.

A thousand questions filled her brain. Agatha had never talked about her time in the city, would always just say simply that she grew up in New York City and moved to the Midwest for a job. Even after years of asking, Bree had never gotten the full story. Did this woman have it?

"You can't put things on the street whenever you want."

Squaring her shoulders, Bree gripped the chair and tried to focus on why she was doing this. Her New York dream started today.

"I saw at least a dozen piles of furniture in front of buildings when I went to the coffee shop and subway this morning."

"It's against the building's rules."

Bree's stomach sank. She'd gotten a whole sheet of papers from the super, but hadn't looked through them yet. Uncertainty and the weight of the chair had her arms shaking.

This could be fate telling her not to mess with anything in the apartment. That she wasn't supposed to make it her own. That she wasn't supposed to stay. Maybe there was some other way to show Aiden she was not a complete disaster, but nothing came to mind.

Of course that would be the exact moment he came up the stairs.

"Mrs. Wilson, are you causing trouble again?"

Like magic, the old woman's expression changed when Aiden appeared at the end of the hall, his hair tousled and lips turned up in a smile. Mrs. Wilson's eyes went soft, and the lines in her forehead smoothed out.

"Aiden, dear, I didn't know you were back in the building."

He gave her a wide smile, his eyes flicking briefly to Bree. Her heart pounded as his critical eye took her in, still standing there with the dining room chair in her hands and the door to her apartment wide open.

"Don't lock yourself out again."

Heat traveled up her neck, and she patted her pocket to show him she had her keys. He nodded and attention shifted back to Mrs. Wilson.

"Now, what's the problem with my friend Bree here doing a little redecorating?"

An excited little flutter went through her chest at the word friend. Mrs. Wilson frowned at it, however, and crossed her arms tightly across her chest.

"A friend, huh? My granddaughter Zara just broke up with her boyfriend, you know."

Aiden leaned against the wall by Mrs. Wilson's door, his attention entirely on the grumpy old woman in the middle of the hallway. "Good for her. He always sounded like a jerk."

"She'll be by this weekend like she always is. You're always welcome to Sunday lunch."

"I'll let you know, Mrs. Wilson. I may have to work."

"You're always working. Doesn't seem fair that woman never paid her fair share of things, leaving it all on you."

Heart racing, Bree looked quickly at Aiden, whose bright expression hadn't changed, other than a slight tightening around his eyes.

What woman? Bree burned with curiosity.

Aiden wasn't rising to Mrs. Wilson's bait, and changed topics as smoothly as Bree did whenever someone brought up politics at the café.

"Even if I can't come to lunch, I'll be staying here for the next few weeks, so you'll see plenty of me, don't worry."

Mrs. Wilson leaned over and patted his cheek affectionately. "Be sure to stop by whenever you have the time." Then the old woman shot a withering glance in Bree's direction. "And talk some sense into this one. Those chairs are antiques. I remember when Agatha's mother bought them. She was so pleased, so proud."

"Why don't you take 'em?" Bree said and pushed the chair toward her, the legs scraping against the hallway's tile floor. "I really don't need them, and I want them to go to someone who'll use them."

"I already have a dining room set." Mrs. Wilson sniffed, and her eyes swiveled back to Aiden, who was looking between the two women like he was trying not to laugh.

Disappointment settled in Bree's stomach. She wasn't doing a great job showing him how capable she was.

"I'd be more than happy to give them to your granddaughter, if she'd like them." It was the first thing she thought of, but once she said it, a sense of rightness replaced the disappointment in her. She could find a solution on her own—no need for Aiden to come to her rescue yet again. She tried not to look too pleased with herself.

Mrs. Wilson was quiet for a moment, but she looked slightly mollified. "How would you get them out to Brooklyn?"

"If you're sure she wants them, then I'll find a way to get them to her." Bree had rented cars and driven all over the states. New York couldn't be that different.

"Tony has a truck, Mrs. Wilson," Aiden said. "He'll let me borrow it."

Hot frustration struck her like a blow. He still thought he had to help her.

"You're an angel. I'll tell her to expect your call. Now, I need to get back to my book."

She waved at Aiden, gave Bree a glare that was only slightly less irritated than earlier, and closed the door.

"I would have rented a truck."

Aiden pushed himself off the wall and walked toward her. "Tony won't mind. It'll take an hour or two, no big deal."

It was a big deal to Bree, but she couldn't even think of how to explain that.

"Well, thanks." Frustrated as she may be, she'd still be polite. She turned to go back into her apartment, chair in hand, then noticed he wasn't heading back toward the stairs. "Did you need something?"

"I wanted to go over the plan for the next few weeks." He reached out and took the chair from her.

Right, a plan. Something this major needed to follow guidelines.

There was a very lengthy contract she'd signed that required specific situations and interactions. Aiden wasn't the type to wing it, the way he still thought Bree would. The way she probably would end up doing it, no matter how much she wished she could change. Today was proof of that.

"This is really happening, huh? I didn't just dream the whole thing when I hit my head?"

The corner of his lip turned up, a small dimple appearing on his chin. A dimple Hayden Carmichael certainly didn't have. Bree's breath hitched. Aiden took a step closer, the chair between them.

"This is really happening," he said.

"Uffda." Bree shook her head and took a step back. "Hayden must really need this break."

Something flickered across Aiden's face, but it was gone before Bree could even guess what it might be.

"Well, come on in and we'll take a look. I have more than enough places to sit, doncha know."

He chuckled, and warmth filled her chest. Maybe this wouldn't be so terrible. Maybe he wouldn't mind spending time with a total disaster.

Then she caught the look of shock and displeasure on his face when he walked into her apartment, and any hope of impressing him today disappeared instantly. He might not want to do this with anyone else, but that didn't mean he'd enjoy spending the time with her.

TWELVE

Two steps into Bree's apartment, and Aiden could see why she wanted to get rid of some furniture. Cramped was an understatement. Between the dark fabrics and outsized pieces, it felt like the walls were closing in on him.

He let the design ideas swirl away in his head as he put the chair back at the dining room table. "How big was your aunt's family?"

"She's not really my aunt." Bree tucked her hair behind her ear. "She was my dance teacher, and I spent a lot of time at the studio. It's where I felt the most at home."

Dance. The word conjured images of Bree twirling around in a tutu with flowers in her hair, moving to a song only she heard. He had an urge to twirl her around himself and draw her against him.

Instead, he leaned on the chair he'd just set down and joined his hands together tightly. "That's nice you had someone like that."

"It was." Bree gave him a sad smile from her perch on the back of the monstrously ugly flower-patterned love seat in the living room. "Anyway, Agatha only had one sister, but she moved out to Minnesota too. She died young, before their parents. Cancer. Agatha got the apartment."

He wasn't sure what to say to that and nodded once, staying silent while he looked around the living room. There were little figurines on the coffee table and shopping bags from Macy's piled on the couch.

Bree cleared her throat, and his eyes snapped back to her. "Anyway, now it's mine, and I want to make it feel like that, but I'm worried with Mrs. Wilson watching me, I can't get rid of even a single spoon . . . "

Something about Bree's accent was very soothing. It was even stronger now than it had been with Mrs. Wilson, and he wasn't sure if she realized that. Aiden felt the corners of his mouth turning up.

She flushed, however. "I'm sorry, I'm just gabbing on and on here. You don't want to hear all this. Let's go over your plan, eh?"

Right, the plan. That's why he was here. Not to find out more about her or listen to her talk in her adorable accent all day or ask her about why she'd spent more of her childhood at the dance studio than at home.

He took a step toward the couch, and rather than move the shopping bags, Bree simply pushed them to the side and sat down. There wasn't very much room next to her, and he didn't know what would happen to him if he got that close to her. Nothing that was part of his plan, that was for sure.

The only option was the chair facing the couch. His eyes fell on a pile of carefully folded paper on the side table next to it, and his hand shot out to touch it before he could stop himself.

"You have a gum wrapper chain?"

"Oh, yeah, I've had it since I was a kid." The smile she gave him was tinged with sadness. "Agatha showed me how. It kept me busy at the studio when I wasn't in a class. I wanted to make the longest one in the world until I found out it was like, a hundred thousand feet."

"I did too." This unexpected similarity shouldn't have meant so much. He did his best to ignore the tightness in his chest it gave him to picture Bree, wild haired in a tutu in the corner of a dance studio, doing the same thing he'd done at his perfectly organized desk while trying to ignore the sounds of his parents fighting. Even if the folds in hers were uneven in some spots and the colors followed no set pattern.

"Really?" Her eyes lit up. "Do you still have it? We could see whose is longer."

"I don't know where it is."

The disappointment on her face made him want to take back the lie. Almost. But why give her more proof how unlike the carefree Hayden he really was? All she'd see in the ruler-sharp edges and alternating strips of white and silver on his chain was the same boring and basic failure that Margot had abandoned at the first opportunity.

Time for a new topic. "How are you feeling about your first official impersonation gig?"

"I'll be fine. I'm not impersonating anyone. I still get to be me, just a fancier version." Her eyes shifted and her bottom lip tucked under her teeth. "Actually, before we get into the plan, could I ask you something?"

He looked at his watch. There wasn't anything he needed to do for a few hours, but that didn't mean he should be here all day. Even if that's what he wanted.

"Sure, what is it?"

"I went shopping this morning."

His eyes dropped to the bags on the floor by their feet. "I guessed."

She flushed. "I don't want to put them away until I'm sure

they're the kind that Hayden's girlfriend would wear. Could you take a look?"

Since she was asking, he let his gaze linger on her simple pair of jeans and long-sleeved blouse. He thought she looked incredible. Sure, the jeans were a little too wide to be on trend, and the blouse was in a pattern that had been stylish a few decades ago. This kind of attention to detail for clothes and trends could be exhausting, but it served him well when imitating Hayden. Though his large capacity for memorizing minutia also came in handy for more useful things, like emergency procedures and the anatomy of different animals.

"I think you look fine."

Her face went well beyond a flush this time, to a bright red. "Thank you. But I want to be sure I'm dressed the way you want."

His heart thumped against his chest.

She looked down at her hands, then back up at him. "I mean, the way Hayden would want. You know him, so could you tell me what he might like best?"

His shoulders slumped. This worry was for Hayden, not for him. Any time they spent together had nothing to do with Aiden. It was just a way for her to get to someone else, someone with more than he had to offer.

Except the way she was looking at him, so unsure, so vulnerable, was impossible to ignore. He'd always wanted to help people. But this was more than that, and he knew it. Within a matter of days, he'd rearranged his life so he could spend more time with her. It was a bad sign and would only end badly for him, like everything in this city did.

"I'm sure they'll be fine." He stood up and looked at his phone. "I'm sorry, I totally forgot I have to be somewhere."

Surprise and—he hated to see it, but there it was—hurt

flashed across her face. She tucked a strand of dark hair behind her ear.

"Oh, okay, that's fine. No worries." She gave a little forced chuckle. "You must be so busy with studying and work and everything."

And with trying to not fall for the one person he absolutely shouldn't.

"I'll text you about where to meet up for our first date."

"Fake date," she said, her singsongy Minnesota accent a little clipped.

"Right." He looked at his phone again and pushed a button like someone was texting him. "I'll let you know."

He managed to walk to the door, but once he was in the hallway, he ran down the stairs and out into the street. There wasn't anywhere he actually needed to be, but he had to get away. As if on cue, the rain started to pour the second he stepped outside, but he didn't go back for a jacket. A walk in the rain would clear his head and hopefully wash away the brain fog that always seemed to descend whenever he talked to Bree.

This had been a terrible idea. He should have insisted he work with a professional actress, someone who would know this was just a job, have the right wardrobe already, not want to hang out outside of their contractual meetups.

Though he was getting soaked, the familiar walk in Riverside Park was one of the best in the city. With the surrounding trees blocking the view of the street as he walked along the paved pathways shiny with the rain and empty of any other people, it was easy to forget he was in the city. At least for a moment, he could pretend he was in a little park in that perfect small town, walking his dog in the rain—a collie, like he'd had as a kid—waiting for her to get back with a stick he'd thrown.

All of it would be possible if things with Bree went according to plan. Being his neighbor added a layer of complexity he hadn't realized would be so hard to navigate. Not to mention she was still irresistible. The effect should have worn off by now, but all it took was a few minutes with her to be overwhelmed by her in the best and worst possible way.

Up ahead, the classical façade of the Grant Memorial loomed over the path. Even in the rain, the benches next to it were bright spots of color. Rolling Bench was one of his favorite parts of the park, not just because of how completely incongruous the whimsy of it was to the stoic and serious memorial, but because of how it was built and restored. The mosaics were there thanks to hundreds of hands, not just artists but regular people, too. Margot had always called them ugly. Bree would probably love them. If it hadn't been raining, he would have sat for a while on the benches, but today, he turned around and headed back to the apartment.

Bree wasn't the first woman he'd been attracted to in the years since Margot had left him. In a city this big, with a face like his, attention from women was a given. He was careful to make it clear who he was and he never pretended to be Hayden to get a date. Sometimes that meant their interest disappeared faster than the city moved on from bakery trends. Hayden was always this week's fancy croissant, while Aiden was just a cronut.

Two women jogged past along the river, rain jackets zipped up tight, their steady stride even and rhythmic. His shoulders bunched up, preparing for the stares he didn't think he could handle right now, but they ran past him without looking beyond their hoods.

Other times, women weren't interested in him but wanted to pretend he was Hayden anyway. For a while, right after Margot had left, he'd let them. He'd wanted to pretend his life was different, too.

With Bree, however, he wanted her to see him as Aiden. He

wanted her to see who he really was. That was the most dangerous thing of all. The bustle of the city greeted him at the edge of the park. He could stay out longer, or even invite Bree to walk with him in the rain. She'd probably love it.

Or he could go back home, get cleaned up, and finish organizing the details for their first public appearance without bothering her at all. Follow the plan he knew would get him where he wanted to go.

He crossed the street and made his way through slick sidewalks to the apartment. He would keep his interactions with her strictly related to the contractual outings. They weren't dates. They were a means to an end. As long as he remembered that, he'd be fine.

THIRTEEN

"You can't wear that. You look like an elementary school teacher."

Leigh's face was twisted into a frown on Bree's tablet, which she'd set up on the dining room table so her best friend could see her entire outfit. There wasn't room in the tiny bedroom to do the same.

"I thought I looked preppy." Bree tugged at the sweater she'd paired with a flowy skirt and the cute Oxfords she'd seen every other woman on the street wearing all week. Surprisingly, they turned out to be just as comfortable as her sneakers. "Aiden didn't say where he's taking me, but it's ten in the morning. I don't think I need to wear a ball gown."

Other than the text from Aiden letting her know when he'd pick her up today, she hadn't heard or seen him the rest of the week. Her nerves had been building day by day, bubbling away like a pot of water ready to boil over. After the way he'd run out of her apartment the other day, she was just waiting for an email telling her the contract was canceled.

"I'm not saying you don't look nice. It would be fine here."

Leigh shook her head. "But you're not in Minnesota, you're in New York. You need to level up."

Bree sighed. This was why she'd wanted Aiden's input on the clothes she'd bought. Despite telling her best friend all the details about her miserable week, Bree hadn't told Leigh about the way he'd rebuffed her request for help. The evidence of his aversion to her was too embarrassing, even days later.

"What's the point when I might not be staying?"

There was enough ongoing proof that the city hated her to keep her suitcases mostly unpacked this week. All she'd made a permanent place for were a few trinkets and the gum wrapper chain that felt more like having Agatha with her than any of the stuffy furniture she still hadn't gotten rid of.

Leigh clicked her tongue. "Don't start with that again."

Bree counted off the events of that week on her fingers.

"The weather is more unpredictable than I am, so no matter what I put on in the morning, it always turns out to be the wrong thing by the afternoon."

"So keep a bag with an umbrella and a cardigan by the door to take with you." Leigh shrugged.

Bree held up another finger. "I tried the bus instead of the subway to get around town, but that was even more of a disaster."

"I'm sure not all bus drivers are that rude when people ask for help. Maybe he was just having a bad day."

"And I got lost again. Twice."

"Once was in Central Park, where I'm sure a lot of people get lost." Leigh shook her head.

"But the second time was on one of the very straight and clearly labeled streets, which I didn't notice was east instead of west." She'd spent an hour trying to find an address, only to realize it was on the other side of the city.

"It'll take time until you get the hang of things. There's no shame in using a map app until then." Leigh's lips turned up. "I'm sure Aiden uses one sometimes."

The mention of Aiden got the nerves simmering in her stomach bubbling away again. Her eyes fell on the gum wrapper chain in the living room. She liked knowing they had something so silly in common, but maybe he saw it as something childish.

"A map app would have been useful, if I hadn't forgotten to charge my phone. Again." She tugged at the bottom of her sweater. "Do I really look like a preschool teacher?"

Before Leigh could answer, there was a knock at the door, and Bree's roiling tension pushed up into her throat.

"He's here. I don't have time to change." She spun around in a panic, as if new clothing would magically appear on her.

"Can I meet him?"

"*No.*" There had been too many mortifying things already this week. "What's he going to think of me if I start the date by showing him off?"

Leigh rolled her eyes. "It's not like it's a real date. You know there'll be another one, no matter how badly today goes."

Somehow, that didn't help. It made it worse, thinking that he'd be forced to spend time with her.

Swallowing the nerves back down, she smiled at the screen. "I'll call you after. Bye."

Bree ended the call just as Aiden knocked on the door again. She hurried over, her shoes clicking on the hardwood floor in the hallway. She smoothed out her sweater and opened the door.

"Sorry, I was just on a call with my friend, and—"

Whatever she was going to say disappeared from her brain.

So far all she'd seen him in were sweats, either on his way to or from the gym. This was the first time she'd seen him wearing jeans, and it shouldn't have been that different, but it was. It was probably also the forest-green cable-knit sweater he was wearing, setting off his eyes so they appeared even greener than usual. He'd styled his hair differently and trimmed his beard as well.

He looked . . . exactly like Hayden Carmichael. The effect was overwhelming, and Bree had to take a step back, leaning on the door for support.

"Hi," she said, her breath leaving her body.

His smile was small, his eyes tight. Bree's stomach churned. He didn't want to be doing this, she could tell. Not with her. She straightened up and turned away.

"I can change, if this isn't right for where we're going."

He reached out a hand and laid it on her arm. A burst of electricity rippled up her arm and down her spine.

"You look fine."

Her stomach fell. *Fine.* Not great, not amazing. But that was okay, since this wasn't a real date.

"Where are we going?" She slipped the strap of her bag over her head and checked twice that her keys were there before following him into the hall.

"It's a surprise." He gestured for her to go down the stairs first.

Despite how anxious she was, this sent a happy flutter through her chest. "I like surprises."

A corner of his mouth twitched. "I thought you might."

"Do I get a hint?"

He opened the front door of the building and held it open for her, the sounds of the city wafting over them. As she passed next to him, he leaned in close.

"Nope," he whispered, his breath tickling her neck, sending shivers down her body.

They made their way down the stairs and out into the bright, sunny morning. She shivered again, mostly in anticipation, but also because of the cool wind that had just blown across her bare legs.

With the ease of someone who'd done it thousands of times, he slung his arm across her shoulders and pulled her close.

"Sorry, I don't have a jacket. The weather's been a little weird this week. I never know what to wear."

Her body relaxed into his. "Me too."

Somehow, this tiny admission that mirrored how Bree had been feeling all week had calmed her racing heart.

He was just a regular person. This wasn't a real date, but it was a chance to get to know someone a little better, someone who may be her first friend in a new city, her new life.

He led her down the street, which was unusually empty for this time of day. There was a brief moment of panic—how would they fulfill the contract if no one saw them?—until she remembered that she was with Aiden. He was taking care of everything. They arrived at a black luxury SUV with tinted windows.

"We're driving?"

He glanced around the vacant sidewalk. "Hayden doesn't take the subway."

"Neither do I, not after what I saw there this week."

Aiden chuckled, and she slid into the dark interior. Two men with short hair and military-style bearings sat up front.

"This is Grant and Marcus," Aiden said when he got in next to her. "They're two of Hayden's actual bodyguards."

"He has bodyguards?" More information on Hayden to tuck away.

The man driving the car chuckled a little. "We stay out of the pictures, but we're always there. I've been with him since he was a teenager."

"He doesn't need you wherever he is?"

"It's a much more secure location." He met her eyes in the rearview mirror and winked. "Private island."

Bree leaned back in the leather seat and let out a breath. Was she totally kidding herself that she had a shot with Hayden? His life was so far away from hers, from everything she'd known.

He's okay with Aiden pretending to date me, she reminded herself, though it sounded a lot like Leigh's voice. He'd taken one look at her in Aiden's apartment and made the offer. He must have liked what he'd seen.

Unlike Aiden, who was sitting as far as possible away from her on the other side of the car. He was so unpredictable. Sometimes sweet, like with the Wi-Fi password and putting his arm around her. Most of the time, he seemed to want to be anywhere but with her. The car drove slowly, Central Park on one side, tall gray buildings on the other. The silence stretched between them.

"Do you ever need to use a map to get around?" she blurted before she could stop herself, shoulders scrunched around her ears like he might yell at her.

He turned his head, and a little frown appeared on his face. "Did you get lost?"

"Maybe."

His eyes were steady on hers, and another beat passed before he spoke. "The east and west sides are divided by Fifth Avenue, so if you're going to Third Avenue, it's on the east side. Streets run east to west, and avenues go north to south. But say uptown and downtown or you'll sound like a tourist."

"Oh. Thanks." Relief washed over her and her shoulders dropped. He was helping her learn about the city, like he'd promised. She felt brave enough for another question—the one she'd been thinking about since she first met him. "Do you really not like the city? You've been here so long."

His lips turned down, like he was debating sharing something. Bree's heart tripped, wondering if she'd misread him yet again. It was so hard to know where she stood with him. Sometimes he said such nice things, and other times, he seemed to loathe the sight of her.

"It's not the city itself, though that doesn't help things." He ran a hand through his hair, and instead of messing it up, it made the style even more Hayden-like. Wild and haphazard, like he'd just jumped out of a plane or rolled out of bed. "It's just . . . it's not the life I pictured for myself."

"Whereas I've been dreaming of living here almost my entire life."

He smiled at this, and his eyes met hers again. Nice Aiden was back. "I know. That's why I'm sure you'll like where we're going."

Bree spent the rest of the short car ride staring out the window. No one even glanced twice at their car, not when there were much fancier, flashier ones to gawk at. When they finally stopped, Bree looked around, but this block looked the same as so many others. They were still next to the park, the green burst of it a calming reminder of the wide-open spaces she'd left behind.

Aiden leaned forward, hands on his knees, his face smooth and serious. "There'll be a few photographers that we tipped off for this, but they should be far away and not come inside."

The earlier nerves were back with a vengeance, as the full impact of what she'd agreed to hit her. Being known as Hayden Carmichael's girlfriend wouldn't come without sacrifices. They were ones she thought she was willing to make to get what she wanted, but now that the moment was here, she wasn't so sure.

There suddenly wasn't enough air in the car. Bree took deep, gasping breaths, her heart racing. Aiden had already stepped out of the car. When he turned and extended his hand to help her out, he looked startled for a moment, then gave her a smile. It was much more Aiden than Hayden, and Bree's breathing slowed.

"I'll be right next to you the whole time." His voice was low and calm, like he was speaking to a scared horse. "They'll be too far away to hear us, so don't worry about saying the wrong thing."

She took his hand and slid out of the car, trying to keep her eyes on him and not turn her head wildly to search for the cameras she now knew were there.

"Try to look a little less terrified. They'll think I kidnapped you, and that's not quite the attention we want." His lips turned up, and she let out a breathless laugh.

"That's better." He slung his arm around her again and steered her down the street. "Lean on me a little."

She did as told, the warmth of his body seeping through his sweater and into hers.

"You should put your arm around me too. It's in the contract, remember?"

Arms around each other, hugs, and holding hands were all things they'd have to do every "date," though constant touching was not. This close to Aiden, with the low rumble of his voice as he pointed out different landmarks in an effort to distract her, it was all she could do not to reach up and plant her lips on his cheek. The fact that the no-kissing clause had been her idea, and that he'd agreed so readily, kept her impulse in check.

The crowds rushed by, busy with their own weekend morning plans. People barely gave them a second glance. The few who did merely looked twice, as if to confirm to themselves what they were seeing. A few may have taken a picture with their phone, but Bree was too concentrated on Aiden to worry about that. Central Park was on their left, but she wasn't familiar enough with the city to know exactly where they were.

"Here we are."

He stopped, and they were standing underneath a columned portico, facing a set of stairs with a red carpet that led to a revolving door, flanked by liveried doormen.

"Is this . . . " Bree's words got stuck in her throat. In her wanderings around the city this week, she hadn't even considered stopping here. It had felt too touristy, too much like something a zealous Hayden fan would do.

"The Plaza Hotel? Yes." Aiden gave her a squeeze and nodded at the doorman. "We're going to have breakfast here."

"Just like . . . " Again, the words failed to make it from her brain and out of her mouth. Someone passed behind them, their expensive perfume engulfing her, and the doorman smiled as the sparkling, shiny couple entered the hotel.

Aiden's voice was soft in her ear. "Just like in *Escape to New York*."

It was one of her favorite scenes in the movie, but how Aiden had known, she wasn't sure. The main character, played by Hayden Carmichael, had inherited a million dollars—a fortune for a fifteen-year-old—and the first thing he did was move into the Plaza Hotel and have tea at the Palm Court. Various shenanigans ensued while his relatives tried to find him to get the money back, and he tried to finagle a kiss from the very cute tourist he took all over the city.

Did the plot make sense? No.

Did Bree watch it whenever she was sick or needed a pick-me-up?

Absolutely.

"How did you know it was my favorite Hayden movie?"

"It's everyone's favorite."

Bree raised an eyebrow.

Aiden rolled his eyes. "Fine, it's my favorite of all his movies." He put his hand on her lower back to ease her up the red carpeted stairs. With a wink at the doorman, he led her through the gleaming gold revolving door. "It's high on the cheese factor, low on the heartthrob meter."

"How many times have you seen all his movies?" His hand on her lower back was a warm pressure that she leaned into as her feet sank into the carpet, and her head tilted up to take in the crystal chandeliers above.

"I'd never seen any until the look-alike work." His arm dropped and he took her hand in his. "Since I started? Probably a dozen times each."

They made their way through a large marble-floored room that hadn't been in the movie, and Bree stopped walking to stare up at chandeliers even bigger than the one in the entrance. Her heart squeezed tightly in her chest. Everything was in shades of cream and gold, the people around them in tailored blouses and jackets, all smooth hair and clacking high heels. It was more beautiful than she'd ever imagined. Not that she'd spent much time imagining herself here, of all places. With Hayden Carmichael, no less.

Not Hayden. Aiden.

"Keep moving," Aiden whispered in her ear. A few people were looking their way from a bar in one corner of the lobby, eyebrows raised and heads close together.

Were they talking about her?

Panic rose in her chest, and she started walking again, her breathing shallow. Barely two minutes into it and she was already doing something wrong. Every flighty instinct inside of her told her it would be better if she left.

"This was a bad idea," she said as softly as she could, while Aiden led her back through the carpeted entrance again.

This wasn't going to work. She was too nervous, too gawking. No one would ever believe Hayden Carmichael was with someone like her. They'd know Aiden wasn't really the actor.

She'd remain a nobody. Hayden would be furious and refuse to pay them. Aiden wouldn't be able to go to vet school. All because she couldn't chill out and act like she was supposed to be there.

This kind of pressure was unbearable, and she felt it breaking her apart from the inside out. This was why she didn't make big plans longer than a few weeks.

Then Aiden squeezed her hand. "You can do this." His voice was a soft tickle in her ear. "Just breathe."

Her shoulders dropped an inch, and she took a gulping breath. He moved her gently through open French doors and into a wide room with a glass-domed roof and leafy plants. Between two marble columns was the entrance to the Palm Court.

From behind his little wooden desk, the maître d's face split into a wide smile.

"Welcome back, Mr. Carmichael."

FOURTEEN

Bree's arm was shaking under his, and Aiden couldn't tell if it was from nerves or excitement. Figuring it was a little of both, he gave it a squeeze. When she looked up at him on their way to their table, he gave her a smile. The effect was almost instantaneous—her shoulders dropped and the lines between her eyebrows smoothed out. The only indication that she still wasn't totally comfortable was the viselike grip she had on his hand.

He leaned down and whispered in her ear, "You're doing fine."

"Th-thanks."

It was the slight stutter that shattered him. Guilt racked his body, every inch of him aching to make her feel comfortable. That was part of this job too. He was playing Hayden, whose girlfriend should be at ease with him, even if she was nervous about being in public together.

They sat down, and now that he could see her face straight on, she looked way beyond nervous.

"I'm sorry, I thought you'd like the surprise." Reaching out a hand, he covered hers. Had the quick peek into the lobby been too much? "We can go home if you want."

"I'm okay, it's just . . . a lot." Beneath his hand, hers tightened and his stomach dropped. The lobby had definitely been too much. "To be here, in this place, with *Hayden Carmichael* is not something I ever thought would happen."

He could hear the emphasis in her voice on the name, and he tensed a little. Their table was set apart from others, and the chatter of the room was a gentle buzz that covered their voices, but that didn't mean they shouldn't be careful.

Speaking of being careful, he should really stop touching her so much. In addition to no kissing, Bree had requested only three physical interactions be required in the contract and was probably annoyed he'd passed that within minutes of being with her. The logical reason, he told himself, was to make the illusion complete that Hayden Carmichael was totally smitten.

But he didn't want to give her any reason to cancel the whole thing and walk out of here, so he quickly took his hand away to pick up his menu.

"Well, it's happening, babycakes." He flashed her a smile but groaned internally. The horrible nickname was what Hayden used in *Escape to New York* with the cute tourist who'd also been staying at the hotel. Lunch at the Palm Court had been their first date. "Get whatever you want."

Was that disappointment in her eyes because of the removal of his hand or his shift from Aiden to Hayden? Or was he just imagining what he wanted to see?

"Let me just head to the ladies' room," she said, and stood up before he could ask her what she wanted to drink.

Knowing she'd want coffee, when the waiter arrived he ordered for them both, the way Hayden would have. He'd gotten a document from Hayden's publicist with details on these kinds of interactions and how the actor usually behaved in public, things Aiden hadn't needed in past gigs.

Which was why Aiden now drew out his phone, just like

Hayden would in this situation. According to the publicist, this kept him from making eye contact with anyone and tacitly inviting them to approach him. For Aiden, it meant he could send a few frantic texts to Tony. NDAs, Aiden had long ago decided, did not apply to your best friend.

> **Aiden**
> This is the worst idea I've ever had.

> **Tony**
> You mean the date you have a minute-by-minute itinerary for? You'll be fine.

> **Aiden**
> I don't think she wants to do this. With me.
> She went to the bathroom as soon as we sat down.

> **Tony**
> Do you think she'd want to do it with me? I'll happily take your place.

> **Aiden**
> Not a chance.

> **Tony**
> Ha, at least give her my number so she knows she has options in this city other than you or the movie star. And you're not even sticking around after this.

Aiden scowled, the jealousy rippling through him. He knew Tony was teasing, but he was right. Once this was over, Bree would still be here in the city, while Aiden would leave. She could have whoever she wanted.

Bree still wasn't back, but he didn't want to draw attention to that. He put his phone down and looked around the packed restaurant without turning his head. Had she changed her mind? Run out the back door to escape lunch with a boring look-alike?

It was another ten minutes before she was weaving her way between the tables and plants to their table. He didn't shift from the relaxed slouch Hayden always had in photos, though every part of him ached to reach for her. "Everything okay?"

She nodded and sat, keeping her head down. Unease roiled in his stomach, and he glanced over her shoulder to where their waitress was hovering discreetly. "We can leave if you want to."

Bree shook her head and he sighed. *It's her first time doing this*, he reminded himself.

When she frowned at the cup in front of her, he realized the coffee must have gone cold during her long absence, and he signaled for another one.

His efforts at conversation were met with one-word answers, which didn't seem like her. The most he got out of her was when the coffee arrived, and she brought the cup to her nose, closed her eyes, and inhaled deeply, a slow smile spreading across her face.

He grinned. "Does it meet your standards?"

She nodded happily and seemed to relax a little. It was still a quiet, awkward meal, and Aiden barely knew what he was eating, so completely absorbed with concern about whatever was worrying Bree.

When they finally walked out of the restaurant, he grabbed her hand, eager for an excuse to touch her again.

"Get ready. The same cameras from before may be there, or they may have left."

"Okay." Her hand gripped his tightly, and her shoulders were inching up toward her ears.

He stopped in the high-ceilinged, echoey lobby and pulled her into an alcove near the door. With an almost unconscious movement, he swept her hair behind her ear.

"What's wrong? I really thought you'd like it here." Realization hit him and a sour taste coated his throat. "Are you disappointed because you did this with me instead of him?"

She looked away.

Oh, hell. That was it, wasn't it? She was still wishing for the real thing.

It shouldn't bother him. It never had before. Hell, when Margot left, he'd welcomed it.

What was it about Bree that made him wish she preferred Aiden Johnson?

"That's not it."

His heart gave a traitorous leap.

"It's just, I overheard a woman in the ladies' room say . . . " Tears suddenly filled her eyes, and a different kind of heat hit his chest. "She said something like, how can he be here with her? She's not even that pretty."

The urge to go punch something—or someone—rose up in him. It was unlike anything he'd ever felt before. In an instant, his mind sorted through the various clauses to get out of the contract, trying to remember which was the fastest. As far as he was concerned, his first job was to protect Bree, and second was the Hayden gig. If he couldn't do one without failing at the other, then he was out.

He wrapped her in his arms and buried his face in her hair as she sank into his chest. Quiet sobs racked her body. Her hair smelled like the strawberry candy Mrs. Wilson had in a bowl in her living room.

"You look incredible. Hayden would be the luckiest man alive if he were the one here with you."

"You don't mean that." Her voice was muffled against his chest, and the heat of her breath warmed him in an unexpected way. "You just said I looked *fine* when you picked me up."

"Of course I mean it. I'm not the best at . . . " He struggled to find the right way to phrase it. No matter how much he had flattered Margot, how much attention or time he'd spent with her, it had never been enough. Words hadn't helped him then. They'd pushed her away, into the arms of someone with the money and status she'd really wanted.

But he had to tell Bree something. "I'm sorry if I didn't tell you how amazing you look when I picked you up. I was nervous."

She sniffed and leaned back to look up at him. "You were nervous? But you do this all the time."

"Not all the time. And not with someone else." He looked around at the chandeliered room, and a harsh huff of a laugh escaped his throat. "Not in places like this."

She shifted her weight, but he held onto her. At this point, the only way he was letting go was if she moved away. It didn't look like she planned on doing that anytime soon.

"This was probably too public for a first outing. I'm sorry." His jaw tightened. The goal had been to impress her, to remind her of all the reasons she'd been excited to move here. Now she was probably even more likely to bail before the end of the week. "I should have just done a walk around Central Park."

"We can still do that, it's right across the street." Her eyes were looking drier, and she sounded excited about the possibility. "Maybe with you there, I won't get lost."

"I used to get lost in there all the time."

The corners of her lips turned up, and his chest squeezed. She stepped out of his arms, wiping a hand underneath her eyes. "Did I streak my makeup?"

He rubbed a thumb across her cheek and shook his head. "You're perfect."

She took a shaky breath, held it for a second, then let it out in a big puff of air. "Thanks for lunch."

"Thank Hayden. He's the one paying for it."

Again her eyes dimmed a little, as if the reminder that he wasn't really Hayden was disappointing.

"Why don't we walk through the park next week for our outing?" Turning toward the door, he held out his hand, heart pounding. If she agreed to that, then at least she'd be here another week. Two outings meant twenty percent of the total payment. Not nearly enough for what he needed, but better than nothing.

After a moment's hesitation that seemed to last for hours, she took his hand. "That would be nice." They stepped into the bright May sunlight.

When they got into the car, Grant confirmed that the paparazzi were still there, but fewer than before. They'd be dropped off a little ways from the apartment, and Aiden would leave her at the door rather than walk in with her, just in case. Then he would circle the block a few times with Grant and Marcus until they were sure no paparazzi were around.

The ride was quiet, and she looked out of the window, sighing a little a few times, so softly he wasn't sure she was even aware she was doing it.

Was she still thinking about leaving? Was she regretting agreeing to this? She was the kind of spontaneous person who followed her heart. As enviably irritating as that was to Aiden, it meant she could change her mind about this whole thing at any given moment.

"The city won't always feel so strange," he said, the words bursting out of him so suddenly she turned with wide eyes to stare at him. "I moved here right after college. It was a lot to take in at first."

"And you figured it out eventually?"

"Eventually, yeah."

Though he'd had someone to help him, someone who loved the city to show him around, it was hard to think of her and not let all the bad feelings that came after rise to the surface, even after so many years.

They were on Central Park West, and the sunlight filtering down through the leaves left dappled patterns of light and dark across the leather backseat. Bree scooted closer to him, put her hand on his, and squeezed. "Thanks for lunch, Aiden."

And just like that, all the bad feelings drifted away.

FIFTEEN

The plan was to meet in a week, and Aiden would text her details about the time and place. Instead, he showed up at Bree's apartment at eight in the morning, two days after their outing at the Plaza.

"You like coffee, right?" he said, without a hello, as soon as she opened the door.

Having only woken up a few minutes earlier, she stared dazedly at him, framed in her doorway and smelling like soap and paint and closets organized by color.

"Is that a serious question?"

"My friend just opened a new café not too far from here. Do you want to go?"

"I thought our next outing would be—"

"Not an outing. Not with Hayden Carmichael." He put his hands in the pockets of his hoodie and shrugged. "Just, like, a neighbor thing."

She raised an eyebrow, still not fully awake enough to understand whatever was happening beneath the surface. The hot and cold moods of Aiden Johnson needed a certain level of caffeination that she had yet to achieve that morning.

"I was going to go to the café down the street."

"That place?" He wrinkled his nose. "They're terrible."

"That's . . . true." Whatever glimmer of recognition she'd seen last week must have been her imagination. They still didn't seem to remember her, even after eight days straight coming in at the same time every morning. She didn't know how long it would take for her to become a regular, or why it was so important to her. "So why did I see you there the other day?"

"I go there because they ignore everyone, which is nice when I want to be left alone."

This was another little fact about him that she added to the slowly growing pile she had collected. It wasn't very big yet, but every new thing she learned was like a tiny spot of light in the mysterious darkness of his personality. Maybe this morning was a sign she should collect even more.

"When do you want to leave?"

He looked at his watch. "I have a training client at eleven, so now is good."

She looked down at her drawstring flannel shorts and plain white t-shirt. "I need to change."

"Why? You look fine."

Again with the "fine." That bothered her more than the baristas still not knowing her order, let alone her name. Bree had been "fine" her whole life. The middle sister of five. Not the tallest or prettiest or smartest. The one who had a steady job, no boyfriend drama, no sibling rivalry because she knew she would never win.

She wanted to be more than fine, and New York was the way to do that. Hayden Carmichael was the way to do that. No one who lived in NYC and was dating a movie star would ever be considered "fine." The NDA meant she could never tell her friends and family the truth, and she didn't want to. As far as they'd ever know, she'd spent her first month in New York dating a movie star.

It was all thanks to Aiden, who said she was "fine" most of the time but had told her she looked amazing at the Plaza. The whisper of fate was hard to hear this early in the morning, but she would still listen to it.

"Alright then, let's go." She stepped out into the hall, but he put his hand on the door to stop her.

"Aren't you forgetting something?"

Heat rushed to her face, and she popped back inside to grab her purse, where her keys were safely tucked inside. "I should put them on a necklace or something."

"That would be far from the weirdest fashion I've seen in this city."

"Oh yeah, what would that be?"

As they walked along, his hat pulled low and head down, he told her about the things he'd witnessed in his decade of living in the city. Head-to-toe flamingo-pink outfits, bathing suits in snowstorms, cats as shawls, dogs as shawls, ferrets as shawls—really, any animal was apparently okay to wear around your neck here. By the time they got to the café, she was laughing so hard she was crying.

"I can see why you've stayed so long." She wiped her eyes. "Never a dull moment."

"Are you kidding?" Shaking his head, he held open the door to the café. "I can't wait to live somewhere boring, where nothing happens."

"You'd love small-town Minnesota, then."

The second she stepped inside and the rich, bitter aroma hit her nose, the disappointment she'd been feeling all week melted away.

"Is this a dream?"

He laughed and made his way to the counter, where a tall man with dark-brown skin waved and gave him a fist bump.

"Hey, Brian. The place looks great."

"Hey, AJ, thanks for stopping by." His eyes flicked to Bree. "Is this who I've been seeing you around town with?"

Bree's heart stuttered. Was it that easy for people to spot the difference?

Aiden simply mimed locking his lips shut, and Brian laughed. "Fine, keep your Hollywood secrets. Can I at least ask your name?"

"Bree." She smiled, not needing Aiden's meaningful look to know her full name wasn't required. Even with all her social media accounts shut down and a relatively common name, it wouldn't be impossible to find her. She didn't want to make it too easy for people. "This is such a cute café. It reminds me of my friend Leigh's coffee shop back in Minnesota."

"Thank you. It's been a lot of hard work." Brian grinned. He seemed to be the kind of person who was always cheerful. Bree wondered how he'd met the grumpy, quiet Aiden.

"I can tell. I helped Leigh get hers ready to open."

The chairs were all comfortable and tufted in different pastel colors. The tables were made from the same wood, but all different shapes and sizes. The blackboard behind the counter was filled with handwritten names and prices of drinks.

But it was more than the décor, it was the feel of it. The unfriendly coffee shop on her street was a cold and clinical operating theater compared to the cozy vibes this place was giving her.

"You're a good friend. Aiden did the same for me and didn't stop complaining the entire time." When Brian smiled, Bree realized it was the owner himself that was responsible for the coziness, just like Leigh brought her own energy into her café. "What can I get for you two?"

They placed their orders and within minutes, they had steaming mugs in hand and moved to a pair of extra large chairs in a corner.

The pair farthest from a window, Bree noticed.

"I don't think anyone would mistake you for him today."

"Why not?"

She thought back to their "date" on Sunday, and the way he'd shifted from Aiden to Hayden. It had been unsettling to see how smooth the transformation had been. Even though she knew he'd been doing it for years, it was still impressive.

"Well, for starters, you shaved. I don't think I've seen a picture of Hayden without some scruff or a full beard in years."

"It's itchy. It'll grow back by this weekend, unfortunately. His doesn't grow as fast."

Now this was a little Hayden detail she hadn't counted on getting this morning. Her pile of facts about him were much smaller, and while she'd been hungry for them at first, there wasn't quite the same thrill as learning more about Aiden.

"It's how you carry yourself too," she said. He sat up at this, and she giggled. "It's not the slouching. It's like, when you're Aiden, you don't care what people think of you."

"Well, I don't. Not really."

"I wish I could say the same. I keep thinking about what I overheard those women say this weekend."

The words were out of her mouth before she could stop them. She hadn't meant to be so open with him. Today was about finding out more about him, not revealing even more reasons he shouldn't be doing this look-alike thing with her.

"They were idiots."

A warm flutter spread through her chest. He'd been the one to ask her to get coffee, she reminded herself, as a "neighbor thing." That meant they were friends, right? There was literally nobody else for her to talk to while Leigh was at work. She'd even considered moving more furniture into the hall, just to get some human interaction in the form of Mrs. Wilson yelling at her.

Aiden took a sip from his mug. "Did you see what the gossip blogs said?"

Her stomach lurched.

"The pictures are out?"

He nodded and held out his phone. "Hayden's publicist sent them over this morning. That's why I came over, but then I remembered how much you like coffee."

The sweetness of this simple thing, remembering this detail about her, gave Bree a glittery, jittery feeling that had nothing to do with the caffeine coursing through her bloodstream.

Bree looked down at the phone in his hand, scooting closer toward him to see better.

It wasn't a picture of them walking, like she'd thought it would be. It was the one of her wrapped in his arms, taken through the glass of a window into the hotel lobby. Her face was buried in his chest, and his head was leaning against hers.

They looked like a couple completely in love.

WHO IS HAYDEN CARMICHAEL'S BOMBSHELL BRUNETTE?

"A bombshell?" Her entire body felt like it was on fire.

"I told you, you looked amazing."

Bree felt herself flush again and buried her face behind her drink.

"They'll probably be a little more alert now, so you might need to start wearing a hat and sunglasses when you go out."

She smiled. "Another reason to go shopping."

For some reason, this made him grin as well, a very Aiden kind of smile. "Don't they have stores back in Minnesota?"

"Of course, but it's not the same. Now if someone asks where I got something, I can say, 'Oh, it's from this little boutique in New York.'" She took a sip of her coffee, closing her eyes for just a moment to savor it. "None of my sisters can say that."

"How many do you have?"

There was a tug of resistance, something holding her back from telling him more about her. The signs all pointed to this being a way to get to know Aiden, not the other way around.

But it would be rude to not answer such a direct question.

"Four."

"Are they going to come out and visit?"

Again she fought against the tug, politeness eventually winning out. "Probably not."

"Really? I had everyone I knew wanting to come visit when I first moved here."

Bree shrugged and sat back in her chair. "They're all really busy with their families. And it's not like I have room for more than one person to crash in that tiny guest room."

"You'd be surprised how many people can fit, if you really try." He shook his head. "Sometimes I get bookings for two, and Mrs. Wilson tells me there were at least eight in there."

The chance to add to her pile of Aiden facts was too tempting to ignore. "What about you? Any siblings?"

"Just me."

"So who comes to visit?"

"My mom." He took a sip of his own drink and his jaw twitched. "My dad's not really in the picture."

"I'm sorry. You don't have to talk about it." Her face heated and she took a hasty sip from her mug to hide her burning cheeks.

He looked at her for a moment. "It's okay. Something about you makes me feel like I can say whatever I want to you."

There was a momentary lightness in her chest, before the disappointed crash of realization smashed through her.

"I get that a lot."

It was the same wherever she went. During her travels, people would tell her things, big things, secret things, because they knew she wasn't sticking around. It was easy to divulge all your thoughts to someone who wouldn't be there in a few weeks to hold them against you.

Aiden wasn't staying in New York, so Bree was safe. It wasn't because he saw her as anything special, or even as a friend, but because she was temporary.

The door of the café opened and a burst of warm air reached them all the way in the back. Brian came out from behind the counter to greet the new arrival with a one-handed hug.

This wasn't supposed to be like all her other ramblings. New York was supposed to be different. She was supposed to be different. Instead of changing topics to something light and unrelated, like Birdbrain Bree would do, she could be New York Bree and talk about herself. Share some of her secrets, some of her past. That was how you formed bonds, how you connected.

But the question that came out of her mouth wasn't deep, or meaningful. And it wasn't about her.

"Where did you meet Brian?"

"In college." He sat back in his chair. "We both were finance majors."

"Finance?" Bree didn't even try to hide her surprise. "But you were studying anatomy the other day at the café."

He shifted in his seat. "I minored in biology, but my dad wanted me to work in finance, like him."

"It's nice he cared so much." Bree ran her finger over the edge of her coffee cup, building up the courage to share some of her truth. "My parents didn't even notice when I dropped out of school my second year to follow my favorite band on tour."

Aiden paused in lifting his own cup to his lips, eyebrows

raised.

"It was totally the right choice," she said quickly. "They broke up right after the tour, so I got to see those last amazing concerts."

"Lucky you." There was the little lift of his mouth that Bree was starting to recognize as a smile he was trying to suppress. "Maybe your parents just knew you were made to live a more interesting life than where college could take you. I just met you and I can already tell that."

There was a burst of steam from the large espresso machine, and the familiar sound sent a twinge of sadness through Bree's chest.

"That's a very nice way of saying I'm a total space case who can't decide on what she wants to do."

"You follow your dreams and you don't apologize for them. That's great."

Now Bree's chest tightened for an entirely different reason. He was trying to make her feel better for all the disasters he'd witnessed in the few short weeks he'd known her.

There was no way he could really believe all these nice things, however. Not when he'd be the only one in the world to, other than Leigh.

Thoughts of Leigh made her heart ache. Bree was so lonely, and here was the perfect opportunity to make a friend, a real one. Not the kind of passing acquaintance Bree had collected over the years in various cities.

All she had to do was share something more serious, something more than the light chatter they'd been doing until now.

"What about your dreams?" she asked.

Or she could turn the focus back on him, the way she always did, the way she knew would make others feel more comfortable. People loved talking about themselves, and they loved Bree for letting them do it.

Aiden slid his coffee cup slightly to one side, then back. "I don't have dreams, just plans."

Bree tried to hide her smirk. That was a very Aiden response. "So what are your plans, then?"

"To get out of New York. Be a vet in a small town somewhere," he said decisively, like he'd been thinking about it forever. The same tone she used to tell people she dreamed of living here. A small smile flashed across his face. "Kind of the opposite of Hayden's movie you love so much."

Sticky embarrassment filled Bree, a confirmation of everything she'd assumed was true up until now. This was just a job for him, and she was no one special. He wanted this so much he'd likely put up with anything to get what he wanted.

Whatever flattery he gave her was just to keep her on board, to make sure she didn't bail the way she always had before. They weren't friends, and he didn't like her any more than he had to in order to get what he wanted, which was as far away from her and New York as he could get.

That was fine, though. She could still get what she wanted out of all of this too. It wasn't just about what Aiden wanted. This was Bree's chance to stand out in a way she'd never been able to do before. It was a shot at spending time with Hayden Carmichael.

"Then let's make sure this look-alike thing goes well so you can go to vet school and I get my date with Hayden." She put her mug to her lips and frowned. "I'm sorry I've been making it so difficult."

"Don't worry about it." His eyes met her, serious and intense. "I always have a plan."

One that probably didn't need her at all, if she got too out of control.

Bree slapped a smile on her face and tried to not let her shoulders sag. "So what's your plan for our next outing?"

SIXTEEN

The spring weather had finally decided to make an appearance, and Aiden couldn't have been happier. He had to admit, there was something magical about these few weeks when it was consistently warm enough to not need a jacket, but before the unbearable heat and humidity of the summer descended and made everything a sticky, disgusting sweat fest.

Something magical . . . he sounded like Bree.

When he got up to her apartment, she was just closing the door, a hand in her purse in what he was sure was gripping her keys.

"Do you want to just leave a spare key at my place, just in case?" The words were out of his mouth before he could stop them.

It was still sitting heavy in his chest days later that she thought she was making things difficult. Like it was her fault that people were mean and Aiden was terrible at comforting her when she—very reasonably—was nervous about a highly atypical situation. Maybe if he made the rest of her life easier, she'd be calmer during their outings.

But was asking for a key too much, too soon?

She smiled instantly, the beauty of it knocking him a little sideways. "That would be great. I'm so terrified I'll forget them every time I leave."

He didn't have the key to anyone's apartment, not even Tony's. That was a level of commitment, attachment, that was just too far for him. If you had someone's key, they expected you to be around.

Contractually, he had to be around for Bree. There'd be time to give her key back before he left the city.

"Can we stop at a place on the way back to make you a copy?"

All he could do was nod, not trusting himself to say anything else. Not while she was looking at him like that with her eyes bright and happiness etched across all of her features.

Not noticing anything was amiss, she bounded down the hall and down the stairs before realizing he wasn't beside her.

"Aiden, come on."

She was holding out her hand, like it was the most natural thing in the world for him to reach out and take it. Which he did, and warmth spread through him as soon as their skin made contact.

They stepped outside, and the late-May sunshine was smooth and snug. She turned her head up to meet it, holding on to her hat, and gave one of her little sighs.

"That finally sounds like a happy sigh."

She looked at him from beneath the wide brim of her hat. It wasn't totally blocking her face the way his sunglasses and cap were him, but it was a start.

"What do you mean, finally?"

They walked along their street, which was only one block away from the park.

The sidewalk was busy, full of people enjoying the Friday afternoon weather. They all looked to be headed toward the park like they were, which would make it both easier to get lost in the crowd and a little harder for the paparazzi to get a clear picture. Grant and Marcus trailed along a discreet distance behind them.

He tugged her hand so she didn't run into a mailbox. "Just that, so far, you seem to be disappointed by your time in the city."

They'd crossed paths a few times in the lobby over the last week, usually when he was heading out and she was heading in. When he asked how she was spending her days, it didn't sound like she was doing much other than wandering around and getting lost until it was late enough to call Leigh.

It was the opposite of how he'd spent his first weeks in the city with Margot. The careful plans he'd made to explore all of the historic and famous places they'd talked about together. Bree seemed to be getting more and more disappointed that her random wanderings weren't leading to anything exciting.

He remembered how much he used to love the city way back when, and tried to tap into that when planning their day in Central Park. Another disaster like the Plaza and she might be on the next flight home.

Today had to go perfectly.

"I'm not disappointed about everything." Bree tucked her hair behind her ear. "I've been getting tons of messages from people back home who saw the photos from the Plaza."

"I've gotten a few too." He navigated them around a group of tourists taking a group photo in front of the low wall that surrounded the park, careful to stay out of the range of their cameras. "Mostly from Tony and Brian."

Their teasing jabs about him getting too famous to hang out with them were all in good fun, but even that was too much for Aiden.

He slipped his arm around Bree's shoulder as they walked into the park at 85th Street. A few people did a double take.

Maybe he'd been too harsh in his opinions about Hayden. This was a complicated life to lead, and Hayden had been navigating it since he was a teenager, without having any major scandals or addictions that so many other stars did. Sure, he was kind of an egotistical megalomaniac, but he still deserved a little privacy. Aiden could deal with this a few more weeks, then go back to a life of blissful anonymity.

"After today, people will know my name, right?" Her eyes were bright.

Bree liked the attention, apparently.

Hayden's publicist had been promising the photographers hints to where "Hayden" would be with his new girlfriend, in exchange for not giving them any details about Bree quite yet. After this outing, they'd let the press know she was "someone he met through mutual friends" and that they were "enjoying getting to know each other." That first photo of Aiden helping Bree on the sidewalk would be seen in a new light, as a caring boyfriend tending to his clumsy girlfriend.

None of it was a lie. Except for the part where Aiden wasn't Hayden, and wasn't really dating Bree, of course.

He ushered her under the Winterdale Arch, moving his hand from her shoulder to hovering over her lower back. Not quite touching, but close enough to steady her if she stumbled.

"After today, outings will be a little less anonymous, so I wanted to show you something special."

She glanced up at him and she flushed. "I have been in the park before."

"Ah, but not all of it. And not my favorite part of it."

They stepped out from under the bridge, and she turned her head sharply to meet his eyes. Her expression was adorably incredulous.

"*You* have a favorite part of the park? I thought you hated the city."

"Not all of it."

She continued to stare, eyebrows raised, with two rosy spots of pink on her cheeks.

"Fine, ninety-nine percent of this city is a trash can fire full of the dregs of society." He took her hand. "But there are a few spots that aren't completely horrible."

The sunlight filtered through the trees, the leaves the rich green of springtime, and the sky was a perfect blue above them. Aiden breathed in deeply, the smell of car exhaust and general stink of the city melting away the farther into the park they got.

"Now who's finally sighing a happy sigh?" Bree giggled and bumped his shoulder, sending little shots of electricity down his arm.

It was perfect weather and they were headed to his perfect spot. It would have been the perfect date, if Bree had actually wanted to be there with him and not Hayden.

He pushed that thought aside, unwilling for once to dwell on the negative. If he wanted her to love the city, he couldn't be in a bad mood.

They rounded a corner in the path, and the tiny gasp she let out was now his favorite sound in the entire world.

"What's that?"

"Belvedere Castle." He turned to take in the full expression of wonder and amazement on her face at the stone façade emerging from the rocks like something from a fairy tale.

"This is so cool! It's like a real castle."

Letting go of his hand, she ran up the stone pathway that led to the wide patio space overlooking Turtle Pond. He followed her at a slightly slower pace, unable to keep the smile off his face.

Her eyes were bright as they took in the view. "Wow."

"I thought you might like it."

"A random castle in the middle of a park in the middle of a city? What made you think this was my kind of thing?" She twirled on the stones under their feet, like a fairy coming home after a day of mischief.

He laughed, joy at seeing the spot mingling with the pleasure of having made Bree happy. There were no nerves like there'd been at the Plaza, no worries about what she was wearing. She was able to enjoy it, finally finding some beauty in the city that had been treating her so harshly.

It's what he had loved most about this place the first time he'd seen it. The pure fantasy of it had been an unexpected treat on a day he otherwise would have tried to forget. The day Margot told him she was leaving.

Bree turned, her smile bright, but then her face fell when she saw what must have been his moody face at the difficult memory. "I'm sorry, I'm probably embarrassing you, acting like a tourist."

Thankful the contract meant he had a reason to pull her in close to him, he took her hands and spun her around. "But you are a tourist."

"I don't want to be." She pouted. "Is it that obvious?"

He slung his arm around her and led her to the edge of the wall. "Don't worry about it. You're with me."

"How can you tell the difference between the tourists and the people who live here?" Bree asked, her teeth digging into her bottom lip.

Momentarily fixated on her lips, it took Aiden some time to organize his thoughts and answer. She wanted attention, but not the irritated kind New Yorkers directed at those slow-walking, subway-seat hoggers who flooded into the city in summer and during the holidays. If she was worried about sticking out, then it meant she wanted to stay.

He would absolutely help with that.

He held up a finger. "First, any American flag gear is a huge red flag."

She groaned at his terrible pun.

"Also, anyone wearing a sports jersey that's not a New York team. Cargo shorts with running shoes, and tall socks on anyone over the age of eight." Two more fingers went up.

She nodded. "Good to know. What else?"

He considered her for a moment, then took her hand again. "I think it'll be easier to just show you."

The plan had been to walk to the *Alice in Wonderland* statue and spend some time there, but on the spur of the moment, he knew that had to change.

Instead of feeling the normal twist of his gut at this kind of last-minute schedule shift, there was an excited flutter in his chest. Teaching Bree how to fit in would make it so much easier for her, and she'd feel more comfortable with the city sooner. What had taken him months to figure out on his own, he could teach her in an afternoon.

"Wait, what's that?" As they hurried past, she pointed with a finger to the statue he'd meant to show her.

"I'll show you next time."

Now that his plan had changed, he didn't want to get off course. This was the perfect time to walk along Fifth Avenue— a beautiful Friday afternoon before a long weekend. It would be full of tourists, with hopefully a few locals to balance things out.

"First lesson." He shifted his grip from holding her hand to an arm around her shoulder. "Always keep moving."

"Okay." Her eyes turned away from the buildings to focus on the street in front of them. "What's next?"

A group of tourists wandered past them, dragging their feet and stopping to take pictures. "No skinny jeans."

"I think I can manage that." Bree nodded, then glanced up at him. "Why are you helping me?"

That was an excellent question. He couldn't exactly tell her that he was worried she'd bail before the end of the contract.

He also couldn't tell her about the lingering sense of danger clinging to Bree that Aiden had been losing sleep over. That every night for the past week as he'd fallen asleep, he'd imagined every single horrible scenario that could happen to a woman living alone in this city, without friends or family nearby. There wasn't much he could do once he left, but he could make sure he did as much as possible now.

"I like teaching people." There, that was a simple, believable answer.

It also seemed to satisfy Bree well enough. "Is that why you're a trainer?"

"No, it's because it allows me to have both a high-earning potential and flexibility to volunteer at the animal shelter or perform more lucrative work on short notice. Like look-alike gigs and apartment stuff."

"Uffda. You thought of all that?"

She stopped in the middle of a crosswalk to stare at him. A cab turned right and honked, and his heart jumped into his throat. He grabbed her hand and tugged her along before the cabbie lost patience and decided his fare was worth a few bruised pedestrians.

"What was the first lesson?" The second they were on the sidewalk again, he dropped her hand like it was on fire and rolled his shoulders.

She turned to look back across the street, her gaze soft, running her fingers absentmindedly across the palm he'd just been gripping tighter than a life raft in a storm. But at least she kept walking. She looked up at him, ignoring his question and waiting for an answer to hers.

"I wasn't always a trainer." He let his gaze drift over the endless stream of cabs along Fifth Avenue and counted at least a dozen with serious suited figures inside. "My dad gave me the money for the down payment for the apartment, but as a condition, I had to have a steady job to pay the mortgage, not go back to school another four years."

It hadn't been an easy choice, but he hadn't had many options back then. Margot wanted to live in the city, and he'd done whatever it took to make her happy.

A bike sped past them, and Bree jumped out of its way, bumping into Aiden and sending a wave of her sweet perfume over him. She blew out her breath in a huff. "Conditions on a gift feels rude."

Maybe in her world, but in his it was pretty standard. Other than Margot, he'd never told anyone about what his dad had done. He hated the constant reminder that he'd never be good enough in his father's eyes, that he'd always see Aiden as someone needing his help.

At least paying it off was something he'd done entirely on his own, no help from Margot whatsoever.

With a gentle pressure on her back that sent tingles up his arm, Aiden guided Bree around a slow-moving group of well-dressed tourists walking out of their five-star hotel. "When the recession hit, I got laid off like most of the people at the bank I worked at."

Now that he'd started the story, it all wanted to come out. He left out the part where his girlfriend, who had been paying half the mortgage, left him a month after he lost his job for someone twice his age and a net worth in the millions.

"I was at the gym almost every day, and when I told them I'd have to stop my membership, they said I could work there to help make ends meet. I studied nonstop to pass the personal trainer certification in just a few weeks, and that plus hosting people in the second bedroom kept me from losing the apartment."

"That sounds so . . . logical." She paused to look up at a red-brick building, the only spot of color on the long avenue of white façades.

He was tempted to launch into a detailed description of the Knickerbocker Club, but somehow Aiden could tell the history of private gentlemen clubs for the very rich and very white in New York wasn't what would keep Bree interested in the city. So he let her stare and enjoy in silence.

But only for a minute, or it'd be obvious she wasn't from the city.

He took her hand and they kept walking. "How did you pick barista as a job?"

"Because my best friend opened a café, and she worked eighty hours a week, so if I wanted to see her, I had to start working there."

He laughed at the simplicity of it. No deliberation, no endless worrying about making the wrong choice and wasting time and money. Just as simple as a friend opening a café and wanting to hang out with her.

"Did you always live alone in your apartment?" she asked.

He stumbled and righted himself quickly before he blocked the flow of sidewalk traffic. With his arm wrapped around her shoulders, he couldn't see her face, but he could hear the curiosity in her voice.

Their gazes were focused on the sidewalk ahead of them, easily slipping around the people streaming past as if they'd done it a hundred times. They were so quick, anyone who bothered with a second look at his famous face didn't even have time to snap a picture.

"You're walking like a natural."

"I *have* been in cities before, just not New York." She

turned her head, and he caught the glimpse of a smile. "And you're avoiding my question."

He inhaled and caught another whiff of her sugary, floral perfume. It was all to make her more comfortable around him, he reminded himself. The more she knew about him, the more she'd realize he wasn't Hayden and the less nervous she'd be.

Even if telling her everything would be too much, he could share a little.

"No, someone else lived with me." He forced his shoulders to drop an inch. "Someone from college."

They walked for another minute in silence before she said anything.

"Where you minored in biology but majored in finance."

His shoulders relaxed all the way. This was why it was so easy to talk to her. She was curious but didn't pry. When something was clearly hard to talk about, she let it drop.

"My dad said it was a more secure future. Maybe he was worried I wouldn't finish vet school, then struggle to pay back the student loans without a job." Or he was just a control freak who hated animals. "Maybe ten years ago he was right. But the recession hit hard and finance wasn't a safe bet anymore."

"So you became a personal trainer because you like helping people and had a background in biology."

Aiden smiled. The odd path his career had taken didn't always make sense to everyone, but Bree seemed to be following along just fine. He was burning with curiosity about her, eager to figure out how someone so sweet, whimsical, and carefree had set her heart on the city of ruined dreams.

"I think that's enough questions for today. Now it's time for me to ask you some."

SEVENTEEN

From the angle of his head beside her, Bree could see individual eyelashes and the tiny pink flick of his tongue when he licked his lips. She swallowed hard. "Is this really the best place for this?"

His eyebrows drew together, and his mouth turned down. "What do you mean?"

"It doesn't feel like a touristy street." She pulled away from him, just a little. "People are walking too fast. Wouldn't somewhere like Times Square or Rockefeller Center be better?"

He glanced around, the frown still on his face while Bree's heart hammered in her chest.

When he said he wanted to ask her questions, she knew they'd be the deep, probing kind she'd asked him. The clear way out of that was the distraction of asking him to change their plans, which she knew he wouldn't want to do. Except now he was actually listening to her, considering her opinion like it mattered.

Like she mattered.

No, that couldn't be what he was doing. She was disrupting his carefully laid plans, and it was stressing him out. Now that she knew how much he needed Hayden's money, he was probably worried that if he didn't do what she wanted, she'd pull out of the contract.

"You haven't been to Rockefeller Center yet?"

Bree shook her head. "I've been staying close to the apartment." The better to avoid getting lost again, but she wasn't about to tell him that.

"We're about ten blocks away."

"I don't mind the walk." Bree tried not to sound too excited. More people would see her.

The glances they'd gotten so far had been like electricity, powering her up and reassuring her this was what she was supposed to be doing. All she'd wanted was to be noticed, and it had been happening nonstop all morning.

"Bree." There was a tone of warning in his voice.

"Ai—Hayden."

Almost using the wrong name seemed to shock him. Like he'd forgotten they were on an outing, and not just the two of them, on a real date.

"We should take the car." He turned and gave a subtle wave at Marcus and Grant, who'd been trailing behind them the entire time. One of them hurried up, and they had a brief conversation about the change in plans.

The hand around her shoulder slipped down her back, and he nudged her toward a crosswalk. "We can wait in the park until they bring it around." He looked around at the crowded street, his eyes tight.

"Sure. As long as you're leading the way, I'll follow."

That seemed to relax him a little. Bree decided to push her luck. "Can we get a hot dog?"

His hand was at her back as he led her across the street back to the park, and she could feel it tense. "Why?"

"I haven't gotten one yet." She leaned back a little, enjoying the safety of his arms. "Is that too touristy? Is that the next lesson? No food from street vendors?"

"Only if your stomach can handle it." He peered down at her, assessing. "Why do I feel like you could eat a ghost pepper and not feel a thing?"

"Surprisingly, my stomach is not as adventurous as the rest of me."

The corners of his mouth ticked up, and a happy little shiver went through her. If she could just get him to loosen up a little, maybe even laugh, then today wouldn't be a total failure.

"I think you should be okay with a hot dog," Aiden said. "But I wouldn't get your hopes up."

They were back in the shade of Central Park, the over-whelming sounds of the city melting away behind them. If she squinted and ignored all the railings and benches, she could almost pretend she was back in Minnesota, surrounded by nature.

"Getting my hopes up is all I've done most of my life. Why stop now?"

Another quiver of his lips. "I just hope you're not too disappointed."

"I'm never disappointed. Fate always pushes me toward what I need."

"Fate, huh?" Instead of the smirk she usually got from this kind of comment, his mouth and eyes turned down in a thoughtful frown.

"Fate, destiny, luck, whatever you call it." Bree shrugged and Aiden's hand pressed into her back a little harder. "It's why I don't let myself make too many plans. That way, when good things come my way, I can take advantage of them."

He was silent for a moment, as if he was really thinking about what she said, and not about to laugh at her or roll his eyes the way people usually did. "Like this contract."

"Right." They turned a corner, and a hot dog cart appeared. She spread her arms wide and grinned at him. "Or like this delicious treat we're about to enjoy."

"It's a hot dog, Bree, not destiny." He took his hand off her back to pull out his wallet. "And it won't be a good thing."

Excitement buzzing along her skin, she watched as the smiling man behind the cart pulled out a sheet of foil and grabbed a bun. He asked her what she wanted on it, and she hesitated. She looked up at Aiden, whose face was carefully blank.

"Nothing will make a difference."

The possibilities were endless. Bree closed her eyes for a moment, then chose the first thing she saw when she opened them.

"Mustard, please."

Prize in hand, Bree let Aiden lead her to a bench in the park a few feet from the cart. Ignoring the fluttering in her stomach from the way his eyes were intensely focused on her, Bree took a bite with trembling hands. Her heart sank.

The hot dog was, in a word, watery.

"This is kind of gross." She made sure to keep her voice down so he wouldn't be insulted. She could barely swallow the piece of it already halfway chewed in her mouth, but she made an effort.

"What did you expect?" Aiden had no hot dog in his hands, only a smug smile on his perfect face.

"New York is known for its food. Hot dogs are a classic food. How can they mess it up?"

"I would argue that New York is more known for bagels."

Bree chewed and swallowed another weirdly spicy yet bland chunk of hot dog.

"Can we go get bagels instead? I don't think I can eat any more of this."

Aiden laughed, and her chest tightened. She'd won the challenge she'd set for herself today, and it was even better than she could have imagined. The deepness of his laugh was still jarring to her ears, so used to the light, staccato laugh of Hayden Carmichael in his movies.

There was no question in her mind now that they were two entirely different people, and it blew her mind to think she ever could have mixed them up.

Aiden was so clearly . . . Aiden. The tilt of his chin, the angle of his smile. While she was glad the paparazzi photos were fooling people, she was amazed that they were successful. It was so obvious to her that Aiden was a different man. Still a completely gorgeous specimen of rugged maleness, but not Hayden Carmichael.

As if on cue, a group of women stopped a few feet away, whispering and shooting looks their way. Bree got the same thrill of excitement from the attention she'd been getting all morning.

"Time to go." Aiden stood up and extended his hand to help her up. "Before we draw too much attention."

"I thought the whole point was for people to see us." She balled up the rest of the hot dog and tossed it into the first trash can they walked by, their every move watched closely by the group of women.

How could Aiden ever get annoyed by this? It was wonderful to have those eyes on her, to have people wondering about her, who she was, what she was wearing. It took everything in her to not wave at them, say hello, and invite them to come walk with them.

"The point is for the paparazzi to see us, not for groups of women to accost me in the park." He took her hand and placed it in the crook of his arm.

It was a natural, easy movement, like they'd done it

hundreds of times before and not only a handful. Like they weren't still mostly strangers who were basically temporary coworkers in the weirdest job Bree had ever had.

It still felt nice to have her hand on his arm.

They arrived in a more secluded area with a bench, and they settled onto it to wait, Marcus at the head of the trail, keeping an eye on things.

"Are you sure you wouldn't rather see more of the park today?"

"You mean there's more than just castles and soggy hot dogs in Central Park?" She put the hand not on his arm over her heart. "What a surprise."

That got something closer to a real smile out of him, but not another laugh. Now that she'd heard it once, she wanted to hear it at least twice more today.

"What have you seen of the park so far?"

"Only the section right off our street. Every time I tried to go further, I ended up getting lost and wandering for hours."

"I thought that's what you like to do?" He raised an eyebrow, but there was no teasing in his voice.

"It is. I just thought New York would be different." She tucked her hair behind her ear and looked away. How had they ended up talking about something so serious? "I thought I'd be different here."

"You are different. You're not like anyone I've ever met."

It was the same thing people had said to her for her entire life, but for the first time, there was no mocking tone. It sounded like he thought it was a good thing she was different. His hand came to rest on hers, and she turned to look into his eyes. There was no trace of Hayden in them, only Aiden, soft and kind the way he'd been from the start with her.

The air coming into her lungs got caught in her throat, and she had to clear it in order to speak again. She pulled her hand away. "That's a nice way of saying I couldn't find my way out of a paper bag."

This got her the laugh she'd been hoping for. It was a full-bodied one, coming from his stomach and lighting up his entire face, as adorable as it was infectious. She couldn't help giggling along with him.

"I just had the visual of you settling into one, like a cat, curling up and deciding that's your new home." He laughed harder at this, bending over double, the laughter coming in short, hard gasps.

He pulled his arm away from her to put both hands on his knees as his guffaws echoed around them.

She sniggered next to him. "Is this your idea of not drawing attention?"

"Okay, I'm sorry." He took a few deep gulps of air and wiped at his eyes. Then he turned to meet hers, and they both burst into laughter again.

"Stop it, or we'll be arrested for disturbing the peace." She shoved his arm, and when he caught her hand in his, he held onto it.

"Wow, sorry, that never happens to me." With his free hand, he rubbed at his eyes, bright with tears of laughter.

"I can believe that."

This seemed to sober him up a bit. The smile was gone from his face, and he met her eyes with a quiet seriousness that was much more familiar than the deep laugh she was in danger of becoming addicted to.

Aiden took a deep breath. "Do you—"

"Ready to head to Rockefeller Center?" Marcus had reappeared, the soundless sign for Bree that whatever was simmering between her and Aiden was not supposed to happen.

Even if what she wanted to do was sit on this bench all day, teasing him and getting him to laugh.

But that wasn't what he wanted—she could tell by the way he was shifting, eager to stand up and finish up the outing. He had his plan to leave the city, and while she might derail him a little, lighten him up a bit with her jokes and teasing, nothing would keep him from it entirely.

His plans had already been interrupted enough today. She wasn't going to add even more disruption to his life. She sighed and stood up, holding out her hand with a smile. "Let's go."

He might think she was the good kind of different, but that didn't make her anything special to him.

EIGHTEEN

For the second time that day, Aiden found himself taking an unplanned detour, and not totally hating it. Bree was doing something to his brain chemistry.

"Do you come here a lot?" Bree asked, looking around with wide, excited eyes. They were walking close together, and her shoulder would bump into his arm every few steps, sending little pricks of electricity through him. It was very distracting. He stepped closer.

"I used to. I had an office job for like, a minute, in the area." Aiden pointed to the building closest to them. "One of my favorite murals is inside there."

During lunch breaks, he'd wander around, enjoying the contrast of the clean lines of the buildings with the organized chaos of the Plaza. There was no pattern to the pathways people took to cross it, but the space itself was well designed, and the multiple focal points kept it from feeling too crowded in any one spot. He hadn't been here in years, didn't have a reason to come once the temp job was over. It was nice to be back, and even nicer to be the one to show it to Bree. Even though the long, lingering glances from people they passed sent prickles up his arms.

"Did I hear the word 'favorite' again, or was I dreaming?" Laughter tugged at Bree's lips, and he couldn't resist wrapping his arm around her and pulling her close.

"Don't start." He laughed into her hair, then felt her tense. "Is this okay?"

"Um, yeah." She slid her arm around his back. "As long as it's not kissing, right?"

She relaxed against him, but his mood had soured. No kissing. Because he wasn't the one she really wanted. There'd be no limits like that when she went out with Hayden when this was all over.

The back of his neck grew hot. The Plaza was more crowded than he remembered it ever being. His pulse ticked up when he realized a small group of people seemed to be following them. They were still a respectful distance away. For now. He looked back and caught Grant's eye. The bodyguard nodded and maneuvered his way a little closer to Aiden and Bree.

After what happened at the Plaza Hotel, he didn't want to alert Bree to the stares they were getting. What if she overheard someone talking about her again? She'd like the attention, but the thought of someone saying something nasty about her gave him stomach cramps the way being late to work did.

To keep her attention away from the crowds, he started talking about the architecture of Rockefeller Center and the history of its construction.

"How do you know all this?" she asked, her voice full of wonder.

"You mean you didn't research the history of every building in the city before moving here?" He gasped dramatically. "I am shocked."

The laugh that burst from her was more of a snort, and it was so cute he gave her a squeeze.

There was an excited titter from somewhere nearby, and his eyes darted around, looking for the source. His heart dropped into his stomach. It wasn't just that the crowd was getting closer. The tone had shifted. What had been curious murmurs were now more insistent. Eager. Aiden peeked over his shoulder and when he couldn't spot either Grant or Marcus, he tightened his grip around Bree, hoping she wouldn't notice.

This was a bad idea. The spontaneous plan had felt relatively safe. He'd been here before several times, and Bree had seemed so excited about it. But every other time, he'd been here as an anonymous worker drone, not Hayden's look-alike showing around his fake girlfriend. His gut was churning with anxiety as his mind raced to come up with an exit strategy that didn't involve freaking out Bree.

"Are you okay?" asked Bree, looking up at him. "You got really quiet all of a sudden. You were telling me about Lee Lawrie."

"Oh, right." Aiden tried to remember where he'd been in his explanation of the various carvings on all the buildings when he heard a squeal behind him.

"It's him!"

Heart pounding in his ears, he didn't wait to see who they were talking about but grabbed Bree's hand and hustled across the Plaza, back toward Fifth Avenue. With his other hand, he reached for his phone, preparing to let loose a very Hollywood-style tantrum.

"Where the hell are Grant and Marcus?"

"Why? What's going on?" Bree's voice was wavering, and he squeezed her hand in what he hoped was a reassuring way.

"Everything is fine."

Bree turned her head and her eyes widened. "That's a lot of people."

As soon as she said it, it was like they were drowning. People were everywhere, asking him questions, blocking his way, shouting his name. He couldn't see, couldn't even breathe.

"Hayden, is that your new girlfriend?'

"Hayden, I love you!"

"Ohmigosh, it's really him! Hayden, smile!"

The crush was overwhelming, and he didn't know where to look first or what to do. Sweaty panic washed over him. He'd been prepared to pose for a few photos, maybe fake a few signatures.

But he'd never prepared for a crowd of this size, couldn't have pictured what he'd do amid the chaos of dozens of people all trying to talk to him, touch him, see him at once.

Fury weaved its way through his panic. It was Marcus's and Grant's job to keep things like this from happening, but they were nowhere in sight. From across the mass of people, he thought he could see the large ginger head of one of the body-guards trying to push through, but then Bree's grip tightened in his hand, and he turned to look at her.

Her face had gone paler than the limestone buildings surrounding them, and her eyes were almost perfect circles in her terror.

Out of nowhere, an arm shot out, shoving a phone into his face and smacking into Bree's nose. Her cry of pain was drowned out by the question the person attached to the arm was screaming at him.

"Hayden, could I get a picture?"

Rage boiled in his veins, and everything went red. Bree was hurt, and it was all his fault.

He should have stuck to the plan rather than think he could just wander off into the city without being recognized. He should have known that he couldn't rely on Grant and Marcus, on anyone other than himself, to make sure this would work.

"Everyone needs to back up right now!" he yelled.

A few people gasped at his harsh words, but for the most part, they acted like he hadn't even spoken. Beside him, Bree was pinching her nose between her fingers while tears leaked from her eyes.

All reason left his body, the urge to protect her taking over every single brain cell. He'd never felt so out of control before. The muscles he spent hours in the gym perfecting strained against his efforts to hold them back, ready to be used against whoever was hurting Bree.

With a tug at his arm, he realized he might be the one causing her some amount of pain, given how hard he was clutching her hand. This cooled his temper more than anything else. If she couldn't feel safe with him, then none of the rest would matter.

Wrapping his arm around her, he set her head against his shoulder. "Don't look at anyone, okay? I've got you."

With the other arm, he started pushing people away. Not hard, but insistently. There was a break in the crowd, and Grant came rushing through, alternating between spouting out profanities and apologies. Marcus was breaking up the rest of the crowd, urging them to keep their distance and reminding them to respect Hayden's personal space, or these kinds of public appearances wouldn't be possible anymore.

If Aiden had his way, he'd never have another.

"This has never happened before," said Grant, moving behind the two of them and shepherding them toward the car, which was parked very illegally on the sidewalk. "At least, not in New York."

"Can I look now?" Bree was still smushed up against Aiden's shoulder, her hair hiding her face.

"Wait until we get into the car."

Later, he'd stress about what a very depressing picture they were painting of Hayden's new relationship with these outings. Even if the photos from the Plaza Hotel with her crying into her shoulder had worked in their favor, it wouldn't do if all the stories in the press were of him comforting her.

Right now, he was about two seconds away from yelling again. At the bodyguards, at the crowd, at Hayden for putting Bree into this situation. At himself, most of all, for letting something like this happen.

If only he hadn't let himself get carried away by random ideas, then things would have gone smoothly. If he'd just followed his original plan, then Bree wouldn't be hurt right now.

Grant ushered them into the car while Marcus slid into the driver's seat.

"I'm sorry," Aiden said into Bree's hair, his fingers fumbling to check for blood on her face. He searched for that sweet, flowery aroma it usually had. Instead, all he could smell was the stink of the crowd, clinging to him like a leech, sucking out every good feeling he'd had today. "That'll never happen again."

"What?" Bree pulled her head out from under his arm and looked at him.

Her hair was a mess, whole chunks escaping the long braid that lay over her shoulder. One of the hundreds of balls of worry in his chest unknotted to see there was no blood, no bruises. Her makeup was smudged, her eyes a black mess of mascara and lipstick smeared along her cheek.

"That was great," she said, eyes shining.

"Great?" His voice echoed in the car, laced with the same panic and anger coursing through his body. "Are you kidding me?"

There was a brightness to her, a sparkle that would have been infectious in any other situation.

This had to be a hallucination. A dream, a nightmare.

"Are you telling me you enjoyed that? You weren't terrified out of your mind?"

Some of her brightness dimmed. "I mean, it wasn't my favorite thing I've ever done." She smoothed a hand over her face and winced. "My nose hurts a little, but it was more shock than pain that had me crying."

The excited stream of her words picked up steam. "Did you see how they reacted to us? They really believed it. They thought you were Hayden and I was his girlfriend, and people wanted to take my picture. They were fighting just to get a chance to see me."

It took several long inhales followed by slow exhales before Aiden could form words. The adrenaline was practically flowing out of her pores, but she hadn't admitted to being scared. Rather than call her out on that, he focused on what she'd seemed most excited about.

All this time he thought Hayden was the main draw for her, with the money as a bonus, but maybe that wasn't true.

"You really like that kind of attention?"

A flush crept up her cheeks, and she looked over at Marcus, who was driving, before her eyes flicked to Grant sitting on Aiden's other side. "I've never had that kind of attention before. Maybe you have, but no one . . . no one's ever looked at me like that before."

"Like they wanted to eat you alive?"

"Like I was important."

It was the softest, saddest voice he'd ever heard from her. Her eyes were still looking away from him, her cheeks still tinged pink. She inhaled, and he stayed quiet, hoping she'd say more but worried what it might be.

"When you're in the middle of five sisters, you have to stand out, you know?"

He didn't, but nodded once.

"New York has always been my thing, and nothing has felt like it's been going right so far, and this finally felt like something was working . . . " She shook her head and looked down at her hands. "I'm sorry it scared you."

"I wasn't scared." The blood was still pounding in his ears, calling out his lie. He'd been terrified. He rolled his shoulders and ran a hand along the back of his neck, trying to ease some of the tension he knew would be there for hours. "I was worried about you."

"Well, I'm sorry I made you worry." She gave him a small smile. "I'm used to Leigh worrying, but no one else ever does."

Something in his chest felt like it was ripping in two. He might have had the more obviously crappy dad, but it didn't sound like Bree's family was sunshine and rainbows the way she was.

"Bree, you wouldn't be in these situations if it weren't for me. Of course I worry. I'm sorry I couldn't keep you safe."

"That's not your job," Grant said beside him, and they both looked his way. "We won't ever let that happen again."

The bodyguard was already an intimidating presence. That was kind of the point. But the serious look on his face was a hundred times scarier than anything Aiden had ever seen before.

Bree put a hand on Aiden's arm. "I never felt unsafe with Aiden."

His arm flexed where she touched it. "Even so, we don't have to keep going. There's a clause about guaranteed safety, and this might be enough to be a breach of contract. We'd still get the whole fee."

Marcus's and Grant's jobs might be in jeopardy, but that wasn't what Aiden was worried about right now. If they couldn't handle a crowd like that, then Hayden shouldn't be using them.

"You want to stop?" At the sound of Bree's voice breaking, he turned to look at her. Her eyes were shimmering with tears. "What if we pull out and don't get everything? You shouldn't have to lose out just because of me."

His heart almost stopped. Was she really worried about his plans? Or did she just not want to miss out on spending time with Hayden and the attention she'd get from him?

She bit her lip. "Maybe we could just do something less public for the next outing."

Public was the whole point, but he knew what she meant. Her tears were like little hammers striking his chest.

This was someone who'd been ignored her entire life, and Aiden had the power to put her in the spotlight, which would make her happy. She had a dream, and he could make it happen.

"*If* we keep going, we have to do it according to plan. No last-minute changes like today."

She nodded quickly, wiping her hands over her eager eyes and smearing her makeup even more. Somehow, she was even more beautiful with it like that. This gorgeous mess of a person who was willing to do anything for the kind of attention being with Hayden would get her. Aiden found himself powerless to do anything other than make sure she got that chance.

With a sigh, he leaned back in his seat and closed his eyes. "Alright. We'll keep going."

Her hand rested on top of his briefly and she squeezed, murmuring a soft "Thank you" that drove those hammers right into his heart to break it in two.

It was pretty much a guarantee at this point that he'd be wrecked at the end of this. All he could do was plan for it and prepare for the pain. Maybe this time it wouldn't be so bad.

NINETEEN

Bree had lied to Aiden.

Her nose hurt a lot.

She spent the morning after the disaster at Rockefeller Center lying on her horrendous couch with a towel full of ice on her face, wishing she'd done it the night before instead of scrolling the endless pictures on social media of the incident until she'd fallen asleep in her clothes. The photos were all fuzzy, but incredible. She looked so scared, and Aiden . . . he looked magnificently furious.

It wasn't the first time she'd gotten hurt in a crowd. But it was the first time someone had been there next to her, trying to protect her from it. He'd been so ready to defend her, and she had no idea what to do with that.

So she'd lied and said it didn't hurt that much, which she regretted now, but not enough to go downstairs to ask for his help or call Leigh. Birdbrain Bree would have changed her mind, but not New York Bree. The decision had been made to suffer alone. Now she'd stick to it.

With no plans for the day other than switching out the ice

once it started to melt, she turned to her default sick day activity: a Hayden Carmichael marathon.

There was an order she usually did this in, but since she was basically living *Escape to New York*, she skipped that one and went right to the second in the lineup, a two-year-old holiday rom-com where Hayden played a time-traveling knight. She settled in to watch, one hand holding the ice against her nose, and the other in a bowl of popcorn.

Halfway through the movie, however, there wasn't the usual rush of comfort from the cheesy plot and slow burn romance. Only an ache, like something was missing.

She paused the movie and looked around the room. Popcorn. Ice. What else did she need?

Her eyes fell to her hands, which somehow had picked up the gum wrapper chain from the side table and started playing with it. Her breath hitched.

The ache was for Aiden.

She liked him, and she'd gotten the impression yesterday that he liked her too. Not a sign, exactly, more of a feeling. A strong one. Even though she was always changing her mind and messing up his plans, he'd agreed to go somewhere else simply because she'd asked. When the fans had mobbed them, he'd protected her and been worried about her in a way only Leigh was.

Then he'd wanted to cancel the contract and still get the full payment. It was sweet that he was concerned about her getting hurt, but he'd only agreed to keep going if they did things his way. No more distractions from Birdbrain.

At the end of the day, it was the money he wanted. That's all this was. Her feelings weren't a sign. They were wrong like they usually were.

With a flick of her hand, the gum wrapper chain fell to the floor, and she turned her attention back to the movie. Hayden was the dream, not Aiden. He had his plan for his life, and she was only a part of it temporarily.

The movie ended without Bree taking in any of the second half, and she started the next movie on autopilot. Her nose was numb, and so was the rest of her.

The opening scene of the jukebox musical that had shown the world that Hayden was a triple threat flashed across the screen. Bree's chest loosened a little, thinking about how she'd learned all his dance moves by heart in Agatha's studio. She'd read an article about his love of dance and known even then that their destinies were somehow intertwined. They'd have so much to talk about when they finally hung out.

The knock at Bree's door was an unwelcome interruption, but she hit pause and dragged herself away. It was probably Aiden, checking to make sure his investment was safe. She quickly ran a hand through her tangled hair before opening it, a smile plastered to her face to prove that nothing hurt anywhere on her body.

The smile vanished at once. Mrs. Wilson stood in the hallway, arms folded tightly across her chest, the deep lines around her mouth fixed in a scowl.

"When will Zara be getting those chairs?"

"I'm sorry?" She frowned but held her ground like New York Bree would.

"It's been over two weeks since I told her Aiden would be bringing them over. He's been too distracted by you to do what he promised me."

Bree's heart gave a little tug at the thought of her "distracting" Aiden.

Then she saw his head appear at the top of the stairs, and her heart stopped entirely.

Aiden glanced at Bree, who'd frozen with her door half-open. He gave the old woman a smooth smile. "Good morning, Mrs. Wilson."

"Don't you 'good morning, Mrs. Wilson' me." She stabbed a finger in his direction. "What are you doing, clomping up here, talking to *her*?" Now her finger swung like an avenging sword toward Bree.

"Is there a reason I shouldn't be talking to Bree?" Aiden leaned against the old woman's doorframe and crossed his arms, his tone light. Meanwhile, Bree's heart had started beating again, a hundred miles a minute.

"She won't stick around. I can tell." Mrs. Wilson narrowed her eyes. "Agatha was my best friend, and she didn't stay. This one has the same look about her."

This finally broke Bree out of her trance. "Why did Agatha leave New York?"

Mrs. Wilson narrowed her eyes. "None of your business."

"And who I talk to is none of yours." Aiden raised an eyebrow. "I'll see if I can borrow Tony's truck this afternoon. You know I don't have a car."

This seemed to mollify Mrs. Wilson somewhat, but not entirely.

"Took you long enough." She sniffed. "Stop by before you go. I'll have some food for you to take over to her as well."

Aiden chuckled. He waited until Mrs. Wilson went back into her apartment before he turned back to Bree. The amused grin on his face disappeared, and his brow furrowed. "I can move them on my own. I'm sure you have other things to do."

There was no point in trying to be New York Bree with him. He'd seen firsthand what a mess she was. "I literally have nothing planned."

His lips curved up again at this, and he leaned on the wall next to her door. "Really? I'm shocked."

She couldn't resist teasing him back. "I can't wait to drive in New York."

The horrified look on his face pulled a laugh out of her.

"You will do no such thing," he growled.

"What? I've helped people move before." She let her hand drop from the door and took a step back, silently inviting him in.

He shook his head. "I need to get to a client. I just wanted to apologize again for yesterday."

"It wasn't your fault. I asked to go there." Something suddenly occurred to her, why he might be feeling this sense of responsibility for her. "You know it wasn't your fault I ran into that door. It would've happened eventually."

He frowned, the look so unlike Hayden, and her breath hitched a little.

"Well, helping me move chairs certainly makes up for it." She did a happy little shimmy with her upper body. "And now I get to see more of the city."

He chuckled, the sound sending warmth through Bree's chest. "You are way too excited about moving furniture. It's unnatural."

"I'll get them all cleaned up." She bustled into her apartment and called out over her shoulder. "Come back when you've got the truck."

And just like that, a new plan for the day had fallen into her lap.

And just like that, another day's plans had been derailed by Bree. At least this time it wouldn't end in them getting attacked by fans in Rockefeller Center.

He hoped.

As they drove through lower Manhattan, Bree craned her

neck to take in the streets, closer together and even more crowded than uptown. When Aiden moved onto a larger road by the river, she let out a little sigh, and he frowned.

"That's one of your disappointed sighs." Yes, he knew them all by now. No, he did not think that was a bad sign or anything.

"I wanted to see more of the city."

"You can see Jersey City on the other side of the river."

To their right, high rises dotted the sky above the dark-blue water of the Hudson.

"Not that city. Can't we go through downtown?"

"No."

"Why not?"

"Because this is Tony's truck, and I hate driving it, and I'd like this to be over as soon as possible." His fingers were almost numb from gripping the steering wheel.

It had been ages since he'd driven anywhere, and he mentally added "get used to driving again" to his endless list of things to do before he left New York. None of the towns he'd scoped out to live in had buses, so he'd have to get used to it one way or another.

"Why didn't you ask Tony to drive?"

"He had a thing."

"A thing?"

Aiden shifted. "A date."

"Oh."

He glanced her way, trying to interpret her expression. A real date. The kind that men and women went on when they were actually interested in each other, not paid to spend time together by a privacy-seeking megastar.

Hayden Carmichael wasn't paying them to do this, however. But it wasn't a date. It was just a neighbor helping a neighbor, driving an hour away to deliver a few chairs to another neighbor's granddaughter . . .

Now Bree let out a happy sigh.

"What's up?" Even though his brain was screaming at him to keep his eyes on the reckless drivers around him, his eyes flicked toward her, like bees toward the sweetest flower of a garden.

It was a vicious circle, feeling anxious about driving, then relaxed when he got a glimpse of her, then panicked when he realized he'd had his eyes off the road again.

He should have done this by himself, but she'd hopped into the passenger's seat the second the last chair was loaded into the back. Like they'd done this a thousand times together already.

"Just thinking that this is the kind of thing that happens back home."

"Driving across an island with a truckload of antique furniture?"

"Not an island, but around a lake, sure. I've helped a ton of people move over the years."

Aiden let himself concentrate on the road for a few minutes as he pondered this.

"You lived near a lake? That must be nice." They hadn't talked much about where she was from. It was like she wanted to erase it entirely, start completely fresh here.

"It was nice, but a lake is still. Unmoving." Bree pointed out the window. "Now a river . . . "

This sigh was deep and full of longing. "I haven't seen the river yet. Not this close."

"Really? It's only a few blocks away from the apartment." It had been one of the first things he'd done. Margot hadn't gone with him. She never had, actually. There wasn't a single memory of the two of them hand in hand, walking along the river. "It's actually one of my favorite things about New York."

"One of your favorite things? Sounds like you have a lot of them."

Another flick of his eyes, and he caught the smirk on her face.

"It's a short list." Though it seemed to be growing the more time he spent with Bree. All the history and beauty that lay just under the surface seemed to burst through whenever she was near. Though nothing about driving to Brooklyn was beautiful, the time with her in the car wasn't the worst way to spend an afternoon.

"I know, it should have been one of the first things I did." She tucked a strand of wild hair behind her ear. "But I focused on the big sights. Times Square, the Empire State Building, all the things that make New York so different from everywhere else."

She was quiet for a moment and stared out the window.

"In Minnesota, you're never far from water. I do miss that."

The urge to reach out and grab her hand was overwhelming.

"We can go to the Hudson River Greenway for our next outing." They still had two outings left. The email the publicist had sent that morning with the pictures also had a few ideas, all restaurants or clubs. None of them had seemed that interesting.

"Does it have to be as Hayden Carmichael and his girl-friend?" Bree took a deep breath. "Could you just take me as a neighbor? Like how you're helping me now?"

He inhaled sharply. Not quite a date, but not quite nothing either. He knew she wasn't interested in him, not like that, but it was something. Something that would turn into absolutely nothing.

"Sure, if you want."

The smile that broke across her face was quickly becoming his absolute favorite thing in New York. A warm ball of light wedged itself behind Aiden's lungs and stayed there for the rest of the drive.

TWENTY

Brooklyn was like Manhattan, but completely different. Bree was sure that Aiden would have a list of what made the two boroughs distinct, with specifics on architecture and historical facts about various landmarks.

All Bree could tell with her untrained eye was that the buildings weren't as tall, and the streets were wider. Or maybe they weren't really wider, but the lack of skyscrapers made it feel like they were.

"You can see the sky here," she said when they got out of the truck.

Aiden frowned and glanced up. "You can see the sky in Manhattan too."

Even though the buildings on their street were the same height as all of these, it felt less overwhelming. There was room to breathe here, and Bree took a deep breath. Then she coughed.

"Not enough sky to blow away all the car fumes, though," said a new voice, and heat traveled up Bree's cheeks.

A gorgeous young woman with dark-brown skin and curly hair walked down the steps of the brownstone that Aiden had parked in front of. Her clothes were the perfect mix of trendy and vintage, her bun effortless and chic on top of her head.

"Hey there, movie man."

There was just a tiny tensing of his shoulders, and his eyes darted left and right before he waved at her. "Hey, Zara."

"You know I have no need for dining room chairs." She folded her arms across her chest, a dozen mismatched bracelets jangling. Something sparkled from the neat row of five piercings in her left ear.

Bree's chest tightened with a familiar burn of envy.

Leaning against the truck, Aiden grinned up at Zara. "Yup."

"You know I'm just going to store them at my studio and only bring them out the next time my grandmother comes to visit."

"Yup."

A smile split Zara's face in two, and Aiden started laughing.

"Next time she comes, keep her, will you?" Aiden gestured to Bree, who had frozen on the sidewalk next to the truck. "Poor Bree needs a break."

"Hi." Bree waved, her arm feeling like a dead weight.

Her voice sounded wooden even to her ears. Aiden looked her way with a furrowed brow but didn't say anything.

Tiny balls of stinging jealousy sat heavy in Bree's gut, blocking any urge to launch into her typical, bubbly midwestern rambling. Here was a woman who was the epitome of everything New York Bree was supposed to be, and she didn't know how to act around her.

Aiden seemed ready to make up for her silence, however, and chatted happily with Zara. The three of them made quick work of getting the eight chairs into the hallway of her building. Bree kept quiet the entire time.

"You don't want us to take them down to your studio?" Aiden wiped his arm across his forehead.

Zara waved a hand. "You've already come all this way. I can get them to the studio."

"You're sure?"

She leveled Aiden with a look that spoke of countless conversations going exactly the same way, of Aiden wanting to help, and Zara insisting she didn't need it.

Bree looked between the two of them. It was a friendly thing, wasn't it? Kind and generous and helpful, Aiden was a good friend.

All thoughts of friendship evaporated when Zara placed a hand on Aiden's arm, however. Bree's body went ice-cold, like she'd just taken a dip in her hometown lake in winter.

"You want to come in for a minute before you drive back?" Zara smiled. "My grandmother would be furious if I didn't repay your kindness with some cookies and tea."

Aiden looked at Bree, and in the long pause that followed, she realized he was waiting for her to answer. He was leaving it up to her what they did.

The floor shifted under her feet, and she steadied herself against one of the chairs they'd stacked in the small hallway. She was sure he had a plan for the afternoon, but he was letting her decide instead. Even after everything that had gone wrong yesterday, he wasn't forcing her to follow his schedule.

Of course, cookies with Zara wasn't a safety risk the way the spontaneous Rockefeller Center visit had been. This was very low risk for him.

Still, to show he understood that at least part of her thrived on spontaneity and leaving herself open to last-minute choices meant a lot. Even if it also meant he still saw her as Birdbrain Bree.

The air in the hallway was stuffy, and she gulped in a lungful of stale air. The itch to leave was strong, but Aiden probably wanted to stay and talk to his friend.

Bree didn't know what to do. She needed a sign, something to make the choice for her.

"We won't be a bother?" she asked.

Zara gave her a friendly smile from her perch at the top of the steps. "Not at all. I have plenty of cookies."

Of course she did.

It wasn't the sign Bree had wanted, and the choice hovered over her, daring her to make the wrong one.

Did she want to stay and watch Aiden's easy exchanges with this cool, perfect New Yorker?

Or did she want to tread the more familiar path of wandering around, letting the mood guide her random turns and discover whatever happened to be down that particular street?

Aiden wasn't anything other than a colleague and a neighbor. They were the kind of friends who helped each other because they had to, not because they wanted to. He hadn't even wanted to drive out here until Mrs. Wilson had bugged him, after all.

"You go ahead, Aiden." Bree took a step back down the stairs and gestured at the street behind them. "I kind of want to walk around, explore Brooklyn a little. We can meet up later."

"You're sure?"

They were the same words he'd asked Zara, but now his voice held a protective tone that reminded her of his arms wrapped around her in the middle of the crowd yesterday.

This protective vibe that made her feel like the way he was checking in with her needs, her desires, letting her interrupt his plans, might be something more.

Except without a sign, there was no way to know for sure.

She shivered and Aiden frowned.

"It's getting chilly, and you don't have a jacket."

Or maybe he was still a total control freak who needed to loosen up.

She rolled her eyes and squeezed past the piled-up chairs. "I'll be fine. I'll meet you back here in an hour."

Then she walked into the Brooklyn sunshine on her own, ready to see what this new part of the city had to offer her.

An hour and a half later, they were driving home from Brooklyn through terrible traffic.

"Zara's just a friend, you know," Aiden said.

Bree kept her eyes out the window and kept her tone casual. "Okay."

And it was. Really. Her time walking alone around Brooklyn had been good for her. For starters, she hadn't gotten lost, which was the clearest sign she'd had in days.

Of what, she didn't know yet. Fate would keep guiding her until it became obvious.

He cleared his throat. "It's just, you seem—"

Before he could finish, her phone rang. Her stomach clenched when she saw who it was.

She gripped the phone tightly to her ear. "Leigh? What's wrong?"

This was the busiest time for her café, and only something major could pull her away.

"Nothing. Something good happened, actually." Leigh's voice was shimmering with excitement.

"Oh?" Now that her heart was beating its normal rhythm again, Bree looked over at Aiden.

He frowned and mouthed, "Everything okay?"

She nodded and the lines in his face smoothed out.

"My parents surprised me with an early birthday present," Leigh said.

"That's nice of them." It wasn't clear yet why a present deserved a phone call in the middle of the afternoon, but it was always nice to hear from Leigh.

Bree wanted to tell her about her day, but not with Aiden sitting next to her. The walk around Brooklyn had stirred up plenty of thoughts about him, but she'd need a whole night alone with Leigh to unpack them.

"Friday's a school holiday, and they showed up to watch the girls . . . and gave me a ticket to New York."

"Are you serious?" A smile broke across Bree's face, and her hand shot out to tap wildly on Aiden's shoulder. "So you're on your way here?"

"I'm here! My plane just landed."

Bree turned to look at Aiden and realized her hand was still on his shoulder. The muscles were tense beneath her fingers. She quickly removed her hand, and he raised an eyebrow, eyes never leaving the road ahead of him.

"You need me to pick her up?" he asked.

Leigh laughed. "Is that Aiden with you?"

"Yeah, we were dropping off some furniture." She glanced at Aiden and put her hand over her phone. He looked so stressed out. "Are you sure? I can take a rideshare. I'm not subjecting her to the subway on her first day here."

There was a quiver to his lips, then he shook his head once and flicked on the turn signal. "LaGuardia or JFK?"

Bree repeated his question to Leigh. "Newark."

A quick nod, and he maneuvered his way across two lanes of traffic to turn left.

Guilt fluttered in her chest. Even she knew it was a pain to get to New Jersey.

Once again, she'd completely messed up his plans for the day. He was a really nice guy, too nice sometimes, and she was taking advantage. This was way more than he should be doing for her.

"I'll bring you a hot dish to thank you for today," she said.

"That's not necessary." He didn't look upset, however, just focused on the road.

"We'll see you soon." She hung up and turned to Aiden. "Do you want me to drive?"

He glowered at her. Clearly he didn't trust her to drive any more than he liked driving himself.

Once again, he'd had to save her. It should have made her feel special, but this was different from protecting her from the crowds. Things usually ended up working out for Bree without worrying too much about the details, but lately it felt less like it was fate helping and more like relying on Aiden.

Depending on Leigh was fine for Birdbrain Bree, but her walk around Brooklyn had given her ideas of how different her life could be as New York Bree. She could picture herself staying, which she hadn't been able to even a week ago.

The details were still hazy, but they felt almost like a plan for the future, not just a dream. It was all bubbling around in her head without settling, like a fizzy drink waiting to explode out of a bottle. Leigh's timing was perfect.

The song on the radio changed, and Bree did a little happy dance. Aiden glanced her way and shook his head. Something that was almost a smile flashed across his face.

Before she could change her mind, Bree asked the question that had popped into her mind while walking around Brooklyn. "Do you think Brian would give me a job at his café?"

"Are you worried about money? Is the contract not enough?"

Bree played with a strand of her hair before tucking it behind her ear. "For a while. I don't want to be scrambling at the last minute."

"That almost sounds like you have a plan." Now he was definitely smiling.

Heat spread across her face, and she looked out the window. A solid wall of cars surrounded them, and they hadn't moved in a few minutes.

"I need more social interaction, and this will end in a few weeks," she said. "Then the only person I'll see on a regular basis will be Mrs. Wilson."

He turned his head to check his blind spot, then flipped on the blinker and squeezed the truck into the right lane before he spoke again. "You'll have your date with the real Hayden. That's social interaction."

"Oh, right." She hadn't even been thinking of that, just that Aiden wouldn't have a reason to see her anymore. "That's only a one-time thing though."

"Don't you want it to be more than that?"

She opened her mouth to say yes, but hesitated. Hayden was what New York Bree wanted, after all. Wasn't it?

Turning in her seat, she let her eyes take him in, really take him in. He was in full Aiden Johnson mode—old jeans and a ragged hoodie, a hat pulled low over his eyes, his sunglasses dangling from the collar of his hoodie. He was magnificent all on his own, with no comparison to anybody.

He took his eyes off the car in front of him and their gazes locked. Something in the air shimmered between them, words unsaid, promises yet to be made, and the explosion of possibilities now felt infinite.

Bree leaned toward him, unsure what she intended to do, but trusting the universe would guide her in the same way it always had to something wonderful. Aiden leaned forward as well, just an inch, but it felt like he was surrounding her, invading her senses. Everything else faded away: New York Bree, Hayden, all of her hazy new plans for Brooklyn.

A car horn blared, and they both jumped back.

"I'll talk to Brian," Aiden said quietly, turning his attention back to the traffic around them.

"Thanks." She brushed her hair away from her face and turned the radio off. The message from the universe had been loud and clear. Hayden was part of her future in New York, not Aiden.

They rode the rest of the way to the airport in silence.

TWENTY-ONE

"We should all get dinner together," Bree said.

They were on the way back from the airport, in the middle of the Lincoln Tunnel, all squeezed in tight into the front seat of Tony's truck. Aiden was using all of his energy to keep his arm from brushing against Bree's.

"Sure," he said.

The decision was just as uncomfortably effortless as all his other recent changes in plans Bree instigated. She asked, he didn't even think about what he'd already scheduled, and he said yes.

"Isn't it too late to go out?" Leigh asked.

Bree's best friend was quieter, more serious than Bree, though she had similar dark, wavy hair. Exactly the kind of person Aiden would be looking for once he started his new life in a small town somewhere.

"It's never too late to go out in New York." Bree was doing her little dance again, the happiness radiating off her like a heat lamp. "Everything's open all the time."

"That's not entirely true," Aiden said. They emerged from the tunnel, and the two women gasped in unison. It wasn't the best view of the city by any means, but with the sun setting behind the buildings and the lights sparkling, it was certainly impressive. There was a surprising pang in his chest to realize he'd miss these sunset views once he left.

"I can give you the name of some places close to the apartment, but I need to get the truck back to Tony."

"But you said you'd have dinner with us." The pout in Bree's voice almost made him miss the turn.

"We can all go tomorrow." Once he'd regained some semblance of control over his decision-making capacities.

"Is that really a good idea?" Leigh asked. She shifted and pulled something from the bag between her feet. Aiden looked over to see a tabloid with a fuzzy photo of Bree and Aiden on the cover. "I think people might recognize you."

Aiden's eyes fell on Bree, who was staring at the picture and biting her lip. The sigh that escaped her lips was one of her disappointed ones. Part of him thought it was because the picture wasn't really of her with Hayden.

But the other smaller, stupider part that had leaned toward her in the truck earlier, hoped her disappointment was for something else.

Aiden's hands tightened on the steering wheel. "I'll figure something out."

In the end, it was Tony who found the solution. When Aiden dropped off his truck after leaving Bree and Leigh at the apartment, Tony reminded him they'd promised his mother a family dinner at her house out in Queens. So while it would undoubtedly be disastrous in its own way, at least Bree would be safe, and no one would be taking their picture.

Less than twenty-four hours later, Aiden was staring into his bathroom mirror, fussing with a tie he only ever wore when he visited Mrs. Russo.

There were approximately eight hundred and five ways that things could go wrong, but Tony had an answer for all of Aiden's worries.

"Someone will recognize me on the train."

"Not dressed like that." Tony walked into the bathroom and raised his eyebrows at Aiden's ball cap and hoodie worn over his navy-blue suit. "You look like you're about to rob a church collection plate."

"You'd know, wouldn't you?"

"Hey, I was four. I thought people were putting money in *and* out."

"I wonder what other stories your mom might tell us tonight."

"Nothing, if she ever wants me to come back." Glancing in the mirror from behind Aiden, Tony ran a hand through his gray-streaked black hair.

"We should get going." Aiden checked his watch. "Your mom will be mad if we're late."

"She's always mad. I haven't given her grandchildren yet."

The possibility seemed more unlikely the longer Aiden knew Tony. Almost a decade older than Aiden, he was at the age where most people had settled down, even in the city.

When Aiden first met him at the gym as a client, he'd had stories to tell almost every day of women he was dating. Those hadn't slowed down at all over the years. Aiden liked to tease that Tony's popularity with women was all thanks to Aiden's excellent training that kept him in peak physical shape.

But the truth was, for some people, that kind of love just wasn't in the cards. Not for Aiden, and not for Tony. As sure as Aiden was that Tony would never leave New York, he knew his friend would remain a bachelor for the rest of his life.

Much to the disappointment of his mother.

"You have, like, eighteen cousins. Don't they all have kids?" A flood of panic shot into Aiden's stomach, and he stopped in the middle of his living room. "They won't all be there tonight, will they?"

Family dinners at the Russo house could get very big, very quickly. Yet another way tonight was a potential disaster.

"Nah, she said it's just us and my aunt." Tony paused at the door, then looked back with a grin. "And her new dog."

Aiden relaxed a little at that. If there was an animal around, he could focus on that.

Tony headed down the hallway. "I hope you warned her how attractive your best friend is so she doesn't accidentally fall in love with me."

The laugh that Aiden forced out of his throat was weak, but Tony didn't seem to notice. He was already hopping up the stairs two at a time. It was one of Tony's favorite jokes, but it was even less funny than the first time he'd made it.

The fear of losing Bree to someone else shouldn't make Aiden this upset. For starters, she wasn't his to be lost. If she could be with anyone, why not with Tony? After all, he had something Aiden didn't—a desire to stay in the city. Tony could be her perfect match.

Except he was all about the easy hookups, and despite Bree's constantly changing whims, she didn't seem like the casual dating kind of woman. But that could just be Aiden's wishful thinking clouding his judgment.

Either way, it didn't shift a single iota of the jealousy rumbling around in his gut.

Tony knocked on the door to Bree's apartment.

"Coming," called Leigh's voice, and they heard the click-clack of heels on wood. A breathless and flushed Leigh opened the door, her dark hair in a topknot on her head. "Sorry, we're just having a small bathroom issue. You should probably wait out here."

Her eyes flicked from Aiden's to Tony's. "Oh, hi there. I'm Leigh Campbell. Nice to meet you."

Beside him, Aiden could feel Tony tense. A quick look at his friend revealed his eyes had gone completely round, and his mouth was hanging slightly open. Aiden had never seen such an adoring expression on Tony's face before.

It was also rare to have Tony be so quiet. When a beat passed and Tony remained silent, Aiden nudged him.

"This is my friend Tony."

"Anthony Russo." The trance broken, he took a step forward and leaned against the doorframe, beaming down a dazzling smile on Leigh. "I'm a contractor. Bathrooms are my specialty."

The corners of her mouth twitched. "Isn't that convenient. Come on in."

He followed Leigh into the apartment like she was leading him through the gates of paradise.

Aiden didn't know if he wanted to laugh or cry. Of all the disastrous possibilities, this had not been on his list. Tony having a fling with a tourist was par for the course, so maybe he should have expected this.

Except, he wasn't looking at Leigh like she was a fling. That unexpected piece of things set a new wave of anxiety washing through him.

"Hi."

He turned toward Bree's voice at his side, blinking away the confusing thoughts, only for everything to go cloudy again at seeing her. Her hair was long and loose around her shoulders, and she was wearing a blue dress that made her eyes sparkle.

"You look great."

She raised an eyebrow. "Not just fine?"

He rubbed his hand on the back of his neck. "Great."

She flushed, then folded her arms across her chest and nodded at the doorway to the bathroom, where the sound of Leigh's singsongy Minnesota accent was mixing with Tony's rougher New York one. "Is he really a contractor or did he just say that to impress her?"

"He's one of the best. Helped me get downstairs into shape."

"Well, it looks amazing down there, so he must be."

"I did a lot too." Inexplicably, Aiden's chest puffed out. "I put together all the furniture and can repair a lot of the smaller stuff."

He'd been working on his apartment all day, getting it ready to sell. Walking into the travesty of Bree's living room again had his synapses firing away on a plan to make it better for her before he left.

"Very impressive." Laughter shimmered in her eyes, and her lips twisted to the side.

The urge to kiss the smirk off her face bubbled up, and he had to ball his hands into fists in his pockets instead.

She stepped toward him, her hands trailing along the back of the couch and her eyes gazing into his. "Maybe you could help me put mine together, once I finally find some?"

His heart hammered in his ears. He took a step back and bumped into a chair. "Absolutely."

He shouldn't be feeling this way. Nothing had changed about their situation. They were still pretending to be dating because of the deal with Hayden, because of the money it would give Aiden and the attention it would get Bree.

Except here he was, taking her to meet the closest thing to family he had in the city, in a suit he'd bought for vet school interviews that Hayden wouldn't be caught dead in. All because she'd asked.

Something had shifted on the ride to Brooklyn. All the plans for his life were taking a new shape, with Bree at the center.

It was nothing like it had been with Margot. They'd been in love in the way all twenty-two-year-olds thought they were. In the way that couldn't survive unemployment and the attention from an older, wealthier option.

Even if Aiden thought she should care a bit more than she seemed to, he knew Bree didn't really care about money. It was the status she craved, the attention and prestige of being attached to someone important.

Aiden could never have that here in the city, but he could in a smaller town. The life Bree seemed to want could fit perfectly into the plan he already had. If she was the wife of the only vet in a close-knit community, everyone would know who she was, say hello to her on the street. He could give all that to her.

Calm down. She just asked you to help put together furniture, not propose to her.

Thankfully, like a good best friend, Tony saved him from doing or saying anything he'd regret later with a perfectly timed interruption.

"I can come by tomorrow to get all this fixed for you." Wiping his hands on a towel, Tony stepped out of the bathroom. Leigh followed close behind, with what could only be described as stars in her eyes.

"I thought we might have an outing tomorrow," Aiden said and looked at Bree. It was as spontaneous a thought as he'd ever had, but her request for help with furniture made the plan fall into place right before his eyes. "There's a big flea market that only happens once a week. I'll talk to Marcus and Grant about the security of the location, but it's nowhere near as popular as Rockefeller Center. We could look for some furniture for you."

"No assembly required?" Her eyes lit up. "That sounds like fun."

Leigh glanced between the two of them with a small smile on her face. "While you do that, I could stay here at the apartment to let Tony in."

"Works for me," said Tony.

It was only because Aiden knew Tony so well that he could see the excitement shining through his friend's suavely inscrutable expression.

"Perfect. When I get back, Leigh and I can go sightseeing." Bree gave Aiden a nudge. "All the super touristy stuff Mr. Carmichael can't take me to see without us getting mobbed."

"I thought that was what you were doing today." Aiden frowned but should have expected the plans Bree had rattled on about on the drive home yesterday wouldn't have stuck. "What did you do all day?"

Bree tucked her hair behind her ear and didn't look him in the eye. "We wandered around Brooklyn for a while."

"Did you have fun?" He looked at Leigh. "I know I always do with Bree."

Leigh smiled at him. "Bree's thinking of moving there."

"Brooklyn?" The hammering in Aiden's heart was back. "Why would you move all the way out there?"

Bree shrugged. "It had a better vibe."

It was such a Bree response, he should have expected it, but the thought still made his chest tighten and palms tingle.

"That's not a reason for picking where you live," he said.

"Why, how do you pick?"

"Return on investment. Proximity to jobs and entertainment and, if you're in a city, public transportation." The evening sunlight streaming through the window glinted off her hair, and he was momentarily distracted.

He blinked, then focused again. "When I bought my place, those were the main search criteria. I didn't even want to visit it, but the realtor highly recommended it."

"Of course you didn't." Casting an *I told you so* look at Leigh, Bree threw up her hands.

"Didn't you move here without knowing anything about the apartment?" He cocked an eyebrow. "How'd that turn out for you?"

Bree opened her mouth, then closed it and squared her shoulders. "It's just a decorating issue."

One he would get solved as soon as possible. "So why look at Brooklyn?"

"It just . . . " She looked around, waving her hands in little circles, lost in thought. "It has better vibes than Manhattan."

His heart sank. It shouldn't bother him. He wasn't staying. But the thought of her anywhere other than this building made his palms sweat and his heart race.

"You still don't like it after everything I've shown you?"

"I like all of that. I like lots of things, though."

Aiden rubbed his hands over his face and leaned against the edge of the chair, groaning. "You're impossible."

Bree giggled, and Leigh joined her from her position near the kitchen.

Aiden looked at his watch. They had time, but not much. "Well, don't move to Brooklyn before our outing tomorrow, okay?"

She smirked at him. "I make no such promises."

"I can show Leigh the sights," Tony said. He'd been unusually quiet during this whole exchange, leaning against the kitchen counter and taking it all in with his eyes fixed on Leigh. "That way, if you get caught up at the flea market, you don't have to rush back."

He winked at Aiden, like he was doing him a favor.

"Oh, that would be so nice of you," Leigh said. She ran a hand over her hair and sent a flirty smile his way.

Aiden exchanged a glance with Bree, who looked like she was trying not to laugh.

It killed him that he couldn't take Bree wherever she wanted to go, not after the disaster of Rockefeller Center. A long list of suggestions rose to the front of his mind, and he only just barely kept them from spilling out of his mouth. Tony knew the city better than anyone, and Leigh would have a good time.

But he wouldn't bother to check the opening times or get advance tickets to avoid the lines or coordinate their itinerary with the sunrise and sunset so that the lighting was best for pictures.

Aiden took a deep breath. Maybe that was okay. Maybe something didn't have to go according to his perfectly laid out plan to still be a perfect day. Yesterday had been an amazing day, and absolutely nothing had been organized more than a few hours ahead. Tomorrow would be just as good because he'd be spending at least part of it with Bree.

He looked at his watch, then nodded once at Tony. "Sounds like a great idea. Now let's head to dinner before Tony's mother gives away our tiramisu to the neighbors."

TWENTY-TWO

Bree and Leigh were in their pajamas, brushing their teeth after what had been the most delicious and entertaining dinner in Bree's recent memory.

Bree peered at Leigh in the mirror. "You know it's not really fair, but I'm not surprised."

"What's not fair?" Leigh asked through a mouthful of toothpaste.

"I've been in New York for a month, and yet you're the one who finds love within hours of getting here."

Leigh spit out her toothpaste onto the mirror and turned, wide-eyed, toward Bree. "What?"

"Isch, gross."

"Sorry." Leigh rinsed her mouth and toothbrush, wiped the mirror with a towel, then turned to stare at Bree. "What do you mean, I'm the one who found love within hours?"

Bree raised an eyebrow. "You're trying to tell me you're not completely gaga for Tony and his family?"

Cool, calm, collected Leigh, who never yelled or got upset, even when a customer had thrown steaming hot coffee on her, was now completely red from head to toe, unable to form a complete sentence.

Bree grinned, triumphant. "Yeah, that's what I thought."

"Well, it's not like it'll go anywhere." Leigh hung up the towel and adjusted it so it sat perfectly in the middle of the rack. "He's a total city guy."

Dinner had been an endless stream of recommendations from Tony, his mother, and his aunt, about where Leigh should visit while she was in New York and where all the best shopping was for Bree. Aiden hadn't said much, instead quietly feeding bits of dinner to the dog who'd lain down immediately at his feet beneath the table.

"So have some fun while you're here." Bree shrugged as she followed Leigh out of the bathroom and into the living room. "You've earned the break."

"Yeah, maybe." Leigh leaned back into the couch cushion and frowned. "This couch is really uncomfortable."

"I know, right?" Bree sat down next to her on the rock-hard and scratchy couch.

The flea market Aiden was taking her to the next day was apparently not on the long list of Russo-approved shopping. He'd politely nodded, but Bree knew he wouldn't change his plans because Mrs. Russo didn't think it was a good place to go.

But somehow, she knew that Aiden would be willing to go somewhere else if Bree was the one to ask.

"Look, you'll have all day together tomorrow, so just enjoy yourself," Bree said.

"And what about you?" asked Leigh.

"What about me?"

"Will you enjoy yourself with Aiden tomorrow?"

"I always do." They were the same words he'd said to Leigh earlier. Did he really mean them? Or was he just trying to make himself look good for her friend?

Either way, it was an unbearably nice thing to say. The thought about what it might mean sent shivers through her. She tucked her legs up underneath a paisley blanket and spread it across Leigh's lap as well.

There was a plate of cookies on the tiny coffee table in front of them, thanks to Tony's mother, and Bree grabbed one for herself and handed another to Leigh.

"I'm so jealous he's taking you to a flea market tomorrow."

"What's wrong with the rummage sales we have back in Minnesota?"

Leigh laughed. "I bet it's much more interesting here. Everything is. I didn't think I'd like the city so much, not with the way you were going on about it."

"Aiden's a good guide to the city. He's been showing me the good parts." Bree bit into her cookie. "I mean, even though he's contractually obligated to go out and about with me, he could have chosen swanky restaurants or something. Instead, he takes me to places he thinks I'll like."

"That's really sweet."

"And then I ruin everything by crying or getting us mobbed by fans."

Leigh looked at her with those mom-who-doesn't-believe-you eyes. "Are you sure there isn't something between the two of you?"

"What?" Bree was so startled, she dropped the cookie, and crumbs sprinkled all over the blanket and rug. At least a small apartment didn't take too long to clean.

"I see the way you two are around each other." Leigh shrugged. "I know it's fake dating, but you seem to get along really well."

"Yeah, but he's super set on leaving New York."

There'd been a long discussion about Aiden's vet school plans at dinner, prompted by Mrs. Russo asking if he'd applied to the program at Long Island University. He had, but only because it was where the vet he'd worked for had gone. Every other school he'd applied to was out of state, and his plan was to go wherever he got accepted—as long as it wasn't in New York.

Bree retrieved the cookie and shoved it into her mouth. "And I'm staying."

"I'm glad to hear it." Leigh smiled. "You needed to get out of our town. Every time you left, I'd be a little sad when I got your call saying you were coming home."

Bree swallowed, her mouth dry, unable to think of a response to that.

"Aiden has nothing to do with your decision to stay?" Leigh asked.

"It can't go anywhere. When all this is over, he's leaving, and Hayden Carmichael said we could hang out."

Cookie halfway to her mouth, Leigh raised an eyebrow.

"Did you get more details in the contract about what that means?"

Looking away from Leigh's intense stare, Bree felt heat creep up her face, and put her hands over her cheeks.

"He'll probably take me to some of his favorite places, the way Aiden's been doing."

Leigh pursed her lips, clearly wanting to say more, but holding back. Aiden did the same thing sometimes, she'd noticed. There were a lot of similarities between her best friend and fake movie-star boyfriend.

The dreaminess of Bree was well-balanced by Leigh's—and Aiden's—pragmatism. Aiden took into consideration what Bree wanted to do, but always kept in mind the how and the what. Instead of a restaurant where they might have been recognized as Hayden and his new girlfriend, he'd found a way for them to spend a relaxed evening together eating incredible food.

In a similar way, Leigh was always careful to not completely squash Bree's ideas, but she also let her know when they were completely ridiculous. Moving to New York had always been supported. Becoming a trapeze artist had been gently discouraged, with multiple reminders of her fear of heights, which Bree always managed to forget until she was actually at the top of something and had to be rescued to come down.

That sparked something in Bree's busy brain. "Did you want to visit the Empire State Building while you're here?"

Standing at the top wouldn't be easy, but she didn't want to deny her friend anything because of her fears.

Leigh shook her head. "I'm sure Tony will take care of things."

The light was back in her eyes at the mention of his name.

Bree couldn't resist a little more teasing. "Oh, I'm sure he'll take care of you." She waggled her eyebrows.

"Stop it!" Leigh shoved her, sending more cookie crumbs to the floor. "We should have taken something to thank his mom for dinner."

"Aiden gave her those gorgeous flowers."

"We should offer to pay him for part of those. They looked expensive."

Of course, he'd had a beautiful personalized arrangement. No last-minute stop at a convenience store to pick up a wilted bouquet of roses, the way Bree would have.

"I'll see which money transfer app he has." Bree picked up her phone.

"Just go down there."

"What, now?" For some reason, her voice was high and squeaky. She cleared her throat and tried again. "I'm in my pajamas. He's probably already in bed."

"Just go. I'm sure he won't mind."

An unusual feeling crept up Bree's chest. The spontaneity should have excited her, made the idea fun and irresistible. Her heart should have been racing with anticipation. Instead, not knowing what she'd do or say was making her gut clench and hands tremble.

For the first time in a long time, she didn't have a plan, and she was scared about it.

"Let's just . . . talk about what I should do when I get down there."

Leigh grinned, then opened her mouth, but she closed it when she saw the look on Bree's face. Scooching closer under the blanket, Leigh gently ran her hands over Bree's hair, smoothing it back from her face. "Sure. Let's talk through it before you do it."

The entire plan would take less time than it had to come up with. First, she'd knock. Then, she'd hand him the money without saying anything. When presented with something, most people would take it. Once he had it in his hands, she'd explain they wanted to pay for part of the flowers. Then she'd run back upstairs before he could say anything or give the money back.

She could do this. She'd learned to water ski in less than a day, and once she'd led an entire arena full of people in the "Macarena" while waiting for the rain to stop and a concert to continue. This would be easy.

Deep breath.

She knocked. There were the sounds of Aiden shuffling to the door. So far, so good. Things were going according to plan. She extended her hand with the folded bills, ready to shove them into his hands. The door opened.

Aiden was shirtless.

Shirtless and in gray sweatpants that hung low on his hips.

Also, he had a tattoo.

A *tattoo*. Right there, on his perfect pec, in handwriting that looked so precise it had to be his own.

Luck favors the prepared.

Everything in Bree's mind went blank. Her extended hand dropped to her side, the money forgotten, the plan forgotten, everything forgotten. The only thought in her brain was the wide expanse of smooth muscles in front of her face. Every exposed inch was honed to perfection, from his bulging biceps to those little V-shapes on the side of his abs.

"Bree?" From a distant corner of her brain, she noticed he was frowning. "Is everything okay? Did something happen?"

The reminder that his default was to assume she needed help shocked her out of her stupor.

"I have a plan." She held out her hand, but it was the one without the money in it, and it smacked into his chest, right below the tattoo. The muscles were just as hard as they looked, and her hand lingered, smoothing over his pecs, over the words that were so perfectly Aiden. His chest felt amazing.

This was why she always went with her first instinct to do whatever felt best.

A small smile spread across his face. "Is this the plan?"

"No." Somehow, she pulled her hand away and took a step back. "Could you maybe put a shirt on? The plan didn't take into account . . . this." She waved vaguely at his half-dressed state.

He took a step forward, the small smile still on his face. "Are you sure? Plans can change, you know. You're kind of an expert at that."

She took a deep breath. This close, she could smell the soap on his skin. The clean, fresh scent of the shower he must have taken as soon as he got home still clung to his body. Even his hair was still a little wet, something she hadn't noticed during her ogling of the shirtless masterpiece that was his body.

She closed her eyes, hoping it would help her focus.

"I just wanted to give you something." Those weren't the words she'd rehearsed with Leigh, but they weren't too far off.

"What is it?" His voice was right by her ear. She knew if she opened her eyes, his face would be close enough to touch. To kiss.

It's just because he looks so much like Hayden, she told herself.

There was a sudden stillness from Aiden, and he took a step back. She opened her eyes and realized she'd said the words out loud . . . and they'd hurt him.

That definitely hadn't been the plan.

Abandoning all attempts at thinking things through, she reached out and wrapped her arms around him.

"I'm sorry."

His skin smelled just as amazing with her face pressed against it. With a deep inhale, their breaths fell into sync. She let herself relax into him, and turned her head slightly so that her lips brushed his collarbone, just above the words he'd had permanently etched into his skin.

The words that could not have been more contrary to the way Bree lived her life. And yet she felt a truth in them that she never would have without Aiden.

She pulled her head back, and her lips were inches away from his mouth. So close she could feel the heat of his breath on her cheeks. With a tiny movement, she brushed her mouth across his. It felt right, in a way nothing else had since she walked down the stairs.

At least it did until Aiden stiffened under her arms and backed away.

Oh, Birdbrain, did you really think he'd want you?

Not daring to look him in the face, she turned, more embarrassed than she'd ever been, and ran back up the stairs without another word.

When she got to her apartment, she shoved the money into her pocket and decided to tell Leigh he hadn't wanted it. That would hopefully keep her friend from asking too many questions, and she could just pretend like this whole thing had never happened.

Just like she hoped Aiden would.

TWENTY-THREE

Bree had kissed him.

The thought consumed Aiden's mind all night after Bree's midnight visit, only taking a break to spin into a mild panic about how awkward it would make the flea market outing.

When he picked her up in the morning, however, she didn't mention it or even look like she remembered. It was entirely possible he'd dreamed it. After all, the words she'd whispered haunted him like a nightmare.

And yet . . . she'd had a plan when she'd come down. That wasn't something Hayden would inspire. It was something she'd done because of Aiden, he was sure of it.

Then there was that whole apology and hug thing, which had been more confusing than anything she'd done thus far, kiss included.

Had she meant to kiss him? It wasn't what he'd expected her to do, but when had she even been predictable?

Today's plan was to get some answers. And some furniture for Bree.

It was the most logical of all of their outings, a way to feed two cats from one bowl. They still had a contract to fulfill, and the Chelsea Flea was popular enough to be seen by a lot of people, but a smaller, more contained area that Grant and Marcus could monitor easily.

Bree needed new furniture that fit her apartment better. Smaller pieces, still classic but more mid-century modern and funky seventies than the massive early twentieth century monstrosities that were in there now.

"Why did you pick this place?" Bree asked, her eyes wide as they walked between the tables loaded with everything from trumpets to sewing machines.

"I used to come here a lot when I was getting the apartment ready to rent." Aiden steered her around an old globe on a stand. "I didn't have much of a budget but wanted it to look nice. I came here week after week, getting to know what the different vendors tended to sell, waiting for that one great piece to appear."

Bree's head turned one way, then the other, like she couldn't decide which way to go next. "That must have taken a lot of patience. And luck."

"Good things are worth waiting for." He slid his eyes to meet hers. "And luck favors the prepared."

Her cheeks turned red, but she didn't say anything in response to the reference to his tattoo.

They walked in silence for a few minutes, looking around at everything on display.

"I feel like Mrs. Wilson is watching me, waiting to yell at me." Bree looked over her shoulder and giggled as her hair shimmered in the late-May sunshine.

Aiden looked back as well, to see that Grant was keeping his distance. After all those close-up fan shots of "Hayden Carmichael" and "his new girlfriend" in the tabloids the past few days, the actor's publicist had released a statement requesting privacy for the couple. It shouldn't have even been necessary, but Aiden wasn't taking any chances with Bree's safety.

One thing about New York was that most people left actors alone, which was why so many of them liked it here.

Hayden Carmichael, however, was not just a regular actor. Even after almost ten years in the city, Hayden had told Aiden about being spotted and stopped all the time. Really, Aiden should have expected and planned for what had happened at Rockefeller Center.

As if on cue, there was a whisper behind them.

"It's him, it's totally him."

Bree caught his eye and squeezed his hand. Of course she was thrilled about the attention. What was more unexpected was how happy he was to see her happy.

Or maybe it was just because he knew she was safer here than she'd been the week before. The bodyguards had also gotten very strict instructions on what to do today.

Grant's voice was quiet but insistent. "Ma'am, please step back. No autographs or photos today."

They stopped at a table full of boxes of old vinyl. While Aiden just flipped through, Bree took her time, staring at each cover carefully.

"Looking for something in particular?"

She shook her head, the dark braid over her shoulder swishing slightly with the movement. "Just wish Leigh could have seen some of these. She loves old records."

"Tony does too." Aiden flipped slower now, pleased when he found one that he knew his friend would like. On the next table was an old record player, and he pointed it out to her. "You should get it."

"It's more Leigh's thing."

They passed by racks of vintage clothes and tables full of jewelry. Paintings and pottery. Cocktail shakers and crystal brandy snifters. "Then what's your thing?"

She shrugged and let her hands play with the fringe of a lampshade. "Whatever. Everything. Anything."

"If that were true, you wouldn't want to redecorate."

"You're the design expert, apparently." Her lips turned up, and her eyes held a challenge. "What do you think my thing is?"

He let his gaze wander around. It was quiet, not too many people milling around this early in the morning. It didn't take him long to spot the little side table with delicate legs, in a lighter wood than the dark mahogany of everything else in her apartment.

"This is nice."

She wrinkled her nose. "It won't match anything that's there."

"That's the point." He chuckled. "Something unique, like you."

Her cheeks tinged pink, and she looked away. "You mean something that doesn't fit in."

"Are you saying you'd rather look like you lived through World War II?"

She snorted a laugh, and a lightness swept through him, the air coming easier into his lungs. This felt comfortable, easy, like they'd been doing it for months. Like it was their regular weekend routine. Much easier than whatever last night had been.

When she knocked on his door, he'd thought . . . well, lots of things. Nothing he could act on in the middle of Chelsea Flea without drawing the wrong kind of attention from people.

Over the next hour, he had to stop himself from taking control and directing her toward the vendors displaying vases and chairs and furniture. The way that Aiden shopped was very different from the way Bree shopped.

A few weeks ago, it would have irritated him, but now he let himself enjoy the slow meander through the alleys formed by the tents, the discovery of unusual items when he let his eyes wander rather than zero in on his target. There was a freeness to it that he hadn't felt in years, not since his first year in New York, exploring and discovering.

It was because of Bree. The way she'd slowly chipped away at his every attempt to control her, control this fake relationship, to set up his usual boundaries and rules that kept him safe. She'd pushed past them and—other than one situation he really should have predicted—everything was fine. Better, even, than he could have ever imagined.

"What about this for my dining room?" She pointed at a gigantic wooden table, at least ten feet long.

"Isn't the point to get smaller furniture?"

"I measured my dining room, it's twelve feet long."

Aiden turned to stare at her. "You measured?"

Her hand smoothed over the braid in her hair. "It would be kind of silly to come all the way out here to buy something and not know how big my space is."

Aiden's heart gave a weird, stuttering thump. If dreamy, unprepared Bree was attractive, prepared Bree was irresistible. When she'd proclaimed so proudly last night she had a plan, it had taken everything in him not to drag her into his apartment.

Happy he had a good excuse to put his arms around her this morning, he did just that, wrapping himself around her from behind and resting his head on her shoulder.

"I'm very proud of your preparedness."

She giggled and leaned back into him. "You want to see my tape measure? I brought it."

I could kiss her right now. He wished it wasn't all pretend, that it wasn't for the cameras that he couldn't see, but he knew were pointed at them.

He should have taken his shot last night instead of backing away. But it had been late. They'd had wine at Mrs. Russo's. And she'd voiced out loud the fear he'd been carrying with him since they started this whole undertaking: she only wanted him because he looked like Hayden. There were lots of very sound reasons he'd stepped back.

Today, in the bright spring sunshine, with his arms wrapped around her at one of his favorite places in a city he was slowly falling back in love with, those reasons were much harder to remember.

"I still think the table is too big. It doesn't feel like you."

"I'm a small table kind of person?" She was smiling, but there was a shimmer of fear in her voice, like she really cared what he thought about her.

He turned her around so he could look her in the eye. "That's not what I meant. It's just that this one is too solid."

Her smile tightened and she bit her lip.

Oh hell, he was really messing this up.

"You're so . . . light. Fun. Whimsical. Your apartment should reflect that. It should be a space that you can dream in. It should feel like a dream. Like you."

"I feel like a dream?" Her mouth twisted to the side. "I'm kind of your nightmare though, aren't I?"

"You're perfect."

The words were out of him before he could stop them. There was a sharp intake of breath from Bree, and their eyes met, the air charging with electricity around them.

He took a small step forward, trying to tell her everything with his eyes, what he felt about her, what he suspected she might feel about him. He lifted a hand, brushed a strand of hair back from her face, and tucked it behind her ear.

Leaning into his hand, she closed her eyes briefly and inhaled deeply, her chest rising and falling slowly. The feel of her skin on his was electric, the smooth warmth of it soothing and exciting all at once.

It was all too easy to forget what they were there to do. Who they were pretending to be. He just wanted to be Aiden, wanted her to want him even a fraction as much as she wanted Hayden and a life in the spotlight.

That's when the whispers started again, just loud enough to reach his ears and break the shimmering tension between him and Bree.

"Shh, that's him, look. It's Hayden with his new girlfriend."

"Should I go up?"

"No, he's about to kiss her. Leave them alone."

They hadn't moved, and his hand was still in her hair, her face still inches from his. He was close enough to see small flecks of white in her blue eyes, which were now wide and searching his for a hint at what to do next.

"Should we kiss?" he whispered. "Give them what they want?"

With a sharp inhale, Bree turned quickly to grab something off the table, and Aiden had his answer. It was what he'd expected, even if it wasn't what he'd hoped for.

"We'd better not mess up the contract." Her eyes were on the table in front of them, and she bit her lip. "This would be great for my living room, don't you think?"

She held out a ceramic vase in the shape of a flamingo, and Aiden ignored the sudden rush of blood in his head to give her a smile.

"It's great. Now let's find a table to match."

Bree paid for the absolutely hideous vase, and they walked away together, close but no longer touching or holding hands.

Close enough any pictures wouldn't look like she'd just stomped all over his heart by rejecting him yet again.

She didn't want him. That was okay. It wasn't the end of the world. It didn't change his plans at all. It was better this way, really.

TWENTY-FOUR

After the longest, quietest, most awkward car ride of her life, Bree hurried back up to her apartment, heart hammering in her ears. Luckily Leigh was still out sightseeing, or she'd have seen straight away when Bree walked in what had almost happened.

Again.

She'd barely hidden from Leigh what had happened the night before. She wouldn't be able to do it a second time. Especially if any of the fans she'd overheard had gotten a sneaky picture and it showed up online or in the tabloids.

The world would see Hayden Carmichael and his new girlfriend sharing a tender moment. Leigh would see just how much Bree wanted Aiden, even though she'd decided to stay. Even though she'd decided she wanted a different life than the one he was planning.

These past weeks had proven she was movie-star-girlfriend material. The press loved her, she was keeping things confidential, and there were no skeletons in her closet for anyone to use as tabloid fodder. It wasn't like she thought Hayden would fall instantly in love with her or anything, but hanging out could definitely lead to more.

Just like it had with Aiden. The weeks they'd spent together had been awkward at first, but as they'd slowly gotten used to each other, it was clear how well they complemented each other. How balanced it felt being around him. Her head was full of him, and after today's almost kiss, all of her ached to know what he really thought of her.

Last night, he'd stepped back from the kiss she'd offered when no one would see. Today, he'd asked to kiss her, but only because people had been watching.

There was a knock at her door, and her chest tightened to a knot right behind her rapidly beating heart.

"Bree? You forgot your vase in the car. Marcus just brought it back."

Of course Aiden had brought it up instead of leaving it by her mailbox or at her door. He was just that kind of guy. The kind of guy who didn't leave things to chance. The kind of guy who said she was perfect.

Nobody thought she was perfect. Because she wasn't. He must have meant something else. He had to have meant something else, or things would get too complicated.

She wasn't Birdbrain Bree anymore, changing her mind every other day. She was New York Bree, who wanted Hayden and was perfect for him.

She opened the door and avoided his eyes, looking down at the vase in his hands instead. "Thanks. You could have just left it."

"You ran off so fast, I wanted to make sure everything's okay." He leaned in close, one arm against the doorframe. "I know we had a lot more attention at the flea market than we were expecting. Nobody said anything to hurt you, did they?"

She looked up and her breath hitched to see his eyes held a dangerous glint. Like he would pummel anyone who so much as looked at her funny. Her heart tapped out a fast staccato rhythm that echoed in her ears.

She stepped back and breathed a little easier with some distance between them. "No, everything I heard was really nice, actually."

There'd been so many whispers about how pretty she was, how good they looked together, how jealous people were. It was everything she'd ever wanted, to have people think she was someone important, someone special enough to be with someone like Hayden.

Only it wasn't really him.

"That's all I heard too." Aiden gave her a small smile. "The publicist already sent an email with pictures. We really have everyone fooled. We're doing a great job together."

"Just one more outing, then you can finally escape." The vase was heavy in her hands, and she clutched it to her chest. "Do you know where you'll go?"

He blinked, as surprised by the question as she was that she'd asked it. Some part of her needed to hear it again: he was leaving, there was no chance for them, and he didn't want her. Then she'd be able to let go of the fantasy that had wormed its way into her decades-long New York daydream. One where a guy like Aiden gave up everything for a girl like her.

But just because it happened in a Hayden Carmichael movie didn't mean it could happen in real life.

"I have a list of potential cities." Aiden put his hands in his pockets and looked away, like he was embarrassed. "I should hear this week where I got accepted, then I'll make my choice."

There it was. The real reason it could never work with him.

If she ended up with just some guy, moving away to what-ever small town he landed in, then she'd be no better than anyone else in her town. The whole point of being here was to be different and special in the same way Aunt Agatha had been.

She'd been "Agatha from New York" her whole life, so everyone knew who she was.

Now, finally, people knew who Bree was.

Thousands, even millions, had seen her in paparazzi pictures, knew her name. She was finally more than just someone's little sister or "one of the Peterson girls." Now she was Bree Peterson, Hayden Carmichael's girlfriend . . . or at least everyone thought she was.

She still had a shot at being that person for real. It was a long shot, but she was a lot closer than she had ever dreamed, even just a few weeks ago.

None of that would be possible if she ended up with Aiden. She'd be a nobody, the same as she'd been her whole life. She could practically hear her family's reaction.

Birdbrain got confused and thought he was Hayden, didn't she?

They'd question if she'd ever even met the real one, assuming any story she told them was exaggerated.

Aiden cleared his throat. "There's another reason I came up. The publicist called me with an update on the contract right after she sent the pictures." He gestured behind her. "Can I come in so we can talk about it?"

She stepped aside, heart pounding. "Are they extending the contract?" More time with Aiden was both what she wanted and what she didn't want.

"The opposite, actually. She told me that Hayden is flying in tonight, a little short notice, but that's how he is." There was a little twitch of his lips that let her know how unhappy he was about a surprise change to his plans.

"Really?" She turned her back on him to set the vase down on the coffee table with shaking hands.

They'd also found a new couch and a new side table at the flea market that would be delivered in the next few days.

Whether she stayed in Manhattan or ended up in Brooklyn, her apartment would look great. Like the apartment of someone Hayden would date.

"Yeah, and she said not to go out while he's here."

"Oh." Disappointment flooded her, which she hadn't expected. She'd been looking forward to whatever Aidan had planned for their fourth outing.

"They'll pay the full fee though."

"That's not what I'm worried about."

"You'll get your time with Hayden too. I already asked."

Yes, Hayden. That's what she wanted.

Turning back to Aiden, she inhaled slowly, then smiled. "That's great. But what about our walk along the river?"

Aiden shrugged and casually leaned against the couch, like it wasn't that big of a deal. Like he wasn't breaking Bree's heart just a little. "We can't be seen together, but Hayden could take you."

"You said you would take me." Unlike Bree, Aiden kept his promises. It was one of the best things about him.

He gripped the edge of the couch, not meeting her eye. "We'll go then, sometime when he's out of the city. It'll be too risky otherwise."

"Too risky?"

"If we're out together and he's also out in the city, then what happens when there's a picture of him in two different places?"

"You mean that's never happened before? No one's taken your picture and printed it, claiming it was him?" Emotion was making her voice shaky, and she didn't understand why. She just wanted to go see the river with Aiden. Like they'd planned. Like she thought he'd wanted to.

Aiden ran a hand along the back of his neck. "Not before this month, no. I don't usually go to the places he goes. I don't usually dress like him."

"So we can't be seen together, or they won't honor the contract."

"Just for a few weeks."

"What about Brian's café?" Surely, they could hang out there, somewhere people would never think to look for Hayden.

He didn't say anything, but he pursed his lips together in what she knew now was his signature move to avoid saying something he didn't want to say.

It was one of his little habits of his she'd noticed over the weeks they'd spent together, storing them away like little treasures, adding them on to her gum wrapper chain of Aiden facts she had only just now realized she wanted to reach a hundred thousand feet.

Tears pricked her eyes, and she made a fist behind her back to keep herself from letting them fall.

What Aiden cared about was the money, not spending time with her. The almost kiss at the flea market had been for the cameras, not because he felt anything for her. She'd been wrong. Leigh had been wrong.

Bree leaned against the wall for support, her legs suddenly weak. The realization hurt more than she'd expected.

"Just for a few weeks . . . " She brushed her hair behind her ear. "But you're leaving once the contract is paid."

"That's the plan."

She knew better than to hope he'd change a plan once he made it, especially for something as silly as a walk along the river with her.

He wanted to get out of the city—away from her—as fast as possible. He could say nice things about her, help her out of the sticky situations she always landed in, but he could never understand what she really wanted.

He got attention all the time from people on the street. Even if it caused him problems, he had something people would always remember him by. He had a plan for a life as a small-town vet. Everyone would know him. He'd be important.

All Bree had was this city and her one shot at a movie-star life. This was everything to her, and he'd helped her get closer than she'd ever thought possible.

"Thank you for everything you've shown me." It came out like she was saying goodbye, her voice hoarse from the effort it took to hold back her tears. "Thank you for all your help."

"Glad I could be of service." Then, without another word, he turned around and walked down the hall to the stairs.

Blood rushed to Bree's head so quickly she swayed on the spot. Closing the door, she leaned back against it and slid to the floor.

Was that it? He could just walk away so easily?

The tears came from deep inside and flowed uninterrupted for nearly ten minutes. It wasn't the loud, racking sobs of a breakup. They were the slow, steady tears of broken dreams. Dreams she hadn't even realized she'd had until today.

Bree let herself cry, then got up and washed her face. By the time Leigh got home, bursting to tell her about the day she'd spent with Tony, Bree had decided to do what she always did.

Any plans she had were thrown away, and she opened herself to whatever would happen next, without getting attached to any specifics. Living that way had never failed her. After all, she was living the New York life she'd dreamed of and had a date with Hayden Carmichael to look forward to. All thanks to a forgotten key and randomly passing Aiden in the street a few weeks ago.

There was no reason to be sad, so Bree simply wouldn't be.

TWENTY-FIVE

Whatever he'd seen in her eyes at the flea market was nothing compared to what had been in her eyes at the news that Hayden Carmichael was in town.

At first, his stupid heart thought she was disappointed he wouldn't be able to walk with her along the river. Then she'd asked about Brian's café, and he realized all she cared about was all the ways Aiden had been helping her get what she wanted. Her dream apartment, her dream job, her dream guy.

Was it really that different from Margot, who'd been thrilled to move to the city with him, but had left as soon as he couldn't give her the life she'd expected there?

Why he thought someone would ever want him—just him, Aiden, for himself—was proof of how off-kilter he'd gotten since Bree had burst into his life like a cloud of bats released into the sky.

He spent the next week getting back on track, sticking to his usual plans, and not deviating from his schedule for anything. The only minor adjustment he allowed himself was skipping coffee at Brian's café. It should have been an easy part of his daily routine to remove, but he had to force his body to walk in the opposite direction every morning.

There was no reason he couldn't still see Bree, other than without the contract, there was no reason she'd want to see him. She'd rejected him at every possible opportunity, and he'd promised himself he'd never make a fool of himself for a woman again. Not one who so clearly preferred someone else.

Another week went by, and Tony showed up at the gym when Aiden was working. They hadn't seen each other since dinner at his mom's, and hadn't spoken other than a few texts once Aiden had gotten paid to ask Tony about apartment stuff to get it ready to sell.

Today, Tony seemed to be in the mood to talk.

"I need to tell you something." His friend's mouth was pressed into a tight line. It was the most thoughtful Aiden had ever seen him.

Aiden raised a curious eyebrow. "Is this a run-around-the-park conversation, or a heavy-weights talk?"

Tony considered for a moment. "Weights."

Uh-oh. The smile fell from Aiden's face. It was something really serious then.

"Is your mom okay?"

"What?" Halfway to the weight room, Tony turned back to him. "Yeah, she's fine. Wanted me to thank you again for the flowers you brought the other night."

They both took a pair of weights from the rack set against the wall and stood to face the mirror. Alternating hands, they pulled the weights up to their shoulders, biceps flexing.

In the mirror, Aiden caught Tony's eye. "So what is it?"

It was another few reps before he answered.

"I'm moving to Minnesota to be with Leigh."

"What?" The sound of Aiden's question echoed in the small

room full of sweaty people. Eight pairs of eyes turned his way, and normally he would have given an apologetic wave, but he was too focused on what his friend—his best friend—had just told him.

"You're leaving New York City." The words came out slowly, each one tasting as bitter as burnt coffee.

The weights were still held tightly in Aiden's hands by his shoulders, immobile, while Tony had already moved on to rows. The coward was bent over and facing the ground instead of Aiden.

"What can I say? I fell in love."

Even though Tony's head was down, Aiden could see the gigantic smile on his face. The proper thing would be to congratulate him, to wish him luck, or something equally supportive.

"You just met her. She was only here for three days and that was . . . " Aiden quickly counted. "Less than two weeks ago." The same amount of time since he'd last seen Bree, but he wasn't thinking about her right now. He was thinking about Tony's absolutely preposterous news.

"We've talked on the phone every single day since she left." He did a few more rows. "For hours, man. I've never . . . this is something so incredible . . . "

He paused his reps to catch his breath, and Aiden took the opportunity to take a few deep inhales of his own.

"How did this even start?"

Tony grinned. "I guess nothing beats a sightseeing tour of New York to make you fall for somebody."

Aiden's chest squeezed tight. He was definitely not thinking about walking around Central Park with Bree.

"You can't be in love with her. You're already in love with the city."

This made Tony stand up and put the weights down on the rack again. He ran a hand through his silver-streaked dark hair.

"Maybe I love it because I've never lived anywhere else. You're the one always saying how terrible it is here. You're the one who's been making plans to leave since the day I met you. Is it so weird that I'd want the same thing?"

"Well no, but . . . " Aiden's hands lifted and fell uselessly at his sides.

Tony made his way to a weight bench.

"I mean, sure, I might hate it. Apparently in Leigh's town there's nowhere that's open past nine at night, and the closest movie theater is twenty miles away." Tony stacked a few more weights to the ends of the barbell. "But she's there. And she makes it sound pretty great. No traffic would be a nice change. A body of water you can actually swim in without getting a tetanus shot first sounds fantastic."

He settled himself beneath the barbell, and Aiden took his place above his head, ready to spot him, his mind racing. There were countless reasons Minnesota was better than New York, all filed away in a spreadsheet he hadn't looked at once since he'd met Bree.

Aiden tried another tactic. "All your family is here."

"My mom wouldn't care if I moved to the moon if it meant she might get grandkids." Tony pulled the weights down toward his chest and pushed them back up with a grunt. "And I don't know if you've heard, but there are these things called airplanes and video calls nowadays."

Aiden ignored the sarcasm to focus on Tony's form. Perfect, just like he'd taught him. For the first time in his life, Aiden wished he wasn't so good at his job so he could yell at Tony for sticking his elbows out or something.

"Your job is here."

"I'm pretty sure they renovate kitchens and bathrooms in

Minnesota too. It's not just something fancy city people do."

"Your friends are here." His voice caught. "I'm here."

"Yeah, but you're leaving soon too. Where did you get into vet school?"

"Iowa and Minnesota." He'd gotten the acceptance letters the day after the flea market. The one from Long Island University came the day after that, but he didn't mention it.

"That's great!" Tony beamed. "Congrats, man. You must be thrilled."

He should be. This had always been the plan, after all. Though in his most recent plans, he wasn't alone in this next chapter. Stupidly, Bree was in this new vision of what his life post-New York would look like. Stupid because she loved the city now, thanks to him. Stupid because once she had her date with Hayden, she'd have everything she'd ever dreamed of, thanks to him.

When Aiden remained silent, Tony sat up on the bench and turned to look at him.

"Wait, are you thinking about staying?"

"No," said Aiden, a little too quickly. Definitely the right choice to not tell him about LIU.

Tony's eyes widened. "Is it because of Bree?"

"Absolutely not."

His best friend burst out laughing and settled back down on the bench.

"You have to tell her." Tony pushed the barbell high over his head, with Aiden standing right behind him, making sure it didn't fall on his face, even though he kind of wanted it to.

"There's nothing to tell. We've had our fake dates, the contract is fulfilled, and we got paid last week. There's no reason to see her again."

"Okay, sure." Tony rolled his eyes as he did his tenth rep.

"I'll save you a seat in my car for when I head out west then, yeah?"

It was a test to see if Aiden was still serious about leaving the city. Of course he was. Why wouldn't he be? There was nothing for him here, and his best friend was moving to the kind of place he'd been planning to for years.

"Absolutely."

There must have been something in his tone, because Tony shut up for a minute. He finished up his set, and they moved on to dead lifts in silence.

"Alright, sorry, man, I didn't mean to upset you or anything. I know this is really sudden, and you don't do great with changes in plans."

"I do okay with them." Especially recently, thanks to Bree.

Tony considered him for a moment before speaking again. "It'd be nice actually, to have you as company for the drive."

"When are you leaving?"

"Next week."

"I won't have everything settled by then." Aiden ran a hand over his face, thinking of his never-ending checklist. "The cleanup work is almost done, and if I call someone today, I could get the apartment listed by this weekend. But even if offers come in a few days after that, it would still be more than a few weeks before the sale would close."

"Hey, no stress, man. I won't have my life totally packed up either, but I don't want to wait any longer. I've been waiting for her for forty-two years."

Aiden gave Tony the look that cheesy line deserved, but his friend just smiled beatifically at him. He was at peace with his decision, happy in the soulmate he'd unexpectedly found in a midwestern woman, willing to change his whole life just to be with her.

"This is completely ridiculous, you realize."

Tony lifted his hands, palms up. "So what?"

For people like Bree and Tony, it really was that easy. Aiden wished he could be that spontaneous. Even if the past few weeks had shown him that it could sometimes work, they'd also shown him that sticking to his original plans was safest.

TWENTY-SIX

Hayden Carmichael was charming, larger than life, drawing every eye in the room to him. Sitting next to him was exactly what Bree had been dreaming of for years.

So why was she bored out of her mind?

"Then the director asked me to do another take, can you believe it?" He was halfway through his third—or maybe fourth—story about filming one of his movies.

It was Bree's fault. Almost a month after Hayden had gotten back to the city, his publicist finally reached out to set up their hangout. It was a last-minute thing, so there'd been no time to prepare.

Which was fine. It was how she liked to operate, but it meant she'd been totally taken by surprise when they sat down and he asked her what questions she had for him. The only thing that came to mind was "What's it like to make movies?"

That was all it had taken to get him started on what she could tell was a well-rehearsed arsenal of behind-the-scenes tidbits. She recognized some of the "secret stories" as things he'd shared in interviews over the years.

Normally, she would have been hanging off his every word.

Or at least pretending to, the way she did with people at Leigh's café, when they told her the same story she'd heard almost every day for years.

It wasn't that she was *un*happy to be there with him. The stares she was getting were the same kind she'd gotten with Aiden, and that was just as satisfying as ever. To be the center of attention—or at least center adjacent—was as exciting and thrilling as she'd hoped it would be.

It was Hayden himself, she realized, who wasn't quite living up to her expectations. He was so different from Aiden. Hayden loved having the focus on him. He hadn't asked Bree a single question about herself, or even where she wanted to go today.

She missed Aiden's quiet observations, his steady presence at her side as he took her to his favorite places in the city. She missed how considerate he was, how curious he'd been about her, even when she'd tried so hard to keep the focus on him.

There was a break in Hayden's story, and Bree took the opportunity to ask another question. "What do you like best about New York?"

"Oh, everything." He flashed her a smile and waved a hand around the trendy but nondescript restaurant he'd taken her to. "Wherever I am is the best part."

It sounded like a rehearsed line, but also rang very true and familiar. Hayden Carmichael was too much like her. He took life as it came without worrying much about a plan, the same as she did. It was charming, how he was interested in everything and could talk to anyone.

After so many weeks with Aiden, however, it was unsettling. Even for the restaurant, Hayden hadn't had a plan. He'd just walked into the first one that looked good. For all he knew, it could have been the worst-rated place in the entire city, full of health code violations.

Fine, it was spotless and the food was amazing, but maybe

he'd just gotten lucky. Hayden was the kind of guy who had luck on his side.

Luck favors the well prepared.

The words tattooed onto Aiden's chest came into Bree's mind.

"Do you have any tattoos?" she asked the actor across the table from her.

He'd been midsentence in his story but didn't seem phased at all by the interruption. "Tattoos? Oh yeah, I've got about a dozen."

Pulling up one sleeve, he leaned across the table to walk her through the five he had on that arm, starting with his first, an iguana on his shoulder that he'd gotten at seventeen right before the sequel to *Escape to New York*. The producers had been furious. Bree smiled at that.

Then he pulled up the other sleeve to explain those.

"This one is new." He pointed to a heart with the letters JM inside. "That's for Jamie."

"Who's Jamie?"

He ran a hand across his mouth, then scratched his chin, considering her. Then, apparently making a decision, he leaned forward and lowered his voice. "You just did this whole thing for me with Aiden, so you're totally trustworthy. Besides, it'll come out in a few weeks anyway. Jamie is the love of my life."

His eyes were shining, and his face lit up like Rockefeller Center at Christmas. "I just spent four weeks in total privacy with her in Bali, all thanks to you and Aiden."

"Three weeks," she corrected automatically.

That's all she'd had with Aiden, then he was just . . . gone. There had been no accidentally running into him in the vestibule, no early morning knocks at her door for coffee. She'd gone to Brian's café every day since the flea market, and he'd never been in once. The only reason he'd been hanging out with her at all was the Hayden gig, apparently.

The movie star responsible for her current mood reached across the table and put his hand on top of hers. "I haven't said it yet, but thank you. We really needed this time together. She's in the business, behind the scenes. I wanted us to be on solid ground before totally turning her world upside down."

He gave her a knowing smile. "You've had a peek at this life, and it's not easy, is it?"

Bree blinked, waiting for the thrill of his hand on hers. But nothing came. There was only the shock of Hayden's news creeping into her brain.

Did Birdbrain think she really had a shot with a real movie star?

Of course Hayden was in love with someone else. Who was Bree, after all? Nobody, just like she'd always been. Not enough for Aiden to want to stay in the city, or even tell her goodbye properly.

"Of course." She slapped a smile on her face. "Glad we could help."

There was a rustle nearby, and they both turned their heads to see a cluster of women standing a few feet away from the table. Clearly tourists, now that Bree knew what to look for. Thanks to Aiden.

"Oh my gosh, Hayden, I can't believe you're really here," said the tallest of the bunch. "This is your new girlfriend, right? Can we get a picture?"

Giving Bree a wink, he smiled at the women. "How about just with me? Bree's still not used to having her picture taken."

Bree leaned back, worried the women would ask her to do it, but they grabbed a passing waiter instead.

The feelings rushing around Bree's chest were too confusing to consider right now. Looking at Hayden and his fans, however, how easy and charming he was with them, made at least one thing clear.

Hayden Carmichael was not the man of her dreams. Maybe he had been once, or the idea of him, at least. The amalgamation of everything he was on screen: sweet, funny, protective. He'd paid two people tens of thousands of dollars just to keep Jamie out of the spotlight. Jamie was the center of his world.

That's all Bree really wanted. To be the center of someone's world.

Leigh was her best friend, but she had her girls and they would always come first, as they should. Her parents had five girls and loved them all, but Bree would never be their shining star. The love she got from them was perfunctory, almost negligent. No matter what she'd done, it hadn't made a difference to the attention she got from them.

"Do you have any other questions?"

Bree shook herself out of her thoughts to look at Hayden. The women had walked off, thrilled with their photo of him, and now he was seeking attention from Bree.

Rather than get upset he hadn't asked anything about her, or even inquired if she wanted something else to drink, she simply smiled. He beamed back at her. He was adorable.

How could she be mad at him? Not when he'd grown up with eyes on him constantly, and didn't know any other way to live.

Bree had thought that kind of life was the one she wanted. But it wasn't attention from the whole world she was looking for. It wasn't even attention from her parents, not anymore, not after this many years. She just wanted to feel important to somebody, to have her be a priority for someone.

There'd only been one person who'd treated Bree like she was the only person in the room, who'd worried about her safety, and thought about what would make her happiest even if it meant going outside their comfort zone.

He looked just like the man sitting across from her, but he was now miles away, gone forever. She'd been so focused on waiting for some enormous sign that Aiden wanted her, she'd missed all the little ways he'd shown her she was important to him.

"I actually think I should get home." Bree stood up, and Hayden's eyes went wide.

"Are you sure? We could totally hang out for longer. I seriously owe you."

She shook her head, but she was smiling. There was still a sweetness to him, the same that had drawn her in the first time she'd seen him on screen. It just wasn't what she wanted. "It's been really great meeting you."

And then, though her starstruck self from a month ago would never have believed it possible, she walked out the door, away from Hayden Carmichael.

TWENTY-SEVEN

"This. Is. Fantastic."

Tony was literally running for joy down the aisle of a supermarket.

"What? The sale on paper towels?"

"Look how empty it is. Have you ever seen a grocery store this empty when it's not midnight? And even then, it still feels packed somehow."

Aiden wished he could match Tony's enthusiasm, but after the two-and-a-half-day drive, he just wanted to sleep and stew in his misery.

There'd been a picture of Bree with Hayden at a restaurant, his hand over hers. He was staring into her eyes like he hadn't just spent a month with someone he'd claimed he was head over heels in love with.

Of course he'd want Bree. She was incredible. Bree wanted Hayden, and now she had him.

Which was why he was here, in Minnesota, what he'd wanted his whole life. Well, not his whole life, and not specifically Minnesota. But he wasn't in New York, and that should have made him as happy as Tony was, running around an empty store like it was paradise.

"When are we meeting Leigh?"

"At three, at her café."

It was only ten. They'd driven for most of the night the past few days. Aiden was dead on his feet. "What are we going to do until then?"

"I set up a few tours of apartments for us. Or houses, I should say." Tony slowed his rambunctious sprint enough to punch Aiden in the arm. "Guess how much a five-bedroom house is out here? Guess. Guess." Each time he said the word, he punched his arm.

"A lot less than it is in New York."

Frowning, Tony stopped. "Hey, you okay?"

"Yeah, fine. Just tired."

"You talk to Bree before we left?"

"Uh, not really, no."

"Wait, you mean to tell me you drove thirteen thousand miles away from the woman you love without saying goodbye?"

"Who said I love her?"

"Are you saying you don't?"

Aiden said nothing, and Tony chuckled. "Better figure it out soon before that movie star snaps her up."

Apparently Tony had seen the pictures too.

"He's all wrong for her."

"Hey, when you know, you know."

"It's not that simple."

Hell, he wished it was. He wished he could just turn up at her door with a bouquet of flowers, spouting cheesy lines like the final scene in one of Hayden's movies, and have her fall into his arms.

Instead, he thought about all the things that could go wrong, all the ways he should plan to make sure it was the perfect declaration. He didn't even know what her favorite flower was.

"Let's just go see these giant houses, okay?"

"Sure, man." And then, amazingly, Tony did exactly what Aiden needed and let it drop.

That afternoon, Aiden walked into Leigh's café and a warm familiarity washed over him. It was the smell of coffee but also the décor, similar to Brian's. There was a coziness that radiated from everywhere.

When Leigh came over to greet them with a smile on her face, it was clear the coziness started with her, and she'd infused it into every nook and cranny of the place.

"I can't believe you're here." She stood a few feet from Tony, drinking him in with her eyes, clearly restraining herself from flinging herself into his arms.

Tony shoved his hands into his pockets, muscles tensing, obviously trying to avoid the same thing. "I can't believe you said yes when I told you my plan."

He'd explained it to Aiden on the endless drive, how he'd get an apartment—or house, apparently—and start looking for contracting work, and they'd see each other a few times a week. Leigh's girls had never seen her with a boyfriend, and she wanted to take things slowly, make sure Tony wouldn't get sick of living in the middle of nowhere and leave in the middle of the night or something before introducing him into their lives in a more permanent way.

One look at Tony's face, however, and there was no doubt in Aiden's mind he was staying for good.

"This place is adorable," said Aiden, to fill the silent love fest happening between Tony and Leigh.

"Hmm?" She pulled her eyes away and then smiled.

"Thank you, Aiden. Bree took me to Brian's place, and I chatted with him a bit. I think we used the same online design account for inspiration."

The mention of her name shouldn't give him such a big pang in his chest, but there it was. Planning for the pain hadn't, in the end, made it any easier to deal with.

"Well, who are these two handsome strangers, Leigh?" A group of three women had just walked into the café and made their way over.

Leigh gave a small, tight smile to the women. "Hi, Mrs. Peterson. Stephanie. Haley."

The women nodded their greeting, and Aiden's heart gave a small jump. Peterson was a common name, but there was too much of a resemblance to Bree for there to not be a connection. The three women were all tall and blond with brown eyes, but they still looked like Bree. Something about the eyes or the nose.

"These are some new folks moving into town from New York City. Bree met them out there and talked so much about how great it is here, they decided it was the right place for them."

The words were short and clipped but delivered so smoothly, Aiden almost forgot the truth.

"It's nice to meet you," the older woman said politely.

Leigh gestured with a hand. "This is Bree's mom and two of her sisters, Stephanie and Haley."

His suspicions confirmed, Aiden's stomach fell. Meeting Bree's family had seemed like a vague possibility in his imagining of being in this town, but he hadn't counted on it happening quite so soon. This was definitely not the small town for him. Luckily, Minnesota was full of them. Or somewhere in Iowa. He hadn't accepted either school's offer yet, but after today, Iowa was looking better and better.

"Nice to meet you all. Bree's such a sweetheart." Tony stuck out a hand, and the women all raised their eyebrows at him before they shook it in turn. "I'm Tony."

"Hi, I'm Aiden."

Even in his two days of travel rumpledness, their eyes still widened at the combination of his name and his face.

"But you're . . . " Bree's mother shook her head. "I saw a picture of you and Bree in Central Park. And just yesterday in a restaurant. Did she bring you home?" She looked around the café. "Is she here?"

Jealousy flared in Aiden's gut at the mention of the restaurant. The photo Mrs. Peterson was referring to was branded on the back of Aiden's skull, a reminder of how he'd been rejected again for someone with more money, more power, more status.

"I'm not him. Similar name, similar face." The words were rote, but they came out a bit harsher than they usually did. "The picture from the restaurant is Hayden Carmichael."

"You mean Birdbrain actually managed to meet him, after all her talk?" said Stephanie or Haley, Aiden couldn't tell.

Birdbrain? Heat pooled in Aiden's chest. He shot a glance at Leigh, whose mouth was a tight, thin line.

"Were those other photos you?" The other sister wrinkled her nose. "She wasn't really dating him, was she?"

Aiden was grateful that the NDA meant he could only shrug. If he'd had to open his mouth, he wasn't sure what rude thing he might say.

The two sisters exchanged looks and tittered.

"She's always been a dreamer, our Bree," her mother said by way of explanation. She waved a hand in the air. "Never amounted to much though, all her talk."

One sister nodded. "If it weren't for Agatha, she'd never have even moved to New York."

"Kept saying for years she was going to leave us all behind for the big city, but did Birdbrain have savings?" The other sister shook her head. "No. Did she have a job or an idea of how to find one? No."

Every muscle in his body tensed. Aiden inhaled deeply and looked at Leigh, whose pursed lips and narrowed eyes seemed to say, *Yup, they're always like this.*

Horrendously insulting nickname aside, there was nothing incorrect about anything her family had said about her. It was some of the same stuff Aiden himself had found most frustrating about his time with her. The lack of planning, expecting things to work out just because she hoped it would.

Guilt seeped into his skin. How could he have ever let her doubt how incredible she was?

"Our flighty little birdbrained Bree." Her mother chuckled. "She'll be back here soon, I'm sure. Pretty girl, but nothing special."

The heat in his chest pumped into his veins, hot and angry. Nothing special? Birdbrain? This was how Bree's own family talked about her?

All her dreams now made perfect sense. Living in a big city. Thriving there. Staying there. Being seen with the completely impractical but very impressive Hayden Carmichael.

It also made perfect sense why someone like Aiden wouldn't fit into that. Not when all he wanted was a quiet life, tending to animals in some small town.

Nothing special.

Except Bree was the most special person to him, other than the lovesick Tony swooning next to him.

The past few weeks with her had been some of the best of Aiden's life. The ways that she'd pushed him to do things outside his comfort zone. The plans she'd ruined yet somehow turned into something better than before. Seeing the city through her eyes had made it seem like somewhere magical again, something special.

He hadn't told her that, though. Hadn't thought it was worth trying, since he was leaving and she wanted someone else. Would it have made a difference if he had? Maybe knowing how Aiden felt would have been enough to show her she didn't need to be with Hayden Carmichael to get the attention she deserved.

One of the baristas came over to ask Leigh a question, and she smiled her apology at them all, then left to attend to her business. Tony's eyes followed her, and once they'd turned back to Aiden's, he nodded toward the door.

Using every ounce of politeness he possessed, Aiden smiled at Bree's family. "It was great to meet you all, but Tony's moving into his new place tomorrow, and we still have a few things to take care of today."

"Well, don't be a stranger." Mrs. Peterson beamed at him, and she sounded so much like Bree that Aiden had to turn away. "We're all friends in this town. Just ask Leigh."

"Oh, I will." Tony smiled widely, and Aiden had to shove him in the shoulder to get him to move.

"Your 'low-key, let people get used to the idea of you and Leigh' plan will be blown in about three more seconds if we don't get out of here," he whispered urgently.

Aiden would blow, too, if he had to keep listening to the Petersons bash Bree.

Back in the truck, Tony turned on him, as close to a pout on his face Aiden had ever seen. "We could have stayed there."

"No, we couldn't, because I need to get back to New York."

"What? Why?" Tony's pout turned into a wicked grin. "Bree?"

Aiden nodded. "It's just . . . I don't have a plan."

The wide emptiness of his brain was scary in its unfamiliarity.

The thought seemed to unnerve Tony as well, who gripped

the steering wheel with white knuckles. "How do you not have a plan?"

Then, his friend burst out laughing.

"It's not funny. This is terrifying."

"Love is supposed to be."

Love. The one thing he hadn't planned on.

"Look, I know Margot did a number on you. It doesn't feel great to be left." Tony gave him a lopsided smile. "Why do you think I always kept things light? My high school girlfriend . . . I thought we were going to get married."

"I didn't know that."

"Why would you? I met you fifteen years after the fact." He paused, ran his hand over the steering wheel. "You know who I told almost immediately about her? Leigh."

"Why?"

"She felt safe." Tony cringed at Aiden's expression. "Not that you don't. It's just . . . I wanted her to know why I was scared but was trying anyway."

"So I should tell Bree about Margot."

"Maybe?" Tony shrugged. He finally turned on the engine and headed out of the café's parking lot back to the motel they'd booked for the night. "Look, I'm no love expert. I just got lucky with Leigh."

"Luck favors the prepared." Aiden said the words automatically, but they didn't feel as weighty as they usually did. He rubbed his hand over the words on his chest, where Bree had touched them too. That midnight visit was one of the oddest things she'd done, but he'd loved it.

He loved her. Every random thing she did, every time she listened to whatever inner voice only she heard to do whatever felt right. He didn't think he even had that voice anymore, but there it was, begging him to get to her as soon as possible.

"You can't prepare for meeting someone who'll change your

life." Tony turned down a side street that was completely empty of cars, something Aiden realized he'd never actually seen in real life. "I got lucky meeting her, but I had to be smart enough to recognize what I was feeling was worth taking a chance on."

Aiden stared out the window. The houses they passed were all the kind he'd been planning for years on living in: a yard big enough for a dog to run around in, biking and hiking trails at the end of the road, a wide-open sky above.

"Chance isn't really how I operate."

"You mean you're scared it won't work out."

"Of course I'm scared. Aren't you?"

Tony shrugged again and pulled into the motel's parking lot. The entire trip had taken less time than it did for him to walk to the nearest subway station from his apartment. "It's scarier thinking about life without her."

Aiden exhaled and ran his hands over his face, then let out a groan. "I'm going to have to wing it, aren't I?"

"Yup." Tony grinned. "Go get your stuff. I can handle moving all my crap myself. I need to get you to the airport."

TWENTY-EIGHT

The front door was opening a lot more than usual. Bree peeked through her apartment's peephole, but there was nobody in the hallway.

Since going to the restaurant with Hayden, Bree had been getting even more attention on the street, and knew it would continue until the story broke about him and Jamie.

Hayden—well, his publicist—had even offered to pay her for a few more weeks because of the annoyance, but Bree had turned it down. Money wouldn't be a problem for a while, and the payment for the original contract was just sitting in Bree's bank account, waiting for her next capricious idea to spend it. Maybe she'd redecorate, but the thought of trawling flea markets on her own wasn't appealing.

The only thing that sounded fun was the job Brian had called her with that morning. Though he hadn't spoken to her in weeks, Aiden had talked to Brian, just like he'd promised.

Bree couldn't start until things calmed down a little, however. At least all the traffic in her building today didn't seem to have anything to do with her.

Poking her head out into the hallway, she was surprised to

see Zara leaning against the staircase's banister, peering down into the entrance hall.

"What's going on?"

Zara turned her head to look at Bree.

"Open house in Aiden's apartment."

"Already?"

He'd acted fast. It had only been a few weeks since they'd gotten paid for the contract. Bree made her way into the hallway to stand next to Zara. There was a line of people out the door, waiting to come into the building.

"Wow, is this what they're always like?"

Zara shrugged. "Pretty much. Especially since he priced it really low. It'll go fast, and above asking, for sure."

Zara handed her a brochure. Looking at the amount was a little staggering. She could get two houses in Minnesota for that price.

"Maybe I should sell, move to Brooklyn."

"Why would you do that?" Zara looked shocked at the idea.

"I don't really feel at home here." *Especially with Aiden gone.*

"You inherited a choice piece of Upper West Side real estate. You don't just give that up."

"Aiden's selling."

"Yeah, but he never even wanted to live in the city. That was all his ex, Margot." Zara shook her head. "She was the one with the big dreams of living here, and he did whatever it took to make her happy."

That sounded just like him . . . and just like her. A niggling guilt burrowed into Bree's chest.

"I just knew this would happen." Mrs. Wilson had joined them in the hallway, a blanket clutched tightly over her thin shoulders. "That apartment is responsible for too many broken hearts. It's cursed."

Zara clicked her tongue. "No it's not, Granny."

"Of course it is." Mrs. Wilson raised her voice, like she hoped the people waiting in line downstairs would hear her and decide to leave. "The boy who lived there with his family loved Agatha."

"What?" Bree looked at the old woman. "Agatha never told me that."

"Why would she? When he died in Vietnam, she was heartbroken." The deep lines around Mrs. Wilson's mouth deepened. "She couldn't stand to be in the city anymore, with all the memories of their time together. She moved to Minnesota and never came back. All I had were letters and phone calls."

She cast a mean look toward Bree, like it had been her idea for Agatha to move to Minnesota. "Aiden better still visit, even if you broke his heart too."

It was like a hand had reached into her chest and wrapped itself around Bree's heart. "I didn't— We were never—"

Zara rolled her eyes. "Granny, Bree's just a friend. He's wanted to sell ever since Margot left him for that Wall Street jackass."

Just a friend. Had they even been that, or just business associates?

"I never liked that Margot." Mrs. Wilson folded her arms across her chest over the blanket, all too willing to give her opinion on Aiden's mysterious ex. "I could tell the first time I saw her she was just looking for someone with more. More money, more power, whatever. Just more." Mrs. Wilson gave an indignant sniff and leaned over the banister. "The way she'd talk to him, like no matter what he did, he wasn't enough."

The guilt had spread to Bree's stomach, heavy and dark. Was that what she'd done with all her talk of Hayden Carmichael? Made Aiden think he wasn't enough for her?

Yes, that's exactly what I did.

"She was such a snob." Zara shook her head at her grandmother, her many earrings catching the light streaming in through the hallway windows. "But they were what, twenty-two when they moved in? Everyone's kind of dumb at that age."

Bree wanted to agree but was worried if she spoke, they'd stop talking about Aiden. She was greedy for details in the same way she'd gobbled up everything he'd ever told her about himself. But he'd never talked about Margot. Now it was clear why.

"There's dumb and then there's mean," Mrs. Wilson said. "She left him to pay the mortgage all on his own. That was mean."

"And he was dumb to put it in his name?" Zara asked.

"No, that was smart. Look at him now. Now that it's all paid off, he can leave the city and set himself up wherever he wants."

For him, it was all so calculated from the beginning. There was his goal, and Bree had just been a way to get there. It was all she deserved for acting no better than Margot.

Zara's eyes cut briefly to Bree, then turned to her grandmother. "He actually just moved to Minnesota with Tony."

"What?" Bree's voice echoed in the stairwell. The line of people all turned their heads to look up at her. All three women backed away from the banister and retreated into the hallway.

"You didn't know?" Mrs. Wilson raised her eyebrows. "Tony moved out there to be with your friend who came to visit. Aiden came by a few days ago to return some Tupperware and told me all about it."

Leigh had said nothing about any of this, and they'd spoken just the previous night.

As if on cue, her phone buzzed with an incoming message.

Call me! Big news!

Her heart rate slowed a little, and she smiled at Zara and her grandmother. "Just going to get all the details now."

Leaving the two women to their gossiping, she slipped back into her apartment and put through a video call.

"You'll never guess who's here." Leigh sounded even more excited than when she'd called from the airport at the start of her surprise visit.

"Tony."

"Wait, did he tell you?" Her eyebrows drew together. "I told him not to say anything to you."

"No, my neighbor did."

"I wasn't sure he'd really come." Leigh's voice was shaking with emotion. "I didn't want to say anything to jinx it or let myself get all excited and then have it not work out."

Bree softened. That was a very Leigh move . . . and an Aiden move. Planning things out but preparing for the worst. Not getting her hopes up too high. Unlike Bree, who told everyone she met her ideas, then shrugged it off when they didn't work out and moved on to the next impractical ambition.

For Aiden, though, she had to have a plan to get him back in her life. If he even wanted that. He'd said goodbye to Mrs. Wilson before he'd left, but not to her.

He *had* called Brian about getting Bree a job, and now he was in Minnesota.

Letting her hopes climb sky-high, Bree clung to the idea Aiden was there because of her, not just because of Tony.

"Tell me all about it."

As Leigh detailed the careful planning she'd done to make sure this thing with Tony really had a chance to work, Bree only had one question.

"I thought he loved the city. He just gave it all up?"

"Well, it's not like I can move there, with my café and the girls here and everything." Leigh's voice took on a closed, husky tone, holding back tears. "He said he'd live anywhere as long as it meant he could be closer to me."

That was what Bree wanted, at her core. The realization hit her hard enough she had to sit down, on the new couch Aiden had helped her pick out at the flea market. Looking around the room, it was impossible to not think of him. She could understand why Agatha would have never wanted to come back to her apartment full of memories of her lost love. It was so painful, she'd never even mentioned it to Bree in all the years she'd known her.

But she'd given her the apartment. She wanted Bree to find her happily ever after.

Was that the city, or was it Aiden?

"I know this is a very big day for you, and I want to be supportive, but uh . . . " Bree wasn't quite sure how to finish her thought without being a total jerk.

Leigh bit her lip. "Did Aiden ask about you? Not exactly." She paused. "Some of your family was here today. They met him."

Bree groaned and put her head on her knees. Heaven only knew what they'd said about her.

"It was fine, don't worry. They didn't say anything they haven't said before."

Except they'd said it in front of Aiden, who already didn't think that much of her.

"Worry is all I can do." Bree sat up and leaned back into the couch. "I don't know what to do."

"That's never stopped you before."

"True, but things are different now. I'm different. Because of him."

There was a brief pause from Leigh. "Who?"

"Aiden, of course."

"No 'of course,' when you were with Hayden just yesterday with his hands all over you."

Bree sat up. "His hands were *not* all over me. He had one

hand on top of mine, and he was thanking me for letting him have the space to be with his new lady love."

"Oh, that's not what your family thought." Leigh gave her a significant look. "Or Aiden."

Dread punched her in the chest, a heavy fist right to the heart. "Even if Hayden hadn't told me about her, I still wouldn't be into him. He's not . . . my Aiden."

Leigh raised an eyebrow. "*Your* Aiden?"

"Not mine. I just mean, you know. Not the other one."

"Why are things different now because of *your* Aiden?" The teasing in Leigh's voice was unmistakable.

"Because I know I can't just go flying back to Minnesota, to him, without a plan."

Surprise rippled across Leigh's face, her eyes going wide and a small smile tugging at her lips.

"A plan? Like a real plan, not just a few bullet points on the back of a napkin?"

"Hey, that was the best Halloween party our town has ever seen, and you know it." Bree sighed, stretched out on the couch, and held the phone above her head. "But to answer your question, yes, a real plan. I need him to know I can do it. No, I need to know I can do it."

It wasn't about him, not in that way. All of her life, Bree had been known as the fickle one, the fun one, the dreamy one, the easily distracted one. It had always worked out for Birdbrain Bree, until New York.

This city, the one of her dreams, took people like her, chewed them up, and spit them out. At first, it had made her hate it, made her think she'd made a mistake.

Then Aiden had shown her what just a little forethought could do. The dates they'd been on—she refused to think of them as mere outings now—had been wonderful, touching, purposeful. They'd meant something to her, because he'd taken the time to think about what she'd like the most.

In order to show him that he was the one she wanted, not Hayden, she could try to do the same thing.

She shared all of these thoughts with Leigh as they talked through some possibilities. When Leigh told her he seemed miserable that afternoon, Bree found that hard to believe.

"No, really, he was super quiet at the café."

"He's a quiet kind of guy." Unlike Hayden Carmichael, who seemed to have a story for everything. It was fun to listen to, but Bree liked to be the one telling the story. Aiden had always listened to her stories. Hopefully he still wanted to.

"This was extra quiet. He didn't seem to like how your mom and sisters talked about you."

"What did they say?"

"Oh, just the usual nonsense they've always said about you. Aiden seemed upset about it."

"Really?"

"Really."

That was enough for hope to spark in her chest, lighting a fire that Bree knew from experience would burn hot and bright. Experience also told her, however, that it would burn out quickly. Panic started to trickle in. Her dreams were short-lived. The only thing she'd nurtured for long was the New York dream. Could she be that dedicated to Aiden?

Her eyes caught on the gum wrapper chain. She thought of the hours she'd spent with Agatha in the dance studio, even once she'd long lost interest in dancing. Bree looked back to her phone at Leigh, who'd been talking to her for close to an hour.

If there was one thing that Bree never lost interest in, it was in the people who stuck by her, who supported her. She could trust that what she felt for Aiden would last.

Now she just had to get to him.

TWENTY-NINE

This is absurd.

Aiden kept repeating the words silently as he stood in the crowded aisle of the plane waiting not so patiently to get out. It did not make him feel better, but it gave his mind something to do other than stress about all the ways this could go wrong and already had, starting with the flight being delayed several hours.

The realtor had called before his plane left to let him know he'd gotten several cash offers well above asking. All he had to do was say yes to one of them and he never had to go back to the city. Yet here he was, fresh off the first flight he'd been able to get to New York.

Well, not exactly fresh.

He leaned down slightly to sniff at his shirt. When given the choice between driving a few hours to Minneapolis to get one of the evening flights or waiting until the next day for the one flight from the closest small regional airport, Tony had driven Aiden to Minneapolis. It meant skipping a shower. At the time, it had seemed like a good idea, but he regretted it now.

At least he wasn't regretting coming back. Not yet.

The people in front of him in the aisle finally reached up for their overhead luggage, and the line began to move. With agonizing slowness, Aiden kept his head down and avoided eye contact, but he still felt a few stares come his way.

This was not the kind of situation where he wanted to be mistaken for the actor, and yet in this scruffy state, he looked like Hayden more than ever.

Finally free from the plane, Aiden headed for the restrooms, only to find the closest one was out of order. Frustration burned in his chest, but he took a deep, calming breath.

Cleaning up now was still more important than getting to her faster. If he showed up rumpled and smelling like he'd been in a truck for three days straight with Tony, it wouldn't matter what he said or did.

A smile tugged at his lips when he realized the ridiculousness of that thought. Bree wouldn't care. Aiden might have been spontaneous enough to jump on a last-minute flight, but he needed to at least feel in control of what he looked like when he saw Bree again.

Not having flown much, Aiden wandered around the airport, unsure which direction would take him to another restroom. He considered asking for help, but at this hour, the airport was nearly empty, and there was no one around except a few long lines of weary-looking travelers waiting to board their flights.

Asking any of them wasn't an option, especially once he noticed a few more eager eyes pointing in his direction. He tried to calm the rising panic in his chest with a slow and careful examination of the walls, concentrating on finding the sign for the men's room.

Up ahead, he spotted one.

He kept his eyes glued to it, weaving around a waiting line that was so long it stretched across two gates. There was a small rippling murmur that made its way through the line when he passed, which he ignored, though his eyes flitted to the crowd, just to make sure no one was approaching him.

Then he saw Bree.

At the other end of the line farthest from him, her hair neatly braided and a small cross-body bag over her shoulder. She looked at her watch, bit her lip, and then her eyes swiveled around, landing on Aiden. He kept walking, not entirely believing what he was seeing, then turned his head to get a second look.

"Bree?"

Her eyes went wide.

Wham!

Aiden stumbled back from the door he'd just run into, stars bursting in his brain. Everything was blurry, but he still saw the shocked look of the custodian who'd opened the door, still heard Bree's voice from behind him.

"Are you okay?" she asked.

He turned, wobbling, and she gripped his arms.

"I had a dream about you," he slurred, and her smile cut through the haze of pain.

"Oh yeah?" Sliding her hand into his, she led him toward a seat. "What was I doing?"

He slumped down into the chair and it dug into his legs, but it brought his face level with hers. "You were a beautiful fairy in a dirty city, and I came to rescue you."

"You did, huh?" From the depths of her bag, she pulled out an ice-cold bottle of water. "How did that work out for you?"

"Not exactly as planned, I must admit."

She held it up to his forehead, and the skin there sang with pain. He closed his eyes and groaned.

"I must be rubbing off on you," she said. "Sorry about that."

His eyes snapped open, and his chest tightened at the sad

look on her face. "You have, Bree. I hope you know how much better my life is for it."

"You always say stuff like that." She waved her hand, bringing it briefly to wipe at her eyes. "You couldn't possibly mean it."

"Why? Because your terrible family doesn't?" He lowered the bottle from his forehead and put it on the little table in between their seats so he could take her hands. "Bree, I wanted to punch them when I heard how they talk about you."

"You'd punch my mom?"

"I'd punch anyone for you. But it's probably better if I teach you to punch so you can do it yourself."

She traced the lines in his hands and didn't look at him. "That's what you've been doing, isn't it? Teaching me how to have more. Not because you think I'm weak or a mess to fix, but because—" Her breath hitched and she took a shy inhale.

"Because you deserve to have whatever you want," he finished for her. "You're so capable, Bree, and so smart and brave, and I'm sorry that I can't get you the attention Hayden can—"

"It's enough." She finally looked up at him, her eyes shining. "I don't need to have the world's eyes on me, just yours."

Heat swelled in his chest, and he ran his hands along her arms, aching to hold her. "If the bruise on my head is any indication, you have them."

She let out a watery chuckle. "I stopped seeing you as Hayden probably after the first day. There's this thoughtful, grumpy face you make . . ." He felt his mouth pull down into a frown, and she laughed again. "Yes, that one. He'd never make such a serious face. When I look at you, I see you, not him."

He took a deep breath and moved as close as he could with the armrests of the seats digging into their legs. "But that night you knocked on my door, you said—"

"I was trying to convince myself I didn't want you, because that would mess up my New York plan." She shook her head, her braid swinging. "At least, I thought it did."

"The plan to date a movie star and get lots of attention?"

"Yes, that plan. You messed it up." The smile on her face was pure Bree—mischievous, fun, and bright. "Luckily, I don't mind when my plans get messed up."

Her face drew closer and he leaned in, breathing her in. Sugar and flowers. "And what was tonight's plan that I messed up?"

"Do you really want to hear it?" Her voice was a whisper against his lips. "It was a really good one. I had a timeline and everything."

"Maybe later."

He brought his hands to her cheeks and pulled her in for their first kiss.

Technically, it was their second kiss, but this was more than a gentle brush of her mouth against his. It was the silkiness of her skin beneath his palms and the tangle of her hair in his fingers. It was the press of her lips on his, and the feel of the sigh in his mouth when she opened to him. It was the unexpected dance of their tongues that deepened the kiss until the chatter of the crowd broke them apart, breathless, and they ignored all the phones pointed at them to dive in again.

It was everything he'd dreamed it would be, and nothing like he'd planned.

He brushed the hair away from her face, warmth spreading through him to see her neat braid now in shambles and her eyes bright with desire he knew was only for him.

He didn't know what would happen next, and that was okay. Whatever dream Bree had for them would be enough for now, and he'd figure out the details later.

EPILOGUE

Minnesota, One Year Later

Bree made a final adjustment to her dress, then went to join Leigh.

"You look amazing," Leigh said, tears in her eyes.

"I think I'm supposed to say that to you." Bree grinned and smoothed out the skirt of Leigh's wedding dress. "You're beautiful."

In a tea-length, A-line white dress with a delicate flower pattern along the hem, Leigh's dress matched those of her two girls, who were busy twirling in a corner under Mrs. Russo's beaming, watchful eye.

"Are you sure I don't look ridiculous?" Leigh touched the flower crown Bree had made her that morning, when the florist had shown up with the wrong order. "This isn't what I'd planned for today."

Everything that could have gone wrong for a wedding had, including a torrential downpour that hadn't been in the forecast.

"You look incredible, and today will be great." Bree added a few more pins to Leigh's hair. "Between me and Aiden, we've got it covered."

Of course, Aiden had come to his best friend's wedding with a backup plan for everything. One that left enough space for Bree's more spontaneous ideas.

Like the wildflower bouquets and boutonnieres, picked fresh a few minutes after the rain had started to fall, from underneath the umbrella Aiden had held over her head.

"Are you sure you two can't spend longer in town?" Leigh pouted a little while Bree touched up her makeup. "Tony and I aren't going on our honeymoon until later in the summer. Stay a few more days."

A year ago, Bree would have immediately accepted the last-minute offer.

"I wish we could, but Aiden has finals next week." She knew if she asked him, Aiden would be okay with her staying, just like she knew he needed the quiet rhythm of their evenings in the city to help him focus.

They were living together in Bree's apartment while Aiden finished school, his days busy with classes and hers with working at Brian's café. On nights and weekends, they explored everything the city had to offer.

Walks along the High Line, concerts in the parks, bookstore browsing, the never-ending search for the best bagels . . . it was everything Bree had dreamed her New York life would look like. Even if no one was taking her picture other than Aiden.

It was still hard to see Leigh disappointed. Bree leaned in close to share the news that was definitely not on any celebrity sites yet.

"You know who else is getting married this weekend?" Bree waggled her eyebrows. "He invited us, you know."

Leigh gasped. "And you came here instead?"

Bree laughed and shook her head. Hayden seemed just as blissful with Jamie as Leigh and Tony were, but there was no question where Bree would rather be today.

The two women finished getting ready and walked to the door of Leigh's house to peek at the tent set up in the backyard.

Aiden was making his way up to them, a wide smile on his face.

"You all look wonderful. The flowers are perfect." He held out his hand to Bree. "Time for us to get into position."

A familiar sense of calm washed over her as he led her to the tent, umbrella held high.

With Aiden's school schedule, this was the first time she'd been back since moving to New York, and she was happier than she'd expected to be. She was able to appreciate the quieter, slower pace of things. Interactions with her family were still hard, but Aiden was there to tell her all the reasons she was great, since she knew they never would.

She leaned in close as they waited for the music to start. "You know, maybe I wouldn't mind living in a small town . . . "

"Really?" His eyes widened, but he kept his head focused ahead so they didn't miss their cue.

"One day."

He chuckled and squeezed her hand.

Now that he'd started school, there was no way he'd make such a big change, and Bree knew it. He lifted her hand to place a kiss on her knuckles and then another on her lips.

Every kiss since the airport was better than the last, each one holding a different meaning. The deep, crushing embraces that they poured all their hearts into. The peck on the cheek before leaving for the day, leaving them both wanting more. The soft brush of their lips to remember the fumbling start to their love.

"We'll figure it out." Aiden's kiss, hard and sweet, was a promise. "You dream it, and I'll make it happen."

The music started and they walked down the aisle.

AUTHOR'S NOTE

Whenever I read a romance novel, I always wonder what's real and what's not.

Yes, I realize the entire point of fiction is that it's made up. But there are always hints of real places, people, and events tucked in between the imaginary dialogue uttered by inexplicably buff and beautiful characters.

Here's a short and incomplete list of what's real and what's not in this book:

- Hayden Carmichael: not a real movie star, unfortunately. He sounds very dreamy, doesn't he? In my mind when writing him, he was a cross between Zac Efron and Henry Cavill. (Though, to be fair, I picture most of my MMCs as Henry Cavill, don't you?)
- Celebrity look-alikes: very real, though probably never quite as perfect a match as Aiden is for Hayden.
- All of the art and architecture they visit in NYC: real! I love the city and majored in art history, so it

was a struggle not to put in every little nerdy detail I could think of.

- The apartment building where Aiden and Bree live: not real. Also, in that area of the city, it would probably not be a condo situation or only have eight apartments, but sometimes romance reasons win over realism. Apologies to my lovely beta reader Sam for any other NYC errors that slipped in!
- Kiosks instead of payphones: real! Like most people, I haven't needed a payphone since I got my first cellphone almost 20 years ago, so this was a fun thing to discover during my New York research.

MORE SWEET CONTEMPORARY ROMANCE

If you enjoyed *Man Of My Dreams* then take a peek at *Houseplants & Hardcovers*, a sweet rivals-to-lovers romance with major *You've Got Mail* vibes and tons of plant puns.

Chapter 1

November

> **JCEdits**
> Hi! Sorry for the random DM. You've been super helpful in the comments, but my current plant situation has gotten overwhelming.

> **Plantsguy95**
> What seems to be the problem? What kind of plants are they?

> **JCEdits**
> Well . . . everything is very, very brown. And they are all, um, green plants? My mother got them for me.

> **Plantsguy95**
> No worries, happy to help with any and all plant problems.

> We'll figure out how to get things back in the green in no time.

April

Pete the prayer plant was dying.

If Juliet was being honest with herself, he had been dying for a while. Then she'd gone into one of her super-concentrated work sprints and did nothing but sleep and copyedit for four days. Now most of her plants looked less than well-loved, sagging sadly over the edge of their pots between teetering stacks of books, but poor Pete had suffered the worst.

Juliet leaned in, examining his leaves in the sunlight streaming through her home office's windows. Unlike Pete, Juliet had gotten some nourishment this week, but only because her mom had sent food over. Almost twenty years since she left home, she still regularly needed to be watered and fed by someone else.

A buzzing from her desk drew her attention away from her plants. Her phone was ringing. She didn't have to look to know it was her mom. No one else called her.

"Did you get the salad?"

"Hello to you too." Juliet tucked the blanket she was wearing over her shoulders even tighter so it draped behind her like a cape. "Yes, I got it."

"Did you eat it?"

"Yes." Not immediately, but within twelve hours. That counted as the same meal, didn't it?

Her mother sighed, as if she'd guessed at Juliet's unspoken words. "It shouldn't be this hard to keep my thirty-seven-year-old daughter alive." The sounds of nature chirped through the phone, along with the babble of a toddler. "Your sister doesn't need this kind of attention. Her small children do."

"So stop sending the salads. I can take care of myself."

"You can't even keep those plants alive."

Juliet had no argument there. Here she was, staring at five shriveled brown leaves on a prayer plant that looked like it was praying to be put out of its misery.

"The plants were your idea. You should be the one to take care of them." The bitterness in her words got another sigh from her mother. Like she needed another reminder about how incompetent she was at managing her own life.

"I water them every time I come over. Or rather, whenever you let me come over."

The itch to get back to her computer and escape this conversation was a thousand writhing ants crawling up her arms. In front of a page, with stylistic errors and typos to be corrected, Juliet was in total control. When online reputations and major financial deals could be ruined forever from a misplaced comma, nothing was more important than the right editor. Her clients' only concern was that she got their manuscripts polished to perfection in record time. They didn't care if she could keep a plant alive.

Juliet tugged gently at the brownest of Pete's leaves, and it slipped off the stem as if attached by only the flimsiest of threads. The prayer plant needed her more than her clients right now, it seemed.

Thank goodness her mother hadn't bought her a cat.

"You can come over tonight, if you want," Juliet said,

turning away from Pete to look at the calendar above her desk. "I just finished a deadline, so I don't have much work for the next few days."

"It'll have to wait, sweetie, Allison needs me to watch the boys overnight."

The sting of rejection shouldn't be as sharp after all these years, but there it was. Her mother complained Juliet never wanted her to come over, but then was too busy when she did invite her. Juliet took a deep breath and the pain in her chest eased a bit, though not completely.

"Well, whenever you have time. I'm always here," she said.

"That's what worries me the most. You should get out of the house more."

"Mom, I work at home."

"Exactly. You live your whole life inside." There was a loud squawk from her mother's end of the phone—one of the kids must have seen a dog or something. "Allison's husband just finished his third Ironman this weekend. He almost qualified for the world championships."

"I know. I saw the pictures." Juliet plopped down in her office chair, curled her legs to her chest, and pulled the blanket over herself.

"You could have seen it in person."

"I had a deadline." Also, it had been a three-hour drive to the mountain town to Tony's race. There was no way she would have been able to do that, even if she still had a car.

"I would have driven you." Again, it was as if her mom had guessed the words she'd held back.

Now if only she could pick up on Juliet's desire to get off the phone and back to her plant disaster.

"Next time. I have to go. I'll call you in a few days."

After saying their goodbyes, Juliet hung up and stood up, the blanket dropping to the floor. Rather than deal with the emotions a five-minute phone call had dredged up, she switched to her camera to take a picture of the dying plant. Then, it was just another swipe of her thumb and a few taps of her fingers to pull open the social media app where normally she'd post about the open space in her editing calendar. Instead, she went into the private-messaging section to send the photo to the one person who could help her right now.

Plantsguy95.

There was already a message waiting for her, a laughing emoji in response to a meme she'd sent him a few days ago. From that initial message a few months ago—when her mother had dropped off five plants and they'd all been drooping within a week—an easy online friendship had blossomed.

Blossomed. She almost groaned out loud at the plant pun. That was undoubtedly his influence. He was funny with words in a way she could never achieve without hours of contemplation first.

The little green dot next to his profile picture—a leafy green *Ficus*—let Juliet know he was online. A reply came almost immediately to her picture of a dying Pete.

Plantsguy95
What happened?

JCEdits
I got busy with work.

Plantsguy95
Isn't this one in the bathroom like I suggested, for the humidity?

Did you not go to the bathroom for a week?

JCEdits
I plead the fifth.

> **Plantsguy95**
> JC, you gotta be nicer to your body. Forget about the plants.

Juliet snorted. Though it went against all sorts of best practices for using social media to grow your business, she didn't share her name unless someone was a client. Plantsguy95 only knew her as JCEdits, her username, which he turned into JC.

> **JCEdits**
> I'm screenshotting that and showing all your 15 million followers you said that.

> **Plantsguy95**
> 15 million?
>
> Wow, it must have gone up by 14.99 million since yesterday.

> **JCEdits**
> You mean you don't check your followers?
>
> You have like, five times as many as me, and people share your stuff all the time.

> **Plantsguy95**
> This isn't my full-time gig.
>
> It's not even a gig. I don't get paid for this.
>
> I just want people to learn about plants.

For someone with close to twenty thousand followers, Plantsguy95 had a very laid-back approach to his account that Juliet couldn't understand. Not for the first time, she wondered what his real job was . . . and his name. Neither of them posted pictures of themselves, so she didn't even know what he looked like. All his photos were plants, sometimes with hands she assumed were his, sometimes his shadow. Her account was entirely copyediting tips and memes, her profile photo a stylized red pen.

She knew he was a *he* from the pronouns in his bio, but beyond that, it was frustratingly bare bones, even more anonymous than Juliet's. At least hers told the world what she did and how to contact her. All his said was "I'm a guy who likes plants. I answer your #solvemyplantproblem questions every Wednesday." No location, no link to a website or even a fundraising campaign.

> **JCEdits**
> Thank goodness you aren't trying to get paid for this.

> The sloppy copy in your posts would make any legitimate sponsors run for the hills.

> **Plantsguy95**
> Well, you refuse to let me hire you, so I'll just have to struggle along without your expert eyes.

> **JCEdits**
> Can I get your expert eyes on my plant please?

> I'll write five posts for free for you if it lives to next week.

> **Plantsguy95**
> Deal.

Juliet never took social media clients, since she charged by word, and it was not the most efficient use of her time. This was a dire situation, however, and exceptions had to be made. Within minutes, he sent a comprehensive list of everything Juliet needed to do, almost hour by hour, to make sure Pete survived. The tension that had built up over the last four days dropped off Juliet's shoulders. It was reassuring to see something so organized. Now that she felt like the plant part of her life was under control, she could get back to work.

Lucas was in the middle of his shift at the hardware store when he got an update from JC about the prayer plant she'd ignored into drought. It was still drooping a week after he'd told her how to save it, but "since it's technically still alive," she said he could send her the posts he wanted her to write.

His lips curved up into a smile wider than the hacksaws he was pricing as he tapped out a reply.

> **Plantsguy95**
> Are you sure your prayer plant doesn't have a death wish?

> **JCEdits**
> The thought has crossed my mind. I thought I was a good roommate.

> No complaints from the others, though.

> **Plantsguy95**
> How many others do you have?

> **JCEdits**
> Roommates or plants?

> **Plantsguy95**
> I already know how many plants you have, since I've had to keep them all from dying from lack of attention.

JCEdits
And how many is that?

Plantsguy95
10.

JCEdits
Ha! I have 12 plants.

I kept the Aloe plants alive all by myself.

Plantsguy95
I'm positively bursting with pride.

JCEdits
Don't get too proud, you haven't saved the prayer plant yet.

She'd avoided the roommate question, and while it might not have been intentional, it did remind him that she wasn't that kind of online friend. Personal details shared were minimal. They never talked much about family or friends. She only mentioned her work when it got in the way of her plant care.

Leaning against a shelf full of boxes of nails, Lucas ran a hand through his hair and stared down at his phone, like he could hypnotize it into giving him the information he wanted.

The internet was an amazing thing. You could look up the answers to literally any question, as Lucas liked to remind his family when they blew up his phone with their bonkers requests at three in the morning. Though at least his grandmother waited until the sun was up.

The internet, however, could not solve the question he'd been wondering about for months, despite the embarrassing amount of hours he'd spent sleuthing.

Who was JCEdits?

All he knew for sure was that she was an editor. A few years ago, he would have traded all his plant advice until the end of time to get professionally written and edited posts. What had started as a failed side hustle had turned into an unexpected way to connect with other plant nerds outside of his small town. It wasn't to make money or get famous, at least not anymore. Not since his ex—and his reason for starting the account—was no longer in the picture. Now, he just wanted to talk to people about plants and help them learn more about them.

A few short months ago, JC had been completely clueless. Even worse than his cousin Marigold—Mari—who'd managed to kill a cactus in two days by mixing up the saltwater she'd put in a bottle for her facial routine with . . . well, it didn't really matter since he'd told her at least five times succulents don't need daily watering.

JC was a quick learner though. Since Lucas loved nothing more than people who asked him questions about the things he loved most, they'd been chatting a few times a week since her first timid message asking for help with her brand-new plant babies.

It was nice, in a way, to have something that was light and low pressure. The opposite of his life with a huge family that lived and breathed drama like they were trying out to be the next reality TV sensation.

And yet . . . he really wanted to know if JC lived with anyone.

Instead of asking again, he looked up from his phone to make sure he was still alone in the aisle, and focused his response to her on the plants, like he was expected to.

> **Plantsguy95**
> Why don't you try your local horticultural society?

JCEdits
I'm sorry, my local what now?

This isn't the 1800s and I am not a romance heroine with nothing to do until an appropriate suitor comes to call.

Plantsguy95
Fine, garden club, if you prefer.

JCEdits
Also not a 1950s housewife waiting for her husband to come home to beat him over the head with a leg of lamb.

He chuckled, and the noise caught his boss's attention. Normally, Henry didn't care about phone use during work. But whenever Henry's dad, who owned the store, was around, the rules suddenly became stricter. So Lucas stashed his phone in his back pocket and got back to pricing boxes of nails under Henry's watchful eye. It was an agonizing three hours before Lucas could reply to JC's message.

His shift finally over, Lucas practically threw his apron at Henry and ran out of the hardware store, passing a row of smaller shops on his way to the back parking lot that employees used. The evening was warm for early spring, and he inhaled a lungful of crisp air as he leaned against the side of his truck and thought about what to tell JC. It was a fine line to walk between revealing too much about himself and coming off as insincere.

The choice to never show his face in the account kept him anonymous. Plants were his main focus on the account, not making it his identity, his business, his life. That hadn't gone very well the first time he'd tried it, as the harsh criticisms of his ex had so generously pointed out.

Besides, Greenhaven was on the smaller side. Five square miles with an adorable store-lined, cobblestone main street that would make Norman Rockwell proud, and a gossip mill that put Hollywood tabloids to shame. Lucas knew word would get around if he put his face out there, then *everyone* would have something to say about it. It was enough trouble as it was to have his younger cousins weigh in on his very outdated use of hashtags.

Now, however, he wished he could tell JC about the garden club in Greenhaven that he'd belonged to since he was old enough to hold a spade.

> **Plantsguy95**
> Google the name of your city + horticultural society or garden club, to see what comes up.

> Most cities of a certain size have one, even if it's just a few people who get together to trade seeds.

> **JCEdits**
> "Trade seeds" huh?

> Is that what the kids these days are calling it?

He laughed out loud at that one, then looked around to make sure no one had seen him. Laughing to himself in a deserted parking lot behind Main Street wasn't exactly his best look. Not to mention if Henry spotted him, he'd probably assume Lucas had nowhere to be tonight and ask him to work a few more hours.

Before he could forget, he drafted a post on garden clubs to share with his followers, giving a bit of the history and importance that they served in communities. It took an enormous amount of restraint to not add anything specific to his town, since he honestly thought they were one of the best in his area. The work they did in Greenhaven was incredible, and not just because his family had done so much of it.

Now dangerously close to having Henry come out and ask him to help close the store, Lucas got into his truck—even years after he passed, it was still hard to not think of it as his grandfather's old truck—to drive to his grandmother's house. On his way, he passed town hall, where the rows of planters were fresh and colorful thanks to the club. Two people chatted away on the nearby bench as the sky turned darker, oblivious to the months of fundraising the garden club had done to get it installed.

Typical. He sighed as he turned onto a side street. *No one appreciates a really good garden.*

There was a family crossing the street to the library, which was lit up inside for some evening event, and Lucas stopped the truck to let them pass. A few buildings down, his cousin Sage's car was parked in front of the garden club, and a light was on.

Their grandmother was still the elected president of the Greenhaven Garden Club, but she'd gotten sick over the winter. Then her best friend had died, and Granny just didn't seem to like being out and about as much. They'd scheduled an election for the next meeting to select an acting president, but for now, the other members rotated duties.

Except Sage wasn't technically a member. She was family, and the Geis family helped each other no matter what. So without a second's hesitation, Lucas pulled into the driveway behind her car, whatever plans he'd had for the evening put on hold in favor of something much more important.

ALSO BY DAPHNE JAMES HUFF

Sweet Adult Contemporary Romance:

Houseplants and Hardcovers

Miller Family Medical:

A Shot At Love

Wedding Games:

The Bridesmaid and the Reality Show

The Bridesmaid and the Ex

The Bridesmaid and Her Surprise Love

Free Wedding Games Prequel Novella:

The Wedding Planner's Second Chance At Love

Young Adult Romance:

Rebound Boyfriend

Leah's Song

This Summer at the Lake

Love Lessons

Carnival Wishes

Home for Christmas